DEM
TRUTH

The Basilica Diaries
Book Three

Richard Kurti

SAPERE
BOOKS

DEMON OF TRUTH

Published by Sapere Books.

24 Trafalgar Road, Ilkley, LS29 8HH

saperebooks.com

ISBN: 978-0-85495-045-4

PART ONE

1: PRAYER

Rome, 1506

Light of the World, Father of All Mercies, who has walked by my side through the years of darkness, I beseech You now to hear my prayer and forgive the blood I have spilled.

So many times did doubt fill my heart. So many times did I fear You had forsaken me.

Yet now I understand: in that silence You were always there, Lord, guiding me with Your loving hands.

Some will not understand the terrible power of Your love. But I have faith in You to know the truth in my soul.

For twenty-three years, I waited.

Twenty-three summers of hope.

Twenty-three winters of despair.

And then You spoke to me, through the miracle of St Peter.

I ask You now, Heavenly Father, to accept the dying body of this priest as an expression of my love and gratitude.

You have kept Your promise, and I have done my duty.

The pain that gripped my heart for so long is soothed by this act of redemption.

I pray that You will always walk by my side to strengthen and guide me, that I may live my life as You have ordained.

By the power of the Holy Spirit.

Amen.

She curls the prayer into a neat scroll, then leans over the body of the priest.

He is breathing, but only just. Every beat of his heart pumps another spasm of warm blood from the gash across his throat, paralysing his body and draining his mind.

"If your right eye causes you to stumble," she whispers, "pluck it out and throw it away from you."

Then she passes her hand gently over his face and presses her thumb onto his eyeball.

"Please......" he gasps. Even this close to death, a last beat of panic grips the priest as he moans for mercy.

"Hush, now," she whispers. "God is with us."

There is nothing he can do except listen to the soft squelch as she gouges his eyeball from its socket.

A strange sob erupts from the priest's mouth, but he no longer has the strength to scream, or even to turn his head away. All he can do is accept.

She waits for the rush of blood to wash away the spilled eye jelly, then delicately she places the small prayer scroll into the man's gaping socket.

"Thy Will be done," she whispers.

Then she hurries away and is swallowed by the darkness of the Vatican's many corridors.

2: BREAKTHROUGH

Six weeks earlier

"You've missed a bit!" Geometra Enzo Castano peered through his floppy fringe of black hair at the cleaner.

"Pardon, sir?" the elderly man blinked in reply.

"I appreciate it is easy to feel insignificant against the vast scale of this great project, but believe me when I say the work you do is of the utmost importance."

"Thank you, sir," the cleaner ventured, unsure what the geometra was talking about.

"Which is why it is imperative that you perform your duties with the utmost diligence." Castano took the bundle of rushes from the cleaner's hand. "Allow me to demonstrate." He knelt low and swung his arm in a smooth arc, sweeping the reeds underneath one of the pews in the Old Basilica, chasing out a layer of grime. "Sweep, step. Sweep, step. That way no dirt will be missed, and you will make steady progress along the length of the pew."

"Yes, sir. I was trying my best."

"*Concilio et labore.* Wisdom and effort. Both are required. You were thrashing back and forth rather randomly, but if you follow my advice, all your effort will be focussed in one direction." Geometra Castano handed the brush back to the cleaner. "Now you try."

The cleaner drew a deep breath, concentrating hard on stopping himself from swinging a fist and punching the geometra in the face. But he needed this job, and if he did as he was told, it would last for years to come. So he bent down and swept under the pew just as the geometra had demonstrated.

"Excellent!" Castano smiled. "Good effort." And he strode away down the nave, confident that the world was running a little more smoothly because of his intervention.

As he walked, Geometra Castano glanced up at the huge canvas sheets that had been slung across the entire width of Old St Peter's, separating this ancient basilica from the chaos that would ultimately devour it. His job was to preserve the sanctity of the Old Basilica while it was slowly torn down and the new one constructed in its place. But a building site and a functioning place of worship made uneasy bedfellows, which is why Castano's life was spent wrangling an army of cleaners, negotiating with foremen to maintain periods of silence during worship, inspecting the ancient walls to make sure there was no collateral damage, and generally worrying about the logistics of the most complex construction ever attempted in Rome.

Castano was one of those priests who had managed to forge a successful career in the church whilst avoiding too much contact with ordinary parishioners, which suited his academic (some would say aloof) nature. Prior to this he had been in charge of co-ordinating the restoration of Vatican frescoes, and before that he had spent many years patiently cataloguing in the Church's vast archives. Perhaps that was why he placed such emphasis on the title of his current role. The chief architect, Donato Bramante, had wanted Castano to be called *L'ispettore*, but Castano had objected because it made him sound like a pedant, when what he really wanted was to be an integral part of this magnificent construction project. *Geometra*, surveyor, sounded nicely technical and esoteric.

He slid through a gap in the canvas screen and moved from the Old Basilica into the building site. What would eventually be the crowning glory of Christendom was currently a cacophony of men and mud. A jangling chorus of noise filled the air, from countless pickaxes hacking into rock to shovels crunching through gravel; scaffolders shouted instructions at each other as they constructed gantries to move enormous slabs of marble around the site; wranglers barked instructions to weary mules who would spend their entire lives labouring on this project. Castano looked at the apparent chaos with quiet satisfaction. Bramante had started the construction work late in the autumn, and now that the calendar was edging towards spring, it was clear that progress was steady.

The initial effort was focussed on a set of gigantic holes. Eventually, the basilica's dome would be supported on four massive piers, each of which required a huge foundation pit twenty-five feet deep and approximately the same in diameter. Three of the pits were still in the preliminary stages, but the northwest hole was nearly at its full depth.

Castano watched as an unending stream of empty baskets was lowered into the gloom, only to emerge on the far side of the excavation bulging with rock and debris. A complex system of pulleys moved the baskets to barrowmen, who trundled the rock away and onto an ever-growing mountain of dirt.

"Where's the foreman?" Castano asked one of the men hauling on a pulley rope.

"Down in the pit."

"Why? Is there a problem?"

The man shrugged. "I just haul rope."

Castano sighed inwardly. It was strange how the Divine was forced to become manifest through the sweat and filth of ignorant labourers; an awkward juxtaposition for theologians to understand.

Suddenly a bell slung from a high scaffold tower started to toll: the *fermare*.

As if by magic, all six hundred workers stopped what they were doing and downed tools. The whole construction site fell eerily silent except for the stern tolling of the bell.

Castano felt a tingle of excitement … and fear. The *fermare* bell had been his idea because there was real danger in these awesome hand-dug pits, not to the labourers (they were disposable) but to the most holy relics in Christendom. The northwest pier was to be sited directly over the ancient burial site of St Peter, so Castano had put protocols in place that required all building work to cease immediately should anything resembling a tomb be discovered.

There had been a number of false alarms over the months as diggers uncovered old Roman water channels and the walls of the Circus of Nero, but Castano would rather stop the work a hundred times than risk damaging the sacred tomb of the Church's Founding Father.

Castano hurried towards the lip of the excavation and peered into the musty gloom, where dozens of workmen had been digging. Now they stood motionless, recovering their breath, the sweat on their bodies glistening in the flickering torchlight.

"What have you found?" Castano called out.

"Bricks. Looks like vaulting," a voice from the depths replied. It was the foreman.

"Are they intact or broken up?"

"Intact. Looks like the top of a chamber."

"Don't move. Touch nothing," Castano instructed, "I'm coming down." He hurried to the top of the first of a series of ladders that zigzagged down the sheer sides of the pit, and scrambled onto the rungs. He could feel the mud under his hands and knew that his cassock would be badly stained, but the normally fastidious geometra didn't care. What was a bit of mud if St Peter's tomb really had been discovered?

After what felt like painfully long minutes clambering down ladders and along narrow gantries, Castano finally reached the floor of the pit. As he picked his way across the uneven surface, the workers parted before him, aware that this man had a direct line of communication to Pope Julius II.

"Show me," he instructed.

The foreman pointed to a small clearing in the dirt that revealed a herringbone pattern of bricks. Castano dropped to his knees and ran his hands over the ancient structure. Were the bones of St Peter really on the other side of this vaulting?

"How far does it extend?"

The foreman and another labourer picked up two shovels.

"Be gentle!" Castano barked.

Carefully the two men scraped at the dirt until a patch of brickwork was uncovered roughly six feet square.

Castano's heart was beating so fast he felt breathless. "Can you remove one of the bricks? I need to see inside."

Someone handed the foreman a hammer and chisel, and he started tapping at the mortar, scraping it away inch by inch, until the brick became loose. Then he wedged the chisel into the crack and levered the brick up.

A pocket of air billowed out as if desperate to be released after a thousand years. Strangely, it didn't smell of decay, but was slightly scented, a bit like the oils used to embalm bodies.

Everyone gazed in silence at the black rectangle in the ground, wondering what mysteries lay beyond.

"Lantern," Castano instructed.

One of the workers hurried forward with a coil of rope, and carefully lowered a small oil lantern into the gloom. Castano lay flat on the ground, his face pressed to the opening, his eyes anxiously scanning the darkness … searching.

No-one moved. They barely breathed.

Then suddenly Castano recoiled. He scrambled to his knees, his face ashen.

"What is it?" the foreman asked. "What's down there?"

"I … I …" but Castano's composure had been shattered.

"Let me see." The foreman tried to peer into the hole but Castano pulled him away.

"No! Evacuate this pit immediately."

"What?"

"Do as I say! Everyone out!" Castano started pushing people back from the brick vaulting. "Stop all work!"

"Six hundred men have to down tools?" The foreman was angry. "Why?"

"Because I say so!"

"This is nonsense." The foreman tried to push Castano aside. "Let me see."

But Castano wrestled him back. "No-one approaches that tomb! On pain of death! Nothing happens until the Holy Father himself has witnessed this."

3: PROTOCOLS

Domenico Falchoni was not happy. As Capitano della Guardia Apostolica, part of his remit was to guarantee the Pope's safety, so when Geometra Castano barged into the papal apartments, covered in mud and clearly agitated, insisting that Pope Julius come with him immediately, Domenico's hackles went up.

"Why can't you just tell us what you saw?" Domenico asked.

"Because I cannot be sure," Castano trembled. "I don't know what I saw. Or what it means."

"Then perhaps you should have found out before coming here?"

"Enough!" Castano snapped. "I'm not talking to you. I'm addressing His Holiness." Castano sank to his knees in supplication. "You must see this with your own eyes, Holy Father. Only you can determine the truth of it."

"Very well," Pope Julius pronounced. "Prepare the construction site. I will come in person."

So easy to say, but quite another thing to execute, Domenico sighed inwardly. There were many arrangements to put in place: a planked walkway would have to be laid so that no mud splashed onto the Holy Father's red leather shoes; a pristine set of tools would need to be provided in case the Pope wanted to examine details of the construction, and anything else that His Holiness might touch would need to be sanitized of all traces of raw effort.

More worrying was the physical danger. Going down into an enormous pit whose walls could collapse without warning was no way to treat God's anointed representative on Earth.

After some hasty discussions with the site foreman, Domenico came up with a solution that involved suspending a mahogany chair from a harness, then attaching it to a long rope which passed through a complex set of pulleys. These were positioned at the end of a boom arm that could be swung out over the excavation site, enabling the chair to be set down at any point in the pit. It meant the Holy Father didn't have to demean himself by scrambling down ladders, but could be lowered into the pit like a descending god. The real beauty of the arrangement was that in the event of subsidence, the Holy Father could be hoisted to safety in moments.

Domenico joined Chief Architect Bramante and Geometra Castano on the floor of the pit, next to the exposed patch of vaulting that had triggered such consternation. Since the initial discovery, Bramante had removed a dozen more bricks to enlarge the hole, and stacked them in a neat pile.

"Did I not leave instructions that nothing was to be touched?" Castano asked sourly.

"You expect the Holy Father to lie on his belly to peer inside?" Bramante replied.

"You had no authority —"

"This is my construction site," Bramante insisted.

"But it is God's basilica. And you are an architect, not a priest."

"Are we ready, gentlemen?" Domenico interrupted, nipping the argument in the bud.

"As ready as we'll ever be," Bramante replied.

Domenico called up, "Safe to proceed!"

All eyes turned to the Pope's temporary throne as it inched up into the air and was swung into the space above the chasm. Pope Julius flinched as the ground disappeared from under him, then quickly clenched his fists — the Warrior Pope could not afford to show fear.

Castano had no such reservations, and for the second time that morning the blood drained from his face. "This is madness," he whispered.

"You insisted he come," Bramante replied.

"I didn't want him suspended like a chandelier!"

"Actually, I think it's a rather ingenious solution."

"Until the rope slips."

"You should have more faith in my men," Bramante chided.

Domenico refused to engage with the bickering because he was focussed entirely on the figure of the Pope that now floated high above him. He listened to the rhythmic creak of the ropes and pulleys, braced for any twitch that might herald disaster. The army of labourers on the surface all gazed in wonder at the bizarre vision of His Holiness Pope Julius II, Supreme Pontiff, Bishop of Rome and Leader of the Papal States, being hoisted like a bull into a ship's hold. It was incredible that no-one laughed, for despite the solemnity, there was something ludicrous about the spectacle.

With incredible precision, the rope-men lowered the Pope until his chair gently touched down on the bottom of the pit. Pope Julius' eyes fell on the black hole in the brickwork. "In there, I presume?"

"We have prepared a lantern, Your Holiness," Castano replied.

Pope Julius stood up and walked the few paces to the brickwork, while Domenico lowered the lantern into the mysterious chamber. The Pope leant forward and squinted as he peered into the gloom.

Silence.

Finally he shook his head. "This is absurd. I can't see anything from here."

"Perhaps Your Holiness would allow me to go down into the chamber?" Bramante suggested.

"This is a spiritual matter," Castano interrupted. "It requires a priest."

"No, it's a technical matter," Bramante insisted. "An engineer needs to assess the safety of the structure."

"What are the risks of collapse?" Pope Julius asked.

Bramante frowned. "Impossible to say, Your Holiness."

"Hardly an inspiring answer," Castano muttered.

"It depends on the size of the chamber, and how well the brick vaulting was constructed."

"And yet it has stood for ten centuries," Pope Julius observed.

"Because it has been undisturbed," Bramante explained. "The moment one starts to excavate, the equilibrium is upset."

Pope Julius turned to Domenico. "What do you think, Capitano?"

"I am happy to go down first, Your Holiness, to make sure it is stable."

"Very well." Pope Julius nodded to Bramante. "You'd better enlarge the hole."

Immediately Bramante set to work with a hammer and chisel, carefully removing more bricks and passing them to Castano, who handled them with ostentatious reverence, as if each brick had been touched by St Peter himself.

Domenico was wary of men like Castano, men who were so obsessed with following the orders of their superiors they made themselves effectively irrelevant. Domenico had discovered early in his military career that one of the myths of soldiering is that a great army is built on complete obedience.

Far from it. Victories in battle often came from the brilliant initiatives of those on the front line, and good generals valued captains who knew when to disagree. It was something the conformists of this world would never understand.

"Is that enough, Holy Father?" Castano beckoned to the enlarged hole.

"Let's find out."

Domenico climbed into the chair and signalled to Bramante, who shouted instructions up to the rope-men. There was a jolt as the chair lifted off the mud, then Bramante gently guided it until Domenico was hanging directly over the hole in the cavern roof.

"Ready?"

Domenico nodded.

"Lower it slowly!" Bramante called up.

The pulley wheels creaked, and Domenico started to descend into the gloom of the unknown.

"Look for any signs of movement or cracking in the walls," Bramante instructed. "There may be trickles of dust or water. All those show structural weakness."

"Understood," Domenico replied.

"But touch nothing," Castano warned. "No relics must be touched until the Holy Father has seen them. You hear me?"

Domenico didn't bother to reply. He just held up the lantern as darkness devoured him.

4: REVELATION

No-one had been in this space for over a thousand years. Perhaps the Roman Emperor Constantine had been the last man to breathe the air in here before the sacred tomb was sealed. It made Domenico feel as if he was walking with giants.

As the chair touched the rough ground and the ropes went slack, Domenico held up his lantern, trying to commit everything to memory before it was disturbed.

Beautifully painted inverted crosses, the symbol of St Peter, had been etched on each of the walls. Underneath them were frescoes depicting scenes from the Bible: a bearded man fishing from a boat (perhaps the Sea of Galilee?), the same man preaching in the catacombs, sharing the last supper with Christ, then ascending to Heaven in the year AD66. Domenico lowered his lantern — broken fragments of pots were scattered across the floor, and in the centre of the space was a simple stone sarcophagus. He peered closer but could see no engravings on the tomb's smooth grey faces.

Domenico's skin tingled. This was St Peter's tomb. It had to be. The evidence here was all consistent with the saint's life, which meant he was now just a few feet from the most sacred relics in Christendom.

"You're looking!" the voice called accusingly from above. "After I specifically forbade it!"

Domenico glanced up and saw Castano's fierce eyes peering through the hole in the roof.

"How can I assess its safety if I don't look?"

"Not the relics!" Castano replied. "Don't look at the relics."

"*Stronzo*," Domenico whispered under his breath, then remembering that he was in the presence of a saint, crossed himself and asked for forgiveness.

He swept the lantern in an arc to inspect the structure of the underground chamber. The walls had been hewn into the rock and smoothed by hand, but there were no piles of fallen stone suggesting subsequent movement, nor any trickles of water flowing from fissures. He studied the vaulted brick ceiling — it had been beautifully constructed in a herringbone pattern, yet despite its age and the enormous weight it had endured, showed no signs of cracking.

"Well?" Castano demanded.

"I think it's safe."

"Think? Or know?"

"It's stable."

"Very well. Step to one side. The Holy Father will descend."

Domenico watched as the chair was hoisted back up through the hole in the ceiling, then moments later reappeared carrying Pope Julius, eyes wide with anticipation.

As it touched down, Pope Julius saw the stone sarcophagus and immediately rocked forward onto his knees in supplication. Suddenly ashamed of having been so casual, Domenico did the same.

Both men stared at the tomb in silence.

"Thou art Peter, and upon this rock I will build my church," Pope Julius whispered. Then he crawled across the rough floor, leant forward and gently kissed the side of the tomb.

Domenico was unsure what was expected of him. Should he do the same, like a pilgrim? Or was kissing the tomb a privilege of popes? Then he noticed that Pope Julius was looking anxious and running his fingers along the side of the tomb lid.

"Is something wrong, Holy Father?"

"It's broken."

"I don't understand…"

"Look closer."

Domenico approached on his knees until he was just behind Pope Julius. "I don't see any cracks, Holy Father."

"Not the stone. The seal." Pope Julius pointed to the dark line where the lid met the body of the tomb. "Once it was sealed. Now all the wax is broken."

Domenico adjusted the lantern and saw fragments of crumbled wax in the gap. "Could it have perished with age?"

"And why are the pots broken?" Pope Julius pointed to the fragments scattered across the floor. "Who disturbed them?"

"What are you saying, Your Holiness?"

"We must look inside."

Domenico felt a shudder of apprehension. "Disturb holy relics?"

"Can you slide the lid off?"

Domenic didn't move. He was caught between fear of the Pope, and fear of the Divine.

"I am ordering you, as Supreme Pontiff of the Universal Church, to remove the lid from this sarcophagus," Pope Julius glared at Domenico. "Remember, God speaks through me."

What choice did Domenico have? He stood up, positioned the palms of his hands on the side of the lid, and pushed.

Nothing happened. The stones had sat next to each other for so many centuries they had started to fuse.

"Use your sword," Pope Julius instructed.

"Are you sure?"

"Do it."

Domenico drew his sword, silently asked St Peter for forgiveness, then ran the blade gently along the crack between the lid and the casket, removing any remaining fragments of wax. He braced his knees against the stone, locked his hands on the side of the lid and tried again. Domenico grunted with effort, the blood vessels on the side of his head pumped and pain shot through his fingers.

A staccato grinding of stone against stone echoed through the chamber, then abruptly stopped. Movement. Domenico looked to Pope Julius for reassurance.

"Go on," Pope Julius instructed. "Do not be afraid."

Domenico braced again and pushed with all his might. Suddenly one end of the stone lid swung round, exposing half of the sarcophagus.

Domenico stepped back fearfully. Pope Julius picked up the lantern, held it over the tomb and peered inside.

There was a strange moment of inflexion in the Pope's bearing, as if disappointment was wrapping its arms around him.

"What is it, Holy Father?" Domenico whispered.

"You've seen death on the battlefield," Pope Julius replied. "Tell me, what do you see here?" He extended his arm, inviting Domenico to approach.

But Domenico couldn't move.

"Tell me," Pope Julius repeated. "Now!"

Anxiously Domenico edged towards the open tomb, leant forward and looked inside. He didn't want to believe what his eyes were telling him. "I don't understand, Holy Father."

"What do you see?"

Domenico shook his head. He could feel tears pricking the backs of his eyes.

"What do you see, Domenico?" Pope Julius' patience was wearing thin.

"A skull. Some ribs. Leg bones. But … these are not human bones. They are…"

"Say it."

"I believe this is a sheep's skeleton, Holy Father."

"There are no human remains, are there?"

"No," Domenico whispered. "I'm afraid not."

"The shrine says St Peter. But the bones say farm animals."

Pope Julius lowered his head into his hands and wept.

5: OBSCURA

Life didn't get much better than this. Cristina Falchoni was alone in her private library, she had locked all the chaos of the world securely on the other side of the mahogany doors, and was now surrounded by hundreds of architectural drawings and engineering plans for the new St Peter's Basilica.

Chief Architect Bramante was keenly aware of how critical Cristina's intervention had been during the design competition, and he knew that without her, his vision for the basilica would never have triumphed. As a mark of gratitude, he had included her on the list of people to whom the ever-evolving designs were circulated. This select group met every Friday morning under the architect's rooftop pavilion to discuss progress, and at first Cristina had enjoyed the vigorous discussions. Sadly, it wasn't long before the meetings became bogged down in pointless arguments, as each man tried to outdo the others. Why did men have to turn everything into a battle for dominance? Why couldn't they show some humility in the face of such an inspiring project?

To preserve her sanity, Cristina retreated to the solitude of her library where she could study the drawings in peace, then put her comments and suggestions in a series of letters which her housekeeper, Isra, hand-delivered to Bramante. Right now, Cristina was preoccupied with the problem of the foundation pits for the great piers: how deep did they really have to be?

She knew how deep Bramante was digging them, but why? How had he made that decision? As far as Cristina could tell, it was all down to tradition and experience. The same went for the dimensions of the piers: they were that size because over the centuries, trial and error had taught builders what worked and what didn't. But Cristina found all this frustratingly vague. You couldn't rely on 'tradition', as the residents of Ely in England had discovered just a few years earlier when the entire northwest transept of their cathedral had collapsed in a spectacular cataclysm.

No, there must be a better way to determine the correct depth of foundations and the true strength of supporting walls. Perhaps the answer lay in mathematics? Could the manipulation of numbers exert real power over the physical world? Were there universal laws of mechanics waiting to be discovered?

Cristina stood up and rubbed her eyes, trying to relieve the tension. For several months Isra had been nagging her to consult a physician in case she needed a pair of eyeglasses, but Cristina refused. She wasn't a vain woman, but felt that thirty-four was too young to start looking like a matriarch.

A short break was all she needed. Once her head was clear she could start again.

Cristina grabbed a beaker of wine and bounded up the stairs to the top floor of the house, then entered the room that faced west over the River Tiber, where she had turned what was once a guest room into an extraordinary optical device: a *camera obscura*

The previous autumn, she had met Leonardo da Vinci on one of his visits to Rome. After discussing several ways of recording the different construction stages of St Peter's, Leonardo had given her a Latin translation of the *Book of Optics*, written by the Arab scholar Ibn al-Haytham five hundred years earlier. It detailed experiments with light, and included a description of a dark chamber which only allowed light to enter through a small pinhole. Intrigued, Cristina set about constructing one for herself…

She painted the floor, ceiling and three of the walls in the top floor guest room black; the wall opposite the bank of windows was painted white, and all the windows were closed off with wooden shutters, except for the middle window, where a small aperture had been drilled in the wood, allowing light to pass through.

The result was impressive: the entire view to the west of the city was now projected in incredible detail onto the white wall of the room. Cristina could observe people walking in the street, birds flying overhead, and trees shimmering in the wind. Crucially, she could see the Vatican, which meant that she could now watch St Peter's grow, stone by stone, while sitting in the privacy and comfort of her own home. The plan was that once a month she would trace an image directly from the projection onto a huge sheet of vellum, gradually building an archive of hundreds of accurate drawings detailing the birth of St Peter's Basilica.

Cristina ran her fingers over the projection, imagining how the Roman skyline would be transformed for all eternity, when suddenly she noticed the army of workers walking off the construction site. She crouched down to look closer — the men were flowing *away* from the Vatican in all directions, like a river that had burst its banks, spreading through the maze of densely packed streets that led down to Castel Sant'Angelo. But it was the middle of the afternoon, construction work should be going at full pitch. Why was the site closing? Had one of the great foundation pits collapsed?

Cristina hurtled down the steps and out of the house without even grabbing a cloak. She barged through the street markets that led down to the Tiber, and pushed past the crowds on Ponte Sant'Angelo.

She had been cooped up in the house for so long, the fresh, cool air billowing up from the river made Cristina feel momentarily intoxicated, but there was no time to pause; she pressed on, running through the dizziness.

As she pushed against the tide of construction workers moving in the opposite direction, Cristina repeatedly tried to find out what was going on, but was met with a barrage of shrugs.

"*No idea.*"

"*They don't tell us nothing.*"

"*Another day's pay lost.*"

"*The usual chaos. Same old, same old.*"

When Cristina finally made it to the basilica, she found the whole of the construction site cordoned off by Apostolic Guards.

"What's going on?" she demanded.

"Move away, signorina."

"Why have they closed the site down?"

"Last warning! Be on your way."

"Listen," she persisted, "my brother is Domenico Falchoni, Captain of the Apostolic Guard —"

"Yeah. And my brother's the Pope."

"I'm serious!"

"So am I. Move away, or you'll be under arrest."

"*Vaffanculo!*" Cristina muttered, and hurried along the cordon to try and find a more amenable guard. At the entrance to the stonemasons' yard, she spotted her brother's deputy, Tomasso, organising his men.

"Tomasso!" Cristina called out as she approached. "What on earth's going on?"

"You can't be here, Cristina. The site's closed."

"But why? What's happened?"

"They're not saying."

"It doesn't make any sense."

"We're under strict orders to clear the whole area."

"I need to find Domenico." She tried to duck under the cordon rope, but Tomasso grabbed her arm.

"Please. Don't."

"Seriously?" Cristina wriggled her arm free.

"Our orders are to arrest anyone who disobeys."

"I'm not just anyone, Tomasso."

"You are today."

Cristina hesitated. Something serious was going on. Serious and bad. "Have the foundation pits collapsed?"

"Stop guessing and go home. Please, Cristina."

"What else could cause such a panic?"

"Our orders are clear. No exceptions."

"Don't tell me they accidentally dug up St Peter's tomb," Cristina quipped.

Tomasso winced. "Why couldn't you just do as I asked?"

Cristina gazed at him. "Wait. What? I was joking."

But Tomasso was already reaching for the hand restraints clipped to his belt.

"Seriously? They've found the tomb?"

"Just. Stop. Talking."

"No!"

"Please!"

"All I did was ask a question."

"The wrong question." Tomasso clamped the irons around Cristina's wrists. "And now you're under arrest. I'm sorry."

6: STAKES

Only the most trusted had been summoned to the Pope's private study. There were no scribes or secretaries, nor any servants or bodyguards.

Domenico, Chief Architect Bramante, Geometra Castano and Cardinal Riario stood in silence, waiting for Pope Julius to marshal his thoughts.

"As I understand it, all those who know the disturbing truth are now stood before me." Pope Julius's eyes moved from one man to the next, assessing each one's integrity. "And that is the way it must stay. If we are to survive, the truth must be suppressed, because the metaphysical core of the Vatican *is* St Peter's tomb. We are called the Holy Roman Church because of his tomb, and if that is compromised..." He fell silent, fearful of completing the sentence and spelling out the consequences.

"Forgive me, Holy Father." Bramante ran his fingers through the mop of curls on the side of his head. "But perhaps this new discovery has been blown out of proportion. My new basilica will truly glorify God. Set against that, does it really matter where a saint's bones are buried?"

Pope Julius glared at Bramante. "Do you not understand the significance of your own design?"

"It was never intended to be a memorial to St Peter —"

"Look at it!" Pope Julius grabbed one of the architectural drawings from his desk and hurled it at Bramante. "Do you not understand what you have drawn? The Dome will rise directly over St Peter's tomb, symbolising the transcendent Christ. The arms of the basilica stretch out in equal length from the dome, symbolising the universal Church reaching out to the four corners of the world. But if all that is centred on nothing but sheep's bones, then your basilica will be mocking God, not glorifying Him!"

No-one dared speak for a few agonising minutes.

The men stood in silence, heads bowed, until the supreme diplomat, Cardinal Riario, judged that the Holy Father had calmed down sufficiently. "Apart from His Holiness, who actually *saw* the sheep's bones inside the sarcophagus? Saw with their own eyes?"

"I did," Domenico replied. "And so did the geometra."

"But only from a distance," Castana explained, "through the hole in the vault's ceiling. I didn't actually get close."

"What about the construction workers?"

"Most of them were too far away," Bramante replied.

"The few who were close enough to realise that something was wrong have been detained in solitary confinement," Domenico added.

"Namely?"

"The foreman. And two of his assistants."

"So in fact," Cardinal Riario's eyes surveyed the witnesses then settled on Pope Julius, "this situation can be contained quite easily. All we need is to guarantee the silence of a few good men."

Castano sank to his knees in submission. "Holy Father, my loyalty to the Church is beyond question. I will only see what you tell me I saw."

"Not quite the absolute silence I was thinking of," Cardinal Riario replied.

Castano blinked. "I don't understand."

But Domenico understood perfectly; Cardinal Riario was talking about assassination to protect a holy secret and prevent a scandal.

The air in the roomed seemed to cool a few degrees.

Domenico had no choice but to bluff. "I have been in the Vatican long enough to understand how things work, Cardinal Riario. Which is why I have written down everything I witnessed today, and lodged the document securely with lawyers. Just in case."

Anger darkened Cardinal Riario's face. "You would dare to blackmail the Holy Father?"

"You would threaten to have me murdered?"

"Don't be absurd!" Cardinal Riario scoffed. "You are being hysterical! Putting words into my mouth."

"If not murder," Domenico persisted, "then perhaps you would have me locked away in some monastery in the middle of nowhere."

"How dare you speak to me like that! I am a cardinal, not some Sicilian thug!"

In other circumstances, Cardinal Riario's anger would have been enough to end a man's career, but the Pope liked Domenico's willingness to speak out. "You have nothing to fear, Capitano Falchoni," Pope Julius reassured.

"Thank you, Holy Father."

"But … as you witnessed what cannot be witnessed, you must also be part of the solution."

"What solution can there possibly be?" Bramante mused. "If the bones aren't there, they aren't there."

"As it happens, I do know someone who we could turn to for help," Domenico suggested.

"Out of the question," Cardinal Riario interrupted. "We cannot widen this circle and let another person know the truth."

"I will hear this," Pope Julius said firmly.

"Her vast and unorthodox learning may provide a solution."

"Her?" Castano said with contempt.

"My sister has devoted her life to defending the vision of a new St Peter's. She has proved her loyalty time and again. She has even put her life in jeopardy for it."

"That maybe so," Pope Julius frowned, "but it does not excuse you for telling her what you witnessed."

"I didn't. Cristina deduced it for herself, Holy Father," Domenico replied. "And I fear she will not be the only one. So I suggest we summon her without delay."

7: DETAINED

It was unclear how official this arrest was.

They had taken Cristina to her brother's office in the barracks under the Vatican and removed her wrist restraints, but they had also locked the door and positioned a guard outside, so any thought of leaving was out of the question.

For the first hour, Cristina sat in silence, eavesdropping on passing conversations in the corridor outside, but that had left her none the wiser. She spent the next hour trying to persuade the guard on the door that there had been a terrible misunderstanding, and if he would let her talk to a lawyer, this whole situation could be swiftly resolved. The guard ignored her. So Cristina lapsed into stoical silence … until she heard Tomasso's voice crossing the parade yard.

She clambered onto one of the desks, peered through a high window and saw him giving instructions to a squad of Apostolic Guards. As they hurried off to carry out their orders, Cristina whistled to him. "Tomasso! Over here!"

He glanced across and shook his head. "You have to be patient, Cristina."

"I thought we were friends?"

"This has come from the very top. Strict orders."

"Won't you at least come and explain it to me?" Cristina pleaded. "Waiting without knowing why is unbearable."

Tomasso looked around the courtyard to check that no-one was watching, then reluctantly strode towards the door leading to the offices. "I really should know better," he grumbled to himself.

Cristina jumped down from the desk and sat in the chair, trying to look obedient. A few moments later a heavy key rattled in the lock, the door swung open and Tomasso entered.

"Thank you for saving me," Cristina smiled.

"I'm not. And you can't leave this office until the Pope allows it."

"The Pope?" Cristina wondered exactly what she had done to ruffle such powerful feathers.

"Have they given you any food?" Tomasso asked.

"I'm not interested in eating. I just want to understand the logic that has put me here."

"I can't say anything, Cristina."

"But think about it," she persisted. "St Peter's Basilica is famous for being built over the saint's tomb. So why would speculating about whether they've discovered it get me arrested?"

Tomasso shook his head. "Don't try and coax any more out of me."

"What exactly were your orders? Which particular words prompted my arrest? Surely you can tell me that much?"

But Tomasso wasn't playing Cristina's game, and when he looked up he didn't try to hide the hurt in his eyes. "Now you want a favour? Now? After ignoring me for the past year?"

"I ... I've not been ignoring you."

"When was the last time we had a proper conversation?"

"Things have been frantic," she frowned. "Do you know how many drawings have been completed for the design? Thousands! Everything from the carvings above the porticos to the precise taper of the columns. And every single one needs to be checked."

"We've all been busy, Cristina."

As she looked at the deputy, Cristina was surprised to find herself wrestling with feelings of guilt. Tomasso was right, she had ignored him, but not just him; she had blocked out the entire world to focus on work. But now that he was sitting in front of her, Cristina realised how much she had missed Tomasso's affable manner. There were no hidden agendas with Tomasso, just a desire to make the best of wherever he found himself. Not so long ago, Cristina would have been contemptuous of such a philosophy, scornful of its lack of ambition. But now she was coming to understand that it took a lot of skill to set your compass to contentment and hold a steady course, no matter what the crosswinds.

"I'm sorry," she said quietly. "I didn't mean to ignore you."

It was like a benign breeze in Tomasso's sails. His eyes seemed to glint as he looked up. "Do you really mean that?"

"I wouldn't have said it if I didn't." Immediately Cristina realised that she sounded too brusque. Isra had warned her about this on countless occasions; *It's like dancing,* Isra loved to say, *you need to repeat moves again and again to show people what you mean. Once is never enough.*

"You're just being nice because you want something." Tomasso turned to go.

"Wait." Cristina reached out and touched his arm. "I'm sorry I've been so reclusive. And I have missed you."

Tomasso looked at Cristina's hand on his arm, then shifted his gaze to her face. "Do you know how much that means to me?" he whispered.

Was this another beat in the dance? Was Cristina expected to repeat her move or change it?

Before she could decide, the door flew open and Domenico strode in. "You've been summoned by Pope Julius. I hope you have some solutions."

Immediately Cristina's mind veered into a different orbit. "You haven't even told me what the problem is."

"The problem is you were right. They've dug up St Peter's tomb."

"But that's incredible news, isn't it?"

"It would be if the tomb wasn't empty."

"What?" Cristina felt her legs weaken and she slumped back into the chair. "That's impossible."

"It's worse than that. The sarcophagus contains animal bones."

"That makes no sense. How could it have happened?"

"That is exactly what the Pope is going to ask you in the next twenty minutes. So you'd better start thinking, Cristina."

8: SAN MARCO

Cristina felt the enormous weight of expectation pressing on her. She stood in the middle of the Pope's private study under the intense gaze of the Holy Father, Chief Architect Bramante, Cardinal Riario and Geometra Castano. The only person who could possibly be said to be on her side was Domenico.

"They're all ears," he whispered to her.

What could she say? How could she solve the problem of the missing relics? If they were gone, they were gone. Nothing she could do would change that. Yet if she said nothing, Cristina knew that Conclave would never again turn to her for advice, and she had fought too hard for acceptance to let that happen. She needed time to think, and the best way to buy time was to talk…

"Holy Father, there are so many legends surrounding the foundation of Venice, it is hard to know which to believe, and which to dismiss as the fabrications of drunken chroniclers."

"Venice?" Pope Julius interrupted. "Why should I be interested in Venice? What is the relevance?"

"*La Serenissima* is so wealthy and its trading arms so long, many rival states have looked at Venice with envious eyes, hoping to discover the secret of its success. In truth, for the first five hundred years of its existence, Venice was a minor city, conquered and reconquered by different powers as their fortunes waxed and waned across the Adriatic. But in the 9th century, everything changed.

"The city rulers decided that to be truly prosperous, Venice needed to be feared and respected. And to that end, its fate had to be bound up with one of the great founding fathers of the Church. But how could that be achieved? When Christ's disciples scattered after the Crucifixion, Venice was just a shambolic collection of huts on wooden stilts, balanced precariously on the mud of the lagoon. It was inconceivable that any disciple would have shown interest in such a godforsaken place.

"Undeterred, the Venetian rulers decided to steal the bones of St Mark from their final resting place in Egypt and claim them for Venice. So one winter's night in the year 827, two merchants, Buono da Malamocco and Rustico da Torcello, landed in the Muslim-controlled city of Alexandria, claiming to seek shelter from a storm.

"It was a lie — there had been no storm, and they were not merchants, but spies. To maintain their cover, Malamocco and Torcello went to the markets every day to trade, but each evening they made their way to the chapel containing the tomb of St Mark. They befriended two of the monks who guarded the relics, and little by little, they started dropping worrying stories into the conversations…

"'You do realise that your Arab governor is planning to destroy all the Christian churches in Alexandria?' they lied. 'He wants to send the marble east to build a fabulous palace in the ancient city of Babylon.'

"At first, the monks refused to believe that anyone would contemplate such a barbaric act of vandalism. But night after night, the merchants repeated their lies. 'Christianity is doomed under Islam.' 'You and your church will be erased from the face of Egypt.' 'The Muslim may smile to your face, but in his heart there is hatred for all Christians.'

"After a month of steadily dripped deception, the monks found themselves caught in a state of fear and suspicion. And that was when the two merchants sprung their trap.

"'There is a way out of this terrible situation,' Malamocco ventured. 'It is dangerous, but that is a risk we are prepared to take.'

"'We are willing to sacrifice our own lives to save the holy relics of St Mark,' Torcello said gravely. 'If that is our Christian destiny, so be it.'

"With great shows of piety, the two merchants offered to smuggle both the monks and the sacred relics out of Alexandria, transport them across the Mediterranean, and give them sanctuary in the heart of Venice where they would be safe. By now, the monks were in such fear, they eagerly agreed.

"So the plans were set; in the dead of night the monks unlocked the chapel gates and fled. Malamocco and Torcello stole the bones of St Mark and hid them in a wicker basket, then covered the relics with cabbage leaves and pork.

"See the two merchants in your mind's eye, Your Holiness, hurrying through the dark, narrow alleys, playing a deadly game of cat and mouse with the night watch, until finally they reached the port only to realise their plans were in disarray. The monks had been tasked with creating a distraction, but they had failed, and now Malamocco and Torcello had to get past the heavily armed customs officers.

"The two merchants held their nerve. As they approached the gates, they obligingly pulled back the awning covering the basket. The first customs officer opened the wicker lid, peered inside and immediately recoiled in disgust.

"'Flesh of the pig!' he screamed. A meat unclean to Muslims. Covering his mouth, the customs officer waved the cart through, glad to see the back of it. Malamocco and Torcello hurried to their ship, loaded the precious cargo into the hold, and slipped their moorings.

"Yet still the merchants were not safe, for as they crossed the Mediterranean, a terrible storm blew up and their ship started to sink. Just when all hope seemed lost, an apparition of St Mark appeared to the sailors, and guided them through the tempest.

"On 31st January 828, the holy relics of St Mark's body landed in Venice. They were placed in the Ducal Palace, where they would remain until a new cathedral was built to house them — the great Basilica di San Marco.

"It was a decisive moment in Venetian history. Blessed by the bones of St Mark, Venice went on to build the formidable empire that it controls today. The wealth, prestige, and power of *La Serenissima* are inextricably bound up with the bones of Saint Mark."

Cristina fell silent. She glanced around the room, and as she studied the mesmerised expressions on the men's faces, she understood what needed to be done.

9: POWER

"And yet," said Cardinal Riario as he scrutinised Cristina, "from what I know about your intellect, the divine power of relics is not something to which you give much credence."

"My personal beliefs do not matter here," Cristina replied. "Whether or not St Mark's bones have any supernatural power is irrelevant. The point is, ordinary Venetians believe the sacred relics make them special, the chosen people of the Mediterranean, and they have lived up to their ambitions. Self-belief can be self-fulfilling."

"Which is bad news for Rome," Pope Julius said grimly.

"Precisely, Your Holiness. Because the reverse is also true: if St Peter's bones have disappeared, the collapse in confidence and morale could be devastating. To many it would feel as if God has turned His back on this city."

"You see?" Pope Julius turned accusingly to Bramante. "She gets it. She understands the significance of all this."

"So you are asking me to steal the bones of another saint? And bury them under my basilica?" Bramante replied petulantly.

"We don't have to," Cristina interjected, hoping to prevent Pope Julius' anger from flaring up. "The real point of the story is *La Serenissima*'s determination. The Venetians refused to be beaten, they moved Heaven and Earth to grasp their destiny, and so must we. But we have an advantage: we *know* that St Peter's bones are somewhere in Rome. He lived here and preached here, he was executed here. He had followers, people who loved him and regarded him as a leader. His body would have been cared for after death. His relics would have been treasured and hidden from the authorities."

"That was fifteen hundred years ago," Pope Julius replied. "A lot has happened in this city since then."

"He is not lost, Your Holiness. I genuinely believe that. He is just hidden."

"Then where exactly do you suggest we start looking?" Cardinal Riario seemed determined to focus on the worst possible outcome.

Cristina brushed off his pessimism and strode to the large map of Rome hanging behind the Pope's desk. "We must be guided by logic, and a close analysis of this city." Cristina pointed to some of the oldest streets and piazzas. "Modern Rome, the city we inhabit, is built on layers of the past. There are traces of ancient history all around us. Building materials have been reused time and again. Ancient stones and inscriptions turn up in modern porticos and palazzos. There is meaning in every monument we stroll past, because everything is built on the ruins of something else. The clues are here." She ran her hands over the map. "We just have to find them, and unravel them."

"But there are over a hundred and thirty churches alone," Castano said wearily. "And countless thousands of graves in the catacombs."

"Then we do not have a moment to lose. We must start searching today."

"And in the meantime, this must be kept a closely guarded secret." As ever, Cardinal Riario's mind was focussed more on the political than the spiritual. "The only people who can know about this crisis are the ones trying to resolve it."

"What about the builders being held in custody?" Domenico asked. "The foreman and his assistants?"

"Keep them locked up and in isolation," Cristina replied.

"But they are innocent. They were just doing their jobs."

"They must have contact with no-one," Cardinal Riario insisted.

"On what charges?"

"On my specific orders," Pope Julius pronounced.

Domenico knew better than to argue with the Warrior Pope. "I understand, Your Holiness."

But Bramante had more practical concerns. "And what of the building work on the piers? That must continue."

"The construction site is to remain closed until we have found the relics," Pope Julius replied.

"But that could take months."

"The Holy Father has spoken," Cardinal Riario scolded.

"I do not accept that!" the architect exclaimed.

"Mind your tongue, Bramante."

"You cannot leave a yawning chasm in the ground! A great building is not a painting that can just be put aside. The walls of the pit will crumble, the entire thing could collapse and take down the Old Basilica with it!"

"In which case," Pope Julius turned to Cristina, "you have two weeks to find the relics."

"But that's not long enough!" Cristina exclaimed.

"It will have to be. Because that's all you have. Search every archive, follow every clue, find St Peter."

"I will try, Your Holiness."

"No. You will succeed. Because we cannot afford to fail." Pope Julius turned his gaze on Bramante. "As for you, shore up the walls of the pits, then close the entire construction site down. This is my command."

10: TEXTS

Naturally, Cristina told her esteemed friend and mentor everything. How could Professor De Luca help solve the problem if he didn't know the true scale of it? In any case, he had been Cristina's trusted confidante for the past fifteen years, educating her in secret when all the doors of academia were slammed in her face simply because she was a woman. Working as a team was the only chance they stood of meeting the Pope's impossible deadline.

Isra turned the library benches into temporary daybeds, so that Cristina and De Luca could take it in turns to grab some rest in between their onerous bouts of research, then she made two huge pots of food which she left simmering over the kitchen fire: a quail stew and a *ribollita*, so there would always be a choice of meal, day and night.

Finally, she placed a box of spare candles in the middle of the table, then looked up at Cristina, who was perched on the stepladder pulling some books from a high shelf.

"Will there be anything else, mistress?" Isra asked, keeping up the public display of hierarchy so that she wouldn't betray their close friendship.

Cristina smiled at the pretence. "Not unless you want to comb through a few hundred pages before dawn. You'd better grab some sleep while you can. And thank you for making us so comfortable in here."

"My pleasure." Isra picked up a lamp to guide her way back down the moonlit stairs, and closed the library doors behind her.

Professor De Luca stretched his arms and looked up at the verge-and-foliot clock, which was now surrounded by a chaotic jumble of hastily scribbled notes that had been stuck to the wall. "It's getting very confusing," he confessed. "I simply can't see a way forward. My mind is just circling around the same ideas."

"We need to organise everything into strands of probability." Cristina slid down the bookcase ladder and started rearranging all the pieces of paper into a new pattern. When she had finished, the clock looked like a strange sun-god with three shafts of paper radiating from its body.

De Luca frowned. "Now I'm even more confused."

"This strand," Cristina pointed to the one on the left, "is unlikely but possible. Whereas this one is credible but unproved. And this one," she touched the shaft of paper notes rising vertically from the clock, "is beyond doubt. If we use reason to build on the known facts, we can't go far wrong."

"Run through them again."

"St Peter was executed at the Circus of Nero, which is now beneath the foundations of the Old Basilica."

"Agreed."

"It was an early Christian tradition that martyrs should be buried as near as possible to the scene of their suffering."

"Also agreed."

"So it is highly likely that St Peter was buried in the necropolis on Vatican Hill."

"I'm not sure that is beyond doubt, Cristina. But it is certainly logical."

"Now, when construction of the Old Basilica began, the necropolis was partially torn down and filled with earth to clear the site. Everyone believed St Peter's tomb was preserved and buried safely under the foundations."

"But everyone was wrong. The tomb was buried, but not the bones."

"So the bones must have been moved."

"But they may have been moved much earlier." De Luca picked up a fragment of paper and handed it to Cristina. "Put that on the wall as well. Fifty years before the first basilica was started, Christian persecution was particularly savage. Under the Emperor Valerian, I believe. So maybe the relics were moved to preserve them from desecration?"

"Perhaps." Cristina added the note to the 'credible but unproved' strand. "But Christians still needed to worship at St Peter's shrine. Surely some clue would have been left for his followers."

"Not necessarily." De Luca frowned. "It could all have been done in secret."

"Either way, the next confirmed mention is in the *Liber Pontificalis*, the Book of Popes," Cristina opened a huge, leather-bound illuminated manuscript and placed it in the centre of the table. "This clearly sets out the embellishments Constantine made to St Peter's tomb. He enclosed the sarcophagus with bronze, and placed a huge gold cross on top of it."

"None of which were found yesterday," De Luca observed.

"Because the Saracens looted all the treasure when they sacked the basilica in the 9th century."

"But they wouldn't dig down into the foundations to steal from a buried tomb, would they? Excavation is not looting. So the *Liber Pontificalis* contradicts all the other evidence."

"Someone must be lying."

"But who?"

They lapsed into silence, their minds wrestling with the competing fragments of evidence.

"What if?" Cristina started pacing the room. "What if … from the very outset, St Peter's tomb contained animal bones?"

"That makes no sense."

"The early Christians could have created a *false* tomb with animal bones, to throw everyone off the scent, while the real tomb was actually located elsewhere."

"It's a possibility," De Luca conceded. "Of course, that means the relics could be absolutely anywhere."

Cristina sighed. "What do we think about Quo Vadis?"

"Remind me again."

"It's in the apocryphal. It describes St Peter fleeing from Rome to escape persecution. On the Appian Way he sees a vision of Christ coming towards him. '*Quo vadis?* Where are you going?' Peter asks. 'I am going to Rome to be crucified again,' Jesus replies. The two men return together. Near that spot where they met, a church was built containing a sacred stone. On that stone are the footprints of Christ."

"Allegedly."

"Surely that church would be a sensible place to hide the relics of St Peter? Outside the city walls, so far less likely to be desecrated."

"We should go and investigate," De Luca replied, "if we can't find a more compelling clue. But it will take up precious time that we do not have."

Suddenly a heavy knocking boomed through the house; someone was hammering on the front doors.

"At this hour?" Cristina glanced at the clock — it was nearly two in the morning.

Boom! Boom! The fists hammered again.

"Are you going to answer it?" De Luca whispered.

"I'm afraid Isra will have to cut her sleep short."

"She won't be happy," the professor muttered. "Mind you, housekeepers never are."

But De Luca didn't really know Isra at all.

Far from sleeping, Isra had been busy hiding weapons at key points throughout the house; she feared this business of the missing relics was going to draw them into dark waters, and wanted to be well prepared.

Cautiously, she slid back the hatch in the front door and held a lantern up to the grille. A monk in a tattered brown habit was standing in the porch, the hood of his cowl pulled down over his face.

"Who is it?" Isra demanded. "Show yourself."

"I have a message for Cristina Falchoni." The man's voice had a strange rasp, as if his throat had been damaged in a fight.

"Do you seriously think I'm going to open this door in the middle of the night?"

"My message is important."

"Come back in the morning."

"You are too distrusting."

"Actually," Isra corrected, "I think I've got just the right level of suspicion."

"What harm can a man such as me do?" The monk raised a hand and drew the hood from his face.

Instinctively, Isra recoiled — the man's skin was cratered with smallpox scars, his eyebrows were missing, and his eyes were milky with blindness.

"What happened to you?"

"I am more sinned against than sinning," the monk croaked. "It is pity I deserve, not fear. Now please, child, fetch your mistress."

11: TIP-OFF

"You didn't recognise him?" Cristina asked as she followed Isra into the kitchen.

"No. And it's a face I would remember."

"Then I'm surprised you let him in at all."

"He wouldn't leave until he'd spoken with you. And to be honest, he didn't seem like a threat."

"Seem? How many times have you told me off for being taken in by first impressions?"

"Well, judge for yourself." Isra swung open the scullery door to reveal the monk sitting patiently on a stool perched between the huge stone washing tub and a sack of lye.

Immediately, Cristina understood what Isra meant; there was an air of sadness, of vulnerability about the monk that lowered your defences. "I believe you wanted to talk to me?"

"Cristina Falchoni?" The man reached out and touched her hand, delicately running his fingers over her jewellery.

She watched as he traced the outline of her rings to confirm her identity. "Have we met before?"

The monk withdrew his hand. "The person who sent me knows you."

"And who is that?"

"He would not reveal his name. Only that he wants to help."

"So where did you meet? Did he summon you to his home?"

"No. He came to me. But he was wearing some kind of mask, to disguise his voice."

"It was inside the city walls, though?"

"You are asking the wrong questions," the monk replied testily. "I don't know what kind of trouble you are in, but the answer lies in Venice."

Cristina and Isra exchanged a baffled glance. "I think you've made a mistake. I am needed here in Rome."

"*Muddy the waters to catch the fish. Go to Venice.* That was the full message."

"Meaning?"

"That is for you to discover."

"I really don't have time for riddles." Cristina turned to go, but the monk's hand flashed in the gloom and gripped her arm.

"Your books will send you round in circles, Signorina Falchoni. The answer you seek lies in Venice."

"That's not possible."

"But it is true."

"What do you know about my books?" Cristina disentangled her arm and stared at the monk's milky-white eyes. Suddenly he no longer seemed so benign. "Do you know what I am investigating?"

The monk shook his head. "Only that it is dangerous. Knowledge like that I can live without."

Was the monk telling the truth? Was he really just a messenger? Or did he have an agenda? "Why should I believe you?"

"Like servant, like mistress," the monk smiled wearily. "So much suspicion in this house."

"That doesn't answer my question."

"You could be a deluded patient for all we know," Isra added. "Escaped from the Hospital for the Incurables."

"Being blind does not make me stupid." The monk's voice became sharp with irritation.

"Nor does it make you trustworthy."

"Give me one good reason why I should believe you," Cristina demanded. "Just one."

"You are engaged in a secret investigation," the monk said. "Only a handful of people in Rome know about it. The person who sent this message is one of those."

"Why couldn't he tell me to my face?"

The monk shrugged. "I have no answers. All I have is the message: *Muddy the waters to catch the fish. Go to Venice.*"

Cristina looked at Isra. "What do you think?"

"Let's see what Professor De Luca makes of it."

"No!" The monk became agitated. "It is for you alone."

"I don't keep secrets from De Luca."

"The person who sent me was adamant. You must tell no-one. The message is for you alone."

"Or else?"

"The answer you seek will slip through your fingers."

Cristina studied the constellation of scars on the monk's face, wondering if it was smallpox that had also robbed him of his sight. "Why must there be conditions on the truth?"

"Because that is how it has been ordained."

"By whom?"

"Go to Venice, Signorina Falchoni. The answers you seek are there, and only there."

While Isra prepared the monk a package of food for alms, Cristina returned to the library where she found Professor De Luca staring at the flurry of paper notes radiating from the wall clock.

"There is another possibility," he said as he heard the door click open. "What if there are more tombs under the foundations? Have they tried making a hole in the side walls of the chamber to see if it is part of some larger catacombs?"

"I'm afraid that was bad news."

De Luca turned to Cristina, who loitered in the shadows by the door. "What on earth has happened?"

"It was a messenger from Arezzo. My father has been taken ill."

"Oh... I'm..." De Luca seemed strangely lost for words. "I'm sorry to hear that."

"I need to go to him."

"Now?" De Luca pointed to the books piled on the table. "In the middle of all this?"

"He's my father."

"Well ... how serious is it?"

"The messenger wasn't clear. But if they've sent for me, I doubt it will be trivial."

"Surely you need more information before you disappear?"

"It'll only be for a few days."

"Two weeks, Cristina! That's all we have!"

"Then the Pope will have to give us more time."

Professor De Luca blinked as he stared at Cristina. "It is not for us to tell the Holy Father what to do."

"The result is what matters. The deadline can be pushed back." She opened one of the bureau drawers and pulled out an iron ring that held two keys. "These are for the servants' stairs. You can come and go as you please while I'm gone. You must make yourself at home."

"And Isra?"

"She's coming with me."

Reluctantly De Luca took the keys from her.

"I'm sorry. I'll be back as soon as I can, but please try to understand, Professor."

"Are you sure this is what you want?"

"He's my father. I don't have a choice."

"Then as your mind is quite set … I will make whatever progress I can in your absence."

Within hours the house was secured and provisions packed onto a pair of strong Arabian horses; by first light Cristina and Isra were on the road. The quickest route was to head east to Pescara, then catch one of the merchant galleys heading up the coast to Venice with their rich cargos of cinnamon and ginger. If the southerly winds held, they could be there in two days.

They rode in silence for the first few hours, both immersed in their own private thoughts. Cristina was wondering who had sent them on this mysterious journey, and why it had to be cloaked in secrecy. Who was in the room when she had told the Pope about the strange odyssey of St Mark's bones to Venice? Domenico, Cardinal Riario, Chief Architect Bramante and Geometra Castano. Which one of those had given her this lead? And why couldn't they have talked to her directly?

12: SERENISSIMA

It began as a grey smudge on the horizon, barely distinguishable from the low-lying marshes running along the stretch of coastline. But for countless thousands of people, that smudge had meant salvation, reunion with loved ones, and the chance to become fabulously wealthy.

Cristina stood on the castle deck at the stern of the galley, mesmerised by the sight of Venice growing more distinct with every passing minute. Gradually, individual church towers became defined, followed by the domes of Basilica di San Marco. Closer still, and she saw other galleys approaching from the north and east, so loaded with luxury goods from the Levant that their hulls sat low in the water. It felt as if the entire world was converging on *La Serenissima*.

"Thank God you had the money to pay for space up here," Isra said as she joined Cristina at the rail. "I just glimpsed below deck — squalid doesn't begin to cover it."

But all Cristina's attention was focussed on the horizon. "This is what Marco Polo would have seen when he returned after travelling for twenty-four years. Imagine, he left in his teens and returned a middle-aged man. What must he have felt, seeing home again after journeying into the unknown for so long?"

"Pity his poor parents," Isra replied.

"His father was just as bad. He left when Marco was a baby, and didn't return for sixteen years."

"Why have children if you don't want to be a parent?"

"Anyone can be a parent," Cristina said dismissively. "The Polo family had a higher calling. They served the God of Knowledge."

"It sounds like abandonment to me."

"Domestic bliss is overrated."

"You'll think differently when you become a mother."

Cristina pulled her gaze away from Venice to look at Isra. "That's quite an assumption."

"Surely you want to have children?"

"Do you?"

"Of course."

Cristina's thoughts spiralled back to that terrible day when her infant brother died.

"Don't you, Cristina?"

Her gaze returned to the horizon. "With so much still unknown, I don't see how there is time to be a good parent."

"But without children, what's the point?"

"Wisdom is its own point. Marco Polo brought back the first detailed account of the Orient, knowledge of paper money, of gunpowder, porcelain —"

"So he gave us new ways to kill each other, and steal from each other. A triumph."

"It's a good job I know you're joking, Isra."

As the galley entered the Venetian Lagoon, the crew sounded trumpets and pipes on deck to announce their arrival, then the sails were lowered and the galley switched to oar power. It was the safest way to navigate one of the most congested waterways in the world, and Cristina immediately understood why the Venetian fleet only used free men who were skilled oarsmen.

One by one, galleys peeled off and tied up at jetties along the Grand Canal, where they were met by swarms of gondolas, some of the ten thousand across Venice, which ferried merchandise away through a tangle of branching canals to warehouses and markets where eager merchants pored over ledgers. The air was thick with shouts in more languages than Cristina had heard in her entire life, and the narrow bridges jostled with life as courtesans pushed past financiers and fiancées to greet the newly arrived galleys.

As she stepped onto the quayside, Cristina felt overwhelmed. It was disorientating to see boats gliding past where you would expect carriages, and to see faces from so many different countries, many adorned with strange tattoos and exotic jewellery. Immediately, she knew she could happily spend weeks here, questioning all these travellers about their voyages and navigation techniques, but Isra jolted her back to reality.

"We don't have time to dawdle, Cristina. We have to do this and get back to Rome."

"There's so much here."

"Tell it to the Pope when our two weeks is up."

But where to begin? *Muddy the waters to catch the fish. Go to Venice.* That was all they had; they'd done the first part, so what did the second part mean?

"What about the city records?" Isra suggested. "Maybe they have archivists who could help."

But Cristina had already thought of a strategy. "Do you know, there are more books published in Venice than in Milan, Florence and Rome put together?"

Isra blinked. "That just makes it harder. There's too much information."

"The people who know what's really going on aren't the bureaucrats. It's the publishers. That's who we need to talk to."

"But we're not looking to buy books."

"Venice is the crossroads of the world, Isra. Information flows through here from all points on the compass. We need to immerse ourselves in those rivers of knowledge."

Isra suspected that Cristina was just finding an excuse to acquire more books, but without a better plan, she followed her across the wooden Rialto Bridge and through the narrow streets of Sestiere di San Polo, until they arrived at Campo Sant'Agostin.

"The information district," Cristina said, turning in a circle to take in the buzz of industry that resonated through the alleys converging on this small square. Every building was somehow connected to the book trade. Shops with beautifully bound volumes on display jostled next to printing workshops that echoed with the clatter of presses. Craftsmen sat hunched on stools as they carved illustrations from wooden blocks, apprentices hauled handcarts stacked high with freshly made paper, leather merchants went from door to door offering samples of their finest hides, and everywhere the sharp smell of ink replaced the pungent damp of the canals. It was from here that Europe's new libraries and bookshelves were being stocked.

"This is the centre of everything," Cristina whispered, but when she turned round, Isra was nowhere to be seen. "Isra?"

Cristina peered through the jostle of people, but suddenly everything seemed very congested. A moment of panic fluttered in her chest, then she heard laughter. She glanced over and saw a dozen children clustered around a small tent where a raucous puppet show was taking place; standing in the back row was Isra, laughing at the slapstick humour.

Cristina hurried across the square. The show was a parody of the crusades, with a fat Englishman wielding an oversized sword, trying to do battle with an Ottoman Sultan who had an enormous white turban and a mischievous djinn trapped in a bottle.

Behind you! Look behind you!

The grotesque masks and bright costumes mesmerised the children, while the coarse humour had them in fits of laughter. Cristina stood right next to Isra, who was busy chanting the magic words to wake the djinn.

Bells and spells my power compels!

Bells and spells my power compels!

Cristina cleared her throat.

"Oh! There you are." Isra tried to look serious.

"I thought we didn't have time to dawdle?"

"This is really quite funny."

"Isra. It's for children."

"Sorry." Reluctantly Isra pulled herself away from the puppets. "So, where do you want to start?"

"It's door to door, I'm afraid. Ask as many people as possible."

Methodically, they started to make their way up and down each of the streets, searching for any sign that might resonate with their clue: *Muddy the waters to catch the fish.*

Their hopes were raised when they found one publisher working under the sign of a dolphin, but when they went inside and started asking about blind monks and the relics of saints, the owner looked at them as if they were insane.

They had similar encounters at another publisher specialising in history books, and a third who was dedicated to publishing the writings of the Fathers of the Church.

Two hours later, they were no closer to a breakthrough, but now they were tired and hungry as well.

Cristina slumped down on the edge of a stone drinking trough and rubbed her feet. "What was I thinking, coming to one of the busiest cities in Europe with nothing but a cryptic clue?"

"While you wait for inspiration, I'm going to see the end of the puppet show," Isra said with a stoic shrug.

"Seriously?"

"He's got some good jokes."

As it turned out, Isra had timed her return well, for the puppeteer was repeating the same show all afternoon, and she was able to pick up close to where she left off.

With the help of the audience, the djinn finally emerged from his bottle in a puff of white smoke which delighted the children, and started wrapping the crusader in a never-ending scarf of magic silk. With every turn of the fabric, the genie uttered a mysterious proverb from the Orient:

Experience is a comb which Nature provides when we are bald.

Patience is a bitter plant yet its fruit is sweet.

Better to light a candle than to curse the darkness.

Muddy the waters to catch the fish.

Isra gasped, barely able to believe her ears. She turned to the child sitting cross-legged next to her. "What did he say?"

"Muddy the waters to catch the fish," the child giggled. "But I don't know what it means. Do you?"

13: PROVERBS

The puppeteer thrust his collection hat at Cristina. "The artist can only be cajoled with a little more gold." Even though the show was over, he seemed unable to stop speaking in rhyme.

Cristina placed a half-ducat in the hat, but the puppeteer looked at it sourly. "Alas, such a miser shall be none the wiser."

"I see greed is your creed," Cristina replied, but she put another ducat in his hat anyway. "We just want to ask about the Chinese proverbs in your play."

"You can't stop me using them," the puppeteer became suddenly touchy. "Language is free, you know."

"I appreciate that, but —"

"How absurd to silence the word!"

"Can't you just speak normally?" Isra sighed.

"Mediocrity is for the aristocracy," the puppeteer declared.

"We don't want to stop you doing anything," Cristina said, trying to soothe his artistic temperament, "we just wondered where you found those Chinese proverbs."

"Why?"

"Because it's such a clever thing to include in a show for children," Isra smiled.

"Oh. Well … they can be very discerning, you know."

"Such a gift to be able to make children laugh."

Cristina watched as the puppeteer's defences crumbled under Isra's compliments.

"So, about the proverbs?"

"Rubbish," the puppeteer declared.

"But —"

"Quite literally. The printers leave baskets full of rubbish in the alleys around here. Proofs, incorrect layouts, faulty pressings. Mountains of paper. They keep it for burning when the weather turns. It's amazing what you can find in their rubbish."

"So you get material for your puppet shows by rummaging in bins?" Isra said.

"I select and perfect what the printers reject." He put the ducats in his pocket and disappeared back inside his striped tent.

After an hour rummaging in the waste baskets of various printers, Cristina and Isra managed to trace the origin of the proverbs to Edoardo Boschi, a self-declared 'Publisher to the Discerning Reader'. In the display cabinet at the front of his shop were two beautifully bounds volumes: *Complete Encyclopaedia of Chinese Wisdom*.

As they entered, a bell clattered on the door but no-one appeared. Cristina looked around the strange room — the retail space at the front merged seamlessly into a printing workshop at the back, where huge cases of type crowded around a long table. Judging by the composition sticks hanging from hooks, this must be where the typesetters worked.

"Hello?" Cristina called out.

They heard the scrape of something heavy being moved in a side room and moments later a middle-aged man with a strangely boyish face appeared. There was a curl of brown hair across his forehead that he took comfort in flicking back into place.

"Edoardo Boschi?" Cristina asked.

"How can I help?"

"Muddy the waters to catch the fish," she replied.

Boschi stared at her blankly. "And?"

"We're from Rome."

"I'm from Mantua. So what?"

"The blind monk sent us."

Boschi flicked his hair back. "Do you want to make a purchase or not? Because I'm a busy man."

"The messenger sent us."

"Look, I don't know anything about monks or messengers, so perhaps it's best you go on your way." He swung open the front door, but Cristina and Isra refused to move.

"I think this is related to the holy relics of St Mark," Cristina said, locking eyes with the publisher.

Suddenly Boschi seemed anxious. "I said I wouldn't publish the diaries. What more do you want?"

"Diaries?"

"Why can't you leave me alone? I swore on the Bible. I took an oath!"

"There's no need to get upset."

"This is entrapment!" Boschi protested. "Sending young women to entice me!"

He tried to bundle Cristina from the shop, but Isra grabbed his arm. "Seriously? This is how you treat customers?"

"Customers?"

"Discerning readers. We came to buy your *Encyclopaedia of Chinese Wisdom*."

"You did?"

"Signorina Falchoni owns one of the largest private libraries in Rome."

Boschi looked at Cristina. "But you're a woman."

"You really do need to work on your sales pitch."

"I didn't mean —"

"Six copies. If we can agree a price," Isra said.

Boschi's eyes fluttered as he calculated the profit. "They are not cheap to produce."

"Do I look like a woman who would be interested in cheap books?" Cristina asked.

"Forgive me. There was a misunderstanding." Boschi pulled up a couple of chairs. "Please, make yourselves comfortable."

"Who did you think we were?" Isra asked.

"It doesn't matter. Some wine?" He started pouring three glasses. "Now, about the encyclopaedias —"

"Entrapment? Censorship?"

"Sounds like you thought we were spies," Cristina observed.

"Venice is a city of spies. In *La Serenissima*, it is unwise to trust even your neighbour."

"And these diaries that have caused you so much trouble?"

"Best we leave all that to one side."

"Surely, six copies of the *Encyclopaedia* earn us more trust than that?" Isra reminded the publisher.

"Were these diaries about the bones of St Mark, by any chance?" Cristina pressed.

"I really cannot say," Boschi looked down.

"Whatever your fears," Cristina stepped closer and lifted his chin, "ours are a thousand times worse. I promise you."

Boschi's gaze flicked from Cristina to Isra, trying to work them out. "May I see your travel documents?" he asked.

"We are travelling legally."

"Indulge me. Please."

Isra rummaged in her leather satchel and pulled out the warrants giving them free passage from Rome. Boschi took the documents to the window, then pulled a magnifying glass from his jacket to study them. But he wasn't interested in the official stamps or signatures, he was interested in the paper itself. He ran the warrants between his fingers, then held them up to the light and examined the texture through his lens.

"Ah … now I understand." He handed the documents back to Isra.

"Understand what?" Cristina asked.

"Why you have come to Venice."

"What did you see in the documents?" Isra was getting irritated now.

"Paper of that thickness in a diagonal weave … it's expensive. Not many people would use it for routine travel documents. You have come from Rome, so this document was most probably issued by the Vatican." He paused to try and read their faces, but Isra and Cristina didn't flinch. "As we speak, huge pits are being dug in Rome to build foundations for the new basilica. And suddenly you turn up in my shop asking about the bones of St Mark? It all points to one thing, doesn't it?"

"I am not at liberty to speak freely," Cristina admitted.

"Now you know the feeling. I'll wager your builders have uncovered the tomb of St Peter. And yet, something is wrong with it. Very wrong."

Cristina concentrated hard on controlling her reactions. "I have never said anything of the sort."

"Not with words. But with your actions," Boschi replied.

"If that happened to be true, would you help us?" Isra asked.

"The security of Christendom is at stake," Cristina added gravely.

"Hyperbole is not helpful," Boschi said. "I'm continually urging restraint on my writers."

"Venetian galleys trade with the Ottoman Empire. You know how powerful the Sultan is, how he would love to conquer Italy."

Boschi considered her words. "I can say nothing. And yet … I suppose I cannot stop you making deductions."

"Can't we just talk plainly?" Isra sighed. "What is it about people here?"

"In Venice, plain talk puts you in prison."

"Fortunately, deduction is one of my strengths," Cristina replied.

"Very well. I can point you in the right direction. But any conclusions you reach about the relics of St Mark will be on your own shoulders."

"Agreed."

"And you will purchase six copies of the *Encyclopaedia*. At full price."

"Agreed."

"Plus shipping."

"Also agreed."

"Then meet me outside Basilica di San Marco tomorrow morning at eight. That will give us one hour before I start the first pressing of the day."

14: UNEASE

As the sun set, the Venetian streets became very cold, very quickly.

Cristina and Isra set about finding somewhere to stay for the night, but the first half dozen locande they tried were fully booked.

"Venice is always full," the unhelpful concierge muttered. "Try Padua. On the mainland." Given that Padua was thirty miles away, this was useless advice.

Instead, they abandoned the main streets and tried their luck in the more obscure alleys and squares.

"Why did you have to say six?" Cristina asked.

"What?"

"Encyclopaedias. One would have been enough."

"We needed to shock him into loosening his tongue. Six will buy him a handsome new summer wardrobe."

"But it would have been cheaper just to bribe him, Isra."

"A bribe wouldn't pander to his pride. And this way, you get to donate some copies to Professor De Luca, and Sapienza University, and the Vatican Archives."

"Which still leaves two I don't need."

"You love books, Cristina. Now you're helping a publisher turn a handsome profit. Everybody wins."

As they headed into the dingy parts of the city, the presence of Venice's notorious pickpockets became more obvious; they seemed to loiter on every corner, and Cristina instinctively tightened her grip on their bags. "We need to find somewhere soon," she whispered.

"There's no shortage of brothels," Isra replied. "We must have passed a dozen already."

"I really want to sleep without sound effects. Especially after that journey up the coast."

"Some of the best hotels are brothels. They just don't like to be reminded of it."

Eventually they found one room left at Locanda Laguna, a small building with peeling paint, halfway down the impossibly narrow Calle de Borgoloco. They handed their papers to the concierge, who started to copy their details into an official-looking ledger. While they waited, Cristina studied the various damp lines on the walls, recording the height of different floods that had overwhelmed the city in the past few years.

"I hope you're not expecting a high tide this week?" Cristina quipped.

"No, no, no." The concierge took everything very seriously, especially the business of recording their details, which was taking for ever. All Cristina and Isra wanted was to collapse into bed and sleep, but the concierge wrote at a painfully slow speed.

"Would you like me to copy the details for you?" Cristina suggested.

"No, no, no."

"It might be quicker."

"No."

And that was the end of the conversation.

When they finally made it to their room, Cristina didn't even bother to unpack, she just flopped onto the bed nearest the window and was fast asleep in moments.

Tired as she was, Isra couldn't bear to leave things in a mess, and felt compelled to hang their clothes in the wardrobe and put their toiletries on the nightstand. This meant that by the time she did climb into bed, Cristina was snoring so loudly it was impossible to relax. Isra tried putting her head under the pillow, but that quickly became too hot. She tried gently tickling Cristina's nose, but that just made the snoring change pitch. Finally Isra nudged Cristina in the back; she rolled over, muttered something in her sleep, and fell silent.

Hallelujah.

Finally, Isra relaxed and felt sleep creeping up her body. Her limbs started to weigh heavily, her breathing slowed, and her mind drifted off in random directions.

She surrendered...

Until a scraping sound pulled her back into the room. Isra snapped open her eyes, but everything was pitch black. Not a shred of moonlight had forced its way through the shutters, and no matter how intently Isra peered into the gloom, it remained dark.

Creak. Then a small shuffle.

Her ears strained to understand what was happening. Something was moving in the room. Was it a mouse? Or was it just the building creaking as it cooled down?

Creak-shuffle.

Part of her just wanted to hide under the covers, but that wouldn't solve the problem. She had to take control, show she wasn't afraid.

Isra steeled herself, then screamed — "GET OUT!!"

Cristina jolted awake. "What? What happened?"

Isra reached for the tinderbox by the side of the bed, sparked it to life and lit a candle.

"What's going on?" Cristina said, still in a sleep-daze.

Isra held the candle up, driving away the shadows. "Something was in here."

Cristina glanced around the empty room. "You must have been dreaming."

But Isra knew what she heard. She clambered out of bed and tiptoed to the door — it was bolted from the inside, just as they had left it. "That doesn't make sense."

"Dreams don't."

"I wasn't dreaming."

"You want to take it in turns to sleep?" Cristina suggested.

"Perhaps we should have gone for a brothel after all. At least the sounds would have been familiar."

"Well, Boschi did say Venice was a city of spies. Maybe someone's watching us."

Isra held the candle up and ran her fingers over the walls, searching for any grilles or hidden panels, but the plaster was solid.

"Whatever it was, I think you've scared it off, Isra."

"Maybe."

"Get back to bed. We've got a busy day tomorrow."

Following her own advice, Cristina rolled over, and was soon snoring again, leaving Isra to start getting back to sleep all over again … only now she had unease to contend with, as well as the sound of snoring.

15: LOST

The following morning, the custode had set a light meal on the table — four rolls of bread, a saucer of butter, and two beakers of small beer. As Cristina and Isra ate, they noticed the custode was studying them intently.

"Do you have mice in the building?" Isra asked.

The custode looked offended. "No, no, no."

"Only I heard some strange noises in the night. As if someone was creeping around."

The custode shrugged.

"Are there any secret passages?" Isra was trying to provoke him. "Spyholes, perhaps? Or hidden doors?"

The custode chuckled to himself. "No, no, no."

"Don't you ever say anything else?"

The custode sniffed petulantly. "Sometimes."

"Bravo," Isra replied.

"Come on, Isra. Time we were going."

"But I haven't finished eating."

Cristina picked up the remaining bread roll and put it in her bag. "You have now."

Succumbing to the spirit of paranoia that hung over Venice like a sea mist, Cristina and Isra didn't go straight to Basilica di San Marco, but diverted through the crowded Rialto market instead, then took a gondola back along the Grand Canal, making it almost impossible for anyone who might have been tailing them to keep up. They arrived in the piazza just as the great Campanile struck eight, and gazed up at the sheer brick walls of the tower which seemed to tremble with the sound of its thunderous bell.

"I wouldn't get too close if I were you," a voice said, "it's pretty fragile."

Cristina and Isra spun round and saw Edoardo Boschi standing close behind them.

"The bell? Or the tower?" Cristina asked.

"The whole thing."

"Looks pretty solid to me," Isra said, admiring the brickwork.

"They've been building it for the last six hundred years, but it keeps getting struck by lightning. They've lost count how many times the spire's burned down."

"Perhaps God is trying to send you a message," Cristina suggested.

"Then perhaps," Boschi smiled, "you could ask the Pope to send our reply."

"If you help us find the bones of St Peter, I'm sure he would be happy to oblige."

"Let me show you what I know." Boschi led them across the piazza until they were standing in front of the arched façade of the basilica. He pointed up at the series of mosaics on the western façade. "This is the story the city tells the world. You see? The theft of the bones from Egypt, crossing the sea, arriving in Venice."

"The craftsmanship is beautiful," said Cristina, craning her neck to admire the detail in the mosaics.

"This is part of Venetian folklore. No expense spared. But what they don't tell you, is that the bones of St Mark were then lost."

"Not another missing saint," Isra muttered.

"It gets worse. When they arrived from Alexandria, the bones were placed securely in the Doge's palace until a basilica could be built to house them. But in 1063, when they were constructing the tomb, the bones simply could not be found."

"Had they been stolen?" Isra asked.

"From under the nose of the authorities? That's ridiculous," Cristina said.

"The archives give no explanation," Boschi said, "but the relics were missing. That much is a fact. Which left the great basilica without its main purpose."

"How embarrassing. And careless."

"They tried to suppress it all, but in Venice, the walls have ears."

"So when did they turn up again?" Cristina asked.

"That's where it gets interesting." Boschi pushed open the massive bronze doors and led them inside the basilica.

It was like walking under a rippling golden sky. Each of the five massive domes was studded with a row of windows which allowed the morning light to shimmer off hundreds of gold-ground mosaics. Cristina knew that plundered treasure from across the Venetian Empire had been used to decorate the basilica for centuries, but she was stunned by the sheer quantity of precious stones and rare marbles salvaged from Byzantium, and the sculptures and columns looted from Constantinople.

"It's certainly not modest," she whispered.

"Modesty is for mediocrities," Boschi replied. "Not something we Venetians know much about."

"Except when it comes to looking after holy relics," Isra replied.

"Ah, yet even there we dazzle, for the solution came in the form of a miracle." Boschi slapped one of the great stone piers that supported the dome of the western crossarm, and listened to the echo decay. "One night, as the builders were finishing their shift, the arm of St Mark himself emerged from one of these pillars and pointed to the location of his lost remains."

"That's impossible," Cristina objected. "Physically impossible."

"All miracles are."

"So are fairy tales. But we don't believe them."

"And yet," Boschi was undeterred by her scepticism, "when the workmen followed the direction of the saint's finger, they found the sacred relics."

"Which pillar was it? And where were the relics? And how many witnessed it?"

"You are missing the point of the story," Boschi warned.

"But details matter. That's where the truth lies."

"Not necessarily. Truth and accuracy can be two different things." Boschi led them towards the high altar, then veered right and creaked open a small door in the corner of the sanctuary. They made their way down some narrow stone steps, the smell of damp stone becoming increasingly overpowering, until they emerged into the low space of the crypt. Boschi plucked a flickering torch from its wall bracket and held it up into the gloom. "That is the point. Right there."

Cristina and Isra gazed at a simple stone sarcophagus that dominated the space. They had been expecting jewelled icons and sacred vessels forged from gold to match the opulence of the main basilica, but this tomb was like a forbidding lump of freshly hewn rock.

And yet, as they gazed at it, they started to understand how the power of the tomb lay in its stark severity. The sheer weight of the stone slabs told the world that St Mark's relics were going nowhere, that they would remain here until the trumpets sounded at the end of time.

"He was lost, then he was found through a miracle," Boschi whispered. "Who could ever doubt that God favours Venice?"

It was a relief to emerge into the fresh air and crisp sunlight of the piazza. Isra decided that street food was the best way to shake off the oppressive gloom of the crypt, and queued up at one of the kiosks in the colonnade of the Procuratie.

While she was gone, Cristina pressed Boschi. "Do you really believe what you just told us?"

"Who am I to doubt?"

"You'd have to be stupid to believe that the living arm of a dead saint could somehow emerge from a stone pillar."

"And yet the whole of Venice does believe it." Boschi scrutinised Cristina. "Perhaps that makes the entire city stupid?"

"I have learnt the hard way," Cristina replied, "never underestimate how many stupid people there are in the world."

Just then, Isra returned with three plates of fried salt cod fillets. "He wants the plates back when we're finished."

"Baccalà. My favourite," Boschi tucked in. "Thank you."

Cristina waited until Boschi had finished eating and was licking his fingers clean. "As an intelligent man, a publisher of learned books, what do you really think happened?"

Boschi studied Cristina's serious face. "I think I don't want to lose my printing licence."

"All I'm asking is for a rational explanation."

"Blasphemy is the surest route to bankruptcy. Better to just go along with the official version."

"I still don't see how any of this helps us," Isra added. "Venice solved its problem. That doesn't solve ours."

"Depends how you look at it," Boschi said carefully.

"What exactly is in those diaries you are no longer publishing?" Cristina pressed. "What scandals do they reveal?"

Again she sensed Boschi become guarded.

"We've come an awfully long way. Whoever sent us clearly believes that you have some answers.

"Let me pose you a question," Boschi said. "Is Venetian power based on the divine protection of St Mark? Or is it based on the brute force of its fleet of fighting galleys?"

Cristina didn't even hesitate. "Given that you have the largest navy in the whole of Europe, I'd say the answer is obvious."

"Then visit the Arsenale and ask to speak to the Master Shipbuilder," Boschi replied. "Speak to him and you will solve the riddle of St Mark's bones."

The Campanile's thunderous bell started to strike nine.

"And now, I'm afraid you'll have to excuse me. The printing press awaits." Boschi handed his plate back to Isra. "It was a pleasure to meet you both."

"Do you really have to be so cryptic?" Cristina called after him.

"In this city, signorina, that is how it works."

Boschi strode away and was quickly absorbed into the crowds of people hurrying across the piazza.

16: ARSENALE

Posing as agents of the Guardia Apostolica, Cristina and Isra managed to secure an audience at the *Arsenale di Venezia* that afternoon. Their cover story was that the Vatican intended to commission twenty new war galleys to strengthen the Papal fleet, and they had been tasked with discreetly gathering information as part of the tendering process. Cristina had specifically asked to speak to the Master Shipbuilder, but instead found herself in a room with Commendatore Gregorio, a retired galley captain turned salesman.

As the commendatore read the beautifully forged letter, Cristina studied the man; there were burn scars on both his hands, and a shallow dent in the middle of his forehead, presumably both were unpleasant souvenirs of the extreme violence encountered in galley combat. Most striking of all, though, was the hair growing from both his ears; it was wiry, grey and abundant.

Cristina noticed that Isra was staring at the growth as well, and the two women exchanged a puzzled glance. Why had his wife not done something about the unruly ear hair? And if Gregorio was not married, surely the tickling must irritate him. Did he never have the urge to pluck? Judging from his beautifully tailored clothes, the commendatore had plenty of money and no doubt several large mirrors at home, so he could not even plead ignorance. Perhaps he thought hairy ears were a statement of fashion; Venice could be curious like that.

Gregorio finished reading the letter and looked up. "Yet you are women?"

"Well observed," Cristina replied. "And it gives us the perfect cover."

Gregorio frowned. "It does?"

"Who would suspect two women of being interested in purchasing a fleet of war galleys?" Isra said innocently.

"Secrecy is vital," Cristina added. "The Vatican does not want anyone to know it is strengthening its naval forces. This conversation is strictly confidential, you understand. It never happened."

"I see," Gregorio nodded. "So, how many shipyards do you intend to visit?"

"I'm afraid that information is also confidential. But I can tell you that we will be busy throughout the summer, visiting Pisa and Genoa to name but two."

Gregorio visibly relaxed. "I have no fear of them. Compared to us Venetians, the Genoese are amateurs."

"You seem very confident, Commendatore."

"Prepare to alter your travel plans." Gregorio rocked back in his chair as he acclimatised to the idea of selling galleys to women. "For I believe you will be so dazzled by what you see in the Arsenale, it will blind you to all other shipyards. Shall we?" He stood up and guided them out of his office and onto a boat that was waiting by the jetty; it was being rowed by two men wearing vaguely military uniforms.

"We aren't walking?" Isra asked.

"Signorina, the Arsenale is a series of interlocking pools, linked by a network of canals. The only way to appreciate its genius, is from the water."

Unfortunately, Gregorio was so large, boarding the boat proved challenging, and the two women had to make sure their combined weight was always balanced on the opposite side of the boat to prevent a capsize. But once on board, weight no longer mattered and the oarsmen steered them effortlessly into the first pool.

It was an overwhelming sight. Sixty galleys at various stages of construction were moored on the water; thousands of workmen teemed along the quaysides and around the lines of workshops. Smoke from boiling tar pots rose in one corner, while clouds of sparks spewed from the foundries; the raucous chorus of instructions being shouted from many different teams made the Arsenale feel more like the Tower of Babel than a shipyard.

And Commendatore Gregorio revelled in it all. "You know, we have been famous for so long, we are even mentioned in Dante's *Inferno.*" Gregorio was clearly a master of hyperbole. "Everyone marvels at the construction of the Pyramids in Egypt, but they are just piles of stones. This…" he opened his arms, embracing the shipyard, "this is genius in motion. Sixteen thousand men working with the perfect co-ordination of an intricate clock."

"Size isn't always everything," Isra observed drily.

"Agreed. But we have turned shipbuilding on its head. That is what is so radical." He pointed to a line of galley hulls that had been tilted on their side to be caulked. "Each of these galleys will move through the shipyard as it is built, floating along the canals to different teams of specialised workmen. In Venice, the mountain comes to Mohammed."

"A strange metaphor, given the Ottoman threat," Cristina said.

"The infidel doesn't stand a chance against Venice," Gregorio scoffed, "and the Arsenale is why."

They rowed behind a galley hull that had just been fitted with masts, and emerged into an even larger pool, bristling with ships.

"Over there the weapons and cannon are fitted." Gregorio pointed to workshops lining the quays. "And in there all the rigging is created. There, the anchor … the oars … the sails, all as the hulls glide from one station to the next. We can produce a fully equipped galley in a single day, a job that would take months in any other shipyard in Europe."

"It is most impressive, Commendatore," Cristina said with genuine admiration.

"It is brilliant. And unique to Venice."

"And all this is the creation of the Master Shipbuilder?"

Gregorio chuckled indulgently. "Signorina, your question tells me that you have not fully grasped the revolution that is unfolding before your eyes. This process is bigger than any single craftsman. Each stage has its own specialised team of workers. The components used in our galleys are standardised and interchangeable. If one of our vessels is marooned off the coast of Tripoli, say, another can sail to its rescue confident that the spare parts it carries will be a perfect fit. We have banished trial and error from the process. The individual object is dead. One day everything will be made this way."

"I find that very hard to believe," Isra said.

"Why?" Gregorio demanded.

"The world needs craftsmen. It always will. People who know how to make something from start to finish."

"You are living in the past, signorina. The Arsenale is focussed on the future." Gregorio beckoned for the oarsmen to head back towards his office. "And in our immediate future, is luncheon."

"I'm afraid we really don't have time," Cristina replied.

"Nonsense! We need to discuss the specific needs of the Papal fleet."

"We are only at the start of the tendering process, so it might be premature —"

"And I have asked the chefs to prepare *bisato su l'ara* in your honour."

"It sounds delicious, but —"

"Eels cooked in bay leaves. A Venetian speciality."

"You really shouldn't have gone to the trouble."

"No trouble, signorina. No trouble at all. And it will give me a chance to tell you about new financing arrangements we have introduced if you commit to placing an order today."

Cristina glanced at Isra, her eyes pleading for help to resist this salesman who could already taste the juice of his commission.

"Commendatore, no-one rushes the Pope," Isra said firmly. "It is the golden rule of working for the Vatican. Ignore it at your peril."

Gregorio looked stung. "But we cannot have a meeting without some refreshment."

"We just did."

In a final bid to persuade, Gregorio leant forward. "You know, here in Venice we have started to import a very special drink. Once you've tasted coffee..." he gave a mischievous smile.

"You must think us very parochial in Rome," Cristina replied tartly.

"Compared to Venice, everywhere is parochial. We are the leading edge."

"And yet, Isra and I have been drinking coffee for several years."

"Rome even has its own coffee shop," Isra added.

"Just the one?" Gregorio shrugged, refusing to be impressed. "How disappointing."

Although the visit had been fascinating, it had also been deeply frustrating. Cristina and Isra had seen nothing linking the Arsenale either to the mosaics or to the relics of St Mark, and far from meeting the Master Shipbuilder, they had discovered that he didn't even exist.

As they walked away from the twin towers that guarded the shipyard's main gate, they paused to watch the newest galley float gently down the canal to start its blood-soaked working life. Even now they could see a small team of inspectors clambering over it, checking everything from the rigging to the rowlocks.

"Do you think he's right?" Isra pondered. "Are we all going to end up as little pieces, doing work that means nothing?"

"I can't imagine Michelangelo would ever be replaced by a system of producing things en masse."

"Because the world only needs one *David*. But what about tables and chairs? And cooking pots? What about carriages and violins?" Isra shivered as an evening chill settled over the canal. "Maybe the world will fill up with things produced at high speed."

Suddenly Cristina burst into laughter.

"You find it amusing?"

"No. Not at all."

"Then what?"

Still laughing, Cristina reached out and hugged Isra. "I think I've found the Master Shipbuilder."

"Where? He doesn't exist."

"And that explains everything."

"What are you talking about?"

Cristina took Isra's hand and hauled her into the alleys leading back towards St Mark's. "It was in front of us the whole time."

17: MOSAICS

They raced through the rapidly darkening alleys, determined to get to Basilica di San Marco while there was still enough light to see the great mosaics above the west doors.

"But we've already looked at those," Isra objected.

"We looked, but we didn't *see*."

"Cristina, you're not making any sense!"

"It's all about category mistakes. That's why we missed it, even though it was right in front of us."

"I really have no idea what you're talking about."

"*He fought the duel with courage and a rapier.* That sentence makes perfect sense. But there's a problem: you can point to the sword, yet you cannot point to courage."

"Agreed."

"Venice is a city of canals, gondolas and mystery." Cristina paused on a narrow bridge and gestured with her hands. "There is a canal, there are some gondolas, but why can't I point to the mystery? It exists, but where is it? I can't see it, or touch it, or hold it in my hand."

"Well ... it doesn't exist in the same way."

"Exactly. And to think it does is to make a category mistake."

"And this is relevant how?"

Cristina grabbed Isra and continued bundling her towards the centre of the city. "A galley is rowed out into the Lagoon, but who built it? Who is the Master Shipbuilder?"

"He doesn't exist."

"Because he is an abstraction. The *process* built the galley, not any individual. The power is in the process, not the object, and Venice has done the same things with the bones of St Mark."

They veered right into Calle de la Canonica, pushed past the spice traders who were packing up for the day, and finally emerged onto the piazza by the north façade of the basilica. "The truth is written on the building itself."

Isra gazed up at the imposing façade, none the wiser. "I'm sorry, I just don't see it."

Feeling suddenly wary, Cristina guided Isra into the shadow of one of the Romanesque arches and lowered her voice. "The bones of St Mark don't exist in a physical sense; they exist only as an idea. Like courage and mystery, you cannot point to them, yet they still have meaning. Eight hundred years ago, the rulers of Venice had that brilliant insight. I don't believe the relics were ever physically stolen from Alexandria; they never crossed the sea or were locked in the ruler's palace; they were never lost then found. All those things happened, but only as ideas, and the people of Venice did the rest: they turned those ideas into reality. Into mysterious physical objects. Holy relics."

Isra frowned. "It's an interesting theory. But you don't have any proof."

"Don't I?" Cristina led Isra round to the western façade and pointed up to the beautiful mosaics Boschi had shown them that morning. "Look again. The first mosaic showing the theft from Alexandria — the body is covered in a shroud. Hidden. We cannot see the saint, yet we assume it is him. Next mosaic, the basket: again, no sign of St Mark. He is an absence. Yet look here..." Cristina pointed to the mosaic in the next arch. "By the time the relics arrive in Venice and are venerated by the Doge, we can already see his face. The myth has been created. We are seeing the birth of the idea. Created from nothing. The Venetians have confessed on the side of their own great basilica."

"So … the authorities lied about the whole thing?"

"It is not a lie, Isra. It is a myth, a legend. It is real but not in the same sense that this stone is real." She slapped the solid marble pillar. "The heroic adventure of the theft, the miracle at sea, the unaccountable loss of the bones, then their miraculous reappearance — the whole thing was an exercise in creating a different layer of reality. Somehow Boschi has stumbled on the truth, probably in those diaries he is so anxious about, but he cannot say it outright. It would be blasphemy. Hence the cryptic clues he gave us. And this, right here…" She looked up at the mosaics. "This is also the answer for St Peter. His relics can become real, even if we cannot find them. A different type of reality."

They were met with the usual glare of surly suspicion by the concierge at Locanda Laguna, but Cristina no longer cared. She had found what she was looking for in Venice, and they would be gone first thing the following morning.

But as they walked down the shadowy corridor that led to their room, Isra suddenly froze.

"What?" Cristina whispered.

"Listen."

Noises seemed to be coming from inside their room — the scrape of furniture being moved, objects being tossed to the floor.

Isra crept closer.

"Wait!" Cristina hissed. "We should tell the concierge."

"You really trust him?"

"We could get ourselves killed."

"So little faith." Isra slid out the dagger that she always kept hidden down the side of her boot, then reached for the door handle. Gently she turned it ... but it was still locked. "Strange," Isra frowned. She beckoned to Cristina. "Use the key. As quietly as you can."

Cristina did as she was told, gently slid the key into the lock and slowly turned it. But the mechanism was badly worn...

Scrape. Squeak.

Cristina froze.

The noises from inside stopped.

A few moments of absolute silence ... then Isra grabbed the key, yanked it to the left and kicked open the door.

All their possessions were strewn about the ransacked room. Furniture had been turned over and the bed lay on its side.

Yet there was no sign of the intruder. He had vanished from inside a locked room.

18: SHADOWS

"I knew there was a hidden way in!" Isra's eyes darted around the room. "You wouldn't believe me."

"There!" Cristina pointed to the fireplace. "Something's wrong with the backplate. See? It's crooked."

Isra dropped to her knees and ran her hands around the fireplace. "There's a gap. It's been opened." She squeezed her fingers into the crack and pulled open the metal backplate to reveal a crawlspace that disappeared inside the wall cavity.

"It's tiny."

"Big enough for an agile man." Isra poked her head into the chasm and listened. She could hear shuffling sounds and the heavy breathing of someone trying to escape through the narrow tunnel. "I'm going after him."

"Don't be absurd!" Cristina exclaimed.

But the top half of Isra's body had already wriggled into the crawlspace. "There's notches in the wall to climb up," her disembodied voice called back. "Must lead to the roof."

"Wait!"

"Find another way up there so we can trap him."

"Isra! This is insane!"

"Go!" With a final slither, Isra's feet disappeared into the wall. "If you're quick we can still catch him."

It was pointless both going the same way, so Cristina did as she was told and ran back down the corridor, searching for a way onto the roof.

Eventually she found a hatch above the stairwell, and by dragging a bureau cabinet across the landing, was able to clamber up and reach the ceiling. She pushed open the hatch and hauled herself into the roof cavity.

It was a cramped space, too low to stand in, lit only by the feeble dusk glow that managed to dribble through the gaps in the rooftiles, but it was enough to see that there were cobwebs everywhere.

There must be a thousand spiders up here. Cristina shuddered. Her body was screaming at her to get out, but she couldn't leave Isra to catch the intruder by herself.

As her eyes adjusted to the gloom, Cristina realised that a series of planks had been laid on top of the ceiling joists, creating a narrow walkway from the hatch to a pair of wooden shutters at the far end of the loft. It had to be the way onto the roof.

She closed her eyes to block out the horror of the cobwebs, and started to shuffle along the planks. Tangles of cobwebs broke across her face, and she felt as if her skin was crawling with spiders, but she didn't dare stop to brush them off. If she stopped, more would overwhelm her.

Something touched her lips and she spat violently, shaking her head to get rid of whatever it was.

Keep going. That was the only way. *Keep. Going.*

After an eternity of crawling through cobwebs, Cristina finally came to the shutters, punched them with her fists and tumbled out onto the rooftop.

Frantically, she ran her hands through her hair and over her body, ridding herself of any spiders, then drew a deep breath to try and regain her composure.

Her eyes darted across the rooftops — chimney pots erupted from the chaos of orange tiles at regular intervals. She picked her way over the undulating roof and listened at the closest pot. Sounds of shuffling and breathing echoed up from inside the vent.

"Isra! Is that you?" Cristina called into the chimney pot.

"Is he up there yet?" Isra's voice echoed out of the darkness.

"No."

"There's a whole network of cavities hidden in the walls and ceilings. It's incredible."

"Leading where?"

"To every room in the building."

"Has he escaped that way?"

"No. I can still hear him crawling."

"So where's he coming out?"

"You tell me."

Cristina's eyes scanned the rooftops — the crawl tunnels had to emerge somewhere. She clambered over the roof, listening at each chimney pot in turn, trying to work out where the sounds of movement were loudest — the intruder seemed to be heading towards the north end of the building. Following the sounds, she picked her way towards the far wall until she was staring down a sheer drop into the Santa Maria canal. Beneath her, a large hoist arm extended from the top floor — this must be a merchant's warehouse. But just as Cristina turned to find a chimney pot to update Isra, the loading doors below her creaked open.

She peered over the edge and saw a figure emerge from the building and slither along the hoist arm like a snake. His hands were stretching out to grab hold of the rope, and Cristina realised he planned to lower himself into a small rowing boat he'd left moored in the canal below.

"You'll never make it," she shouted. "I swear to God I'll cut the rope with you on it."

The figure froze, then quickly slithered back into the safety of the warehouse.

"He's on the canal side!" Cristina yelled into the nearest chimney pot. "Top floor! We've got him."

She hurried around the edge of the roof until she found a small skylight that was covered with years of sticky pigeon excrement. Choking back her disgust, she scraped off as much as she could with her boot, then hauled open the skylight and peered down into the storeroom. It was piled to the rafters with barrels, crates and huge sacks of aromatic spices.

Slowly, Cristina lowered herself through the skylight until her feet tiptoed on the highest layer of crates. Taking care not to topple the whole pile, she clambered down the stack and reached the floor just as Isra emerged from a fireplace on the far wall.

"He's in here," Cristina whispered. "Somewhere."

But that wasn't much help — there were hundreds of crates, maybe thousands, and he could be holed up in any of them.

"Do we really have to search every barrel?" Isra sighed.

The answer came in the form of a sneeze. An uncontrollable sneeze from somewhere on the opposite side of the room.

The women waited, eyes peering into the gloom, barely able to believe their luck.

Another sneeze tore through the silence, this time accompanied by a nasal whistle.

Cristina couldn't help smiling. "Wherever he's hiding, he's obviously allergic to it."

Guided by the sneezes, Isra homed in on a pile of sacks containing frankincense. "So that's what's set you off," she muttered, creeping closer and gripping her dagger tightly. She waited for one final confirmatory sneeze.

Achoo!

Isra hauled the front sack aside and raised her arm to plunge in the dagger —

Then froze, mid-strike.

Cowering in front of her, eyes streaming, was a skinny boy who couldn't have been more than thirteen.

"What the hell are you doing?" Isra gasped.

Achoo!

Cristina looked down at the boy, incredulous. "This is who's been snooping on us?"

"I didn't take nothing!" he cried. "I swear!"

Isra turned to Cristina in dismay. "What are we going to do with him?"

"Well, we only have one friend in Venice."

19: ESPIONAGE

Edoardo Boschi was not pleased to see them standing in his printing workshop again. In particular, he seemed irked by the presence of the enigmatic boy.

"At least in Rome, thieves have the decency to confess when they're caught." Cristina pushed the lad towards Boschi. "This one swears he's stolen nothing, but refuses to offer any explanation for his disgraceful behaviour."

"He's just trying to prove himself," Boschi said wearily.

"As what? A promising young criminal?"

"Some career paths are less obvious than others. This is how those without connections get started in life."

"What's wrong with an apprenticeship at the Arsenale? Half the city seems to work there."

"True, we have a formidable fleet, but at heart, Venice is a city of spies. Isn't that right, *ragazzo*?"

The boy looked uneasy, as if Boschi had rumbled him.

"He's a child spy?" Cristina exclaimed. "Does this city have no shame?"

"The thing is," Boschi explained, "if this boy can deliver useful information to the authorities, it may open the door to being recruited by the intelligence services."

"So we were just an audition? A trial run?" Cristina glared at the boy. "And what did you find out about us?"

The boy just shook his head defiantly.

"He won't tell us anything," Isra intervened. "If he cracks under interrogation, no-one will ever recruit him."

Cristina suddenly felt her indignation turn to caution. The *ragazzo* may be young, but he could still be dangerous. She glanced at Boschi. "Now we've brought him here, will he report you as well?"

But Boschi was an old hand at this game. "Report me for what? You came to study the mosaics at St Marks so that you can offer advice to the architects now rebuilding St Peter's. There is nothing suspicious in any of that."

"There's also nothing wrong with ambition," Isra said, putting her hand on the boy's shoulder. "He was just trying to get on."

Cristina crouched down so that her face was level with the boy. "Will you report us for anything?"

The boy shook his head. "I didn't find nothing. Waste of time."

Cristina felt a twinge of sympathy. Who knew how difficult his life was, or how much he needed a chance to get on.

"Maybe we can give him something," Isra suggested. "A useful nugget to help him."

Cristina nodded. "If you must report a scandal, then have this one: I came to Venice to find a publisher who would take on the scandalous memoirs of the artist Vito Visconti. A liar, a cheat and a fraud, who fooled the whole of Rome. Unfortunately, no-one wants to touch it. 'Too risky,' they say. 'Too many reputations will be destroyed.'"

The boy's eyes twinkled as he listened — this was information that had currency.

"Even a publisher as broadminded as Edoardo Boschi rejected the manuscript," Cristina continued. "So alas, the story will remain lost in oblivion."

Boschi smiled and shook his head. "It was an intriguing narrative, but I doubt readers will engage with it. The central character is too unlikeable."

Cristina looked at the boy. "Will that do?"

"Thank you."

"Remember that the next time our paths cross."

The boy nodded and hurried from the workshop, clattering the door shut behind him.

"And did you get what you came for?" Boschi asked.

"It's like the puppet show that plays in the piazza outside," Cristina chose her words carefully. "Are the puppets real or not? They talk and move, we empathise with them, yet at the end of the day, the puppeteer puts them back in a box for the night. Reality is not as simple as it seems."

"Indeed it isn't." Boschi stood up, crossed the workshop floor and opened the door. "And now I think you need to leave Venice immediately. For everyone's sake."

20: APOPLEXY

Cristina wasted no time.

Still covered in dust from the journey back to Rome, she left Isra in charge of returning their horses to the stables so that she could go straight to Sapienza University.

Even though her access to the hallowed halls had been unquestioned for over two years, Cristina still attracted disapproving glances whenever she walked along these corridors, and it didn't help that today she looked like a bandit freshly arrived from the hills. She didn't care. All that mattered was sharing her breakthrough with Professor De Luca.

But the moment she entered his mahogany-panelled study, Cristina knew something was wrong. Not only was there no sign of the professor, but it looked as if he hadn't been here for several days. The desk was unusually tidy, the customary clutter of half-read books had been gathered into neat piles, and there were no paper scatterings of hastily written notes.

Cristina checked the clock — 11.35. At this time in the morning De Luca should be dancing with the whirlwind of academic pursuit, his office should be a place of chaotic energy. She ran her finger along the surface of his desk — someone had even polished the wood, a very bad sign.

The door clattered open and De Luca's fresh-faced clerk hurried in.

"Federico, where is the professor?"

The young student's face clouded with worry. "You haven't heard, Signorina Falchoni?"

"I've been away. But I need to see him. Urgently."

Federico opened his mouth to speak, but was overwhelmed with emotion. He lowered his head and sobs heaved up from his chest.

"What on earth's happened?"

Federico wiped his eyes and struggled to compose himself. "It was so sudden. There was no warning. He was going through the volumes he'd taken from your library the previous evening, and I asked if he was going to attend the chapter meeting in faculty, but he said he didn't have time. So I went next door to prepare some cantuccini and a small glass of wine, because I knew it was nearly time for his morning snack..." Federico gulped down his tears. "I just heard a slump. Like ... like something falling over. I came back into his study, and there he was, lying on the floor, just there." He pointed to the woven rug. "Struck down in an instant."

"Was he conscious?" Cristina asked. "Was he breathing?"

"His eyes were open, but I don't think he could see me. And he was trying to speak, to say something. But it just came out as a groan. From the back of his throat, as if his tongue had been cut out." The memory of his stricken master overwhelmed Federico again and his voice stuttered into silence.

"Is he alive? Tell me!"

Federico nodded.

"Where did they take him?"

"The doctors couldn't agree —"

"Where did they take him?" Cristina demanded.

"It was nothing I did!" Federico gasped. "I do everything I can to look after him!"

Cristina grabbed Federico's face and forced him to look into her eyes. "Last time: where is Professor De Luca?"

As she hurried through the streets towards the Hospital for the Incurables, a sense of unreality engulfed Cristina. These streets that were so familiar suddenly seemed paper thin, as if they were just painted on a canvas that was tearing into pieces, threatening to plunge her into oblivion. De Luca was the cornerstone of her life, the Archimedean point about which she leveraged the world; if he was gone, she would be lost.

Cristina pushed her way through the crowded corridors of the *Incurabili*, accosting every nursing sister she saw, demanding to know where the professor had been taken; finally she was directed to a small room at the back of the hospital.

She entered the sparse room and saw De Luca lying on his back, eyes closed, mouth open, breathing in strained gasps. Cristina was so relieved to see that he was still alive, she hurried over and clasped his hand tightly. "Thank God I found you."

Not a flicker of response. She touched his forehead to see if he was running a fever. "How are you feeling? What medicines are they giving you?"

But he was not there, not in any meaningful sense. De Luca's body was alive, but his spirit seemed completely absent. Cristina leant over the bed to look into his face. "Professor, it's me," she whispered.

His vacant eyes registered nothing, they just gazed at the same spot on the ceiling. He was unreachable.

Cristina felt panic boiling up inside her. She gripped the bed rails until her knuckles were white.

Think, Cristina. Think.

Should she pray? Would that help? But the nursing sisters would have already done that, and God didn't appear to be listening.

Quickly, Cristina cast her mind across the various books she had read about medicine and healing: the Greeks, Galen and Hippocrates, the balance of the four humours, the great Byzantine *Compendium* ... finally she remembered the writings of Abu Bakr al-Razi, an Islamic scholar from the Golden Age. Four years earlier she had been shown a half-finished translation of his text 'On Surgery', and had been fascinated by his radical approach to medicine. Now she recalled that al-Razi had hypothesised about hearing being the last sense to die, even after all else was gone.

She looked at the insensible figure of De Luca; perhaps he was still there, trapped inside his own body. Perhaps he was silently asking her to tell him what she had discovered in Venice, to keep their investigation moving forward. And perhaps he knew this was the only way that Cristina could cope.

So she drew up a stool next to the bed and talked to De Luca as if he was just reclining in his study.

"Professor, I believe I have found a solution to the lost relics of St Peter," she whispered. "And you will love its ingenuity. Its daring cleverness. It demonstrates the power of pure intellect to solve an intractable problem." She squeezed his hand. "When you awake, old friend, you will be sorry to have missed it. So I will do this in your name."

"Most of them never wake up, you know."

The brittle voice jolted Cristina from her reverie. She turned and saw an elderly nursing sister with a downturned mouth, standing in the doorway.

"Most is not all."

The nurse shrugged. "The surgeons have lost interest in this one."

"Do not refer to him like that." Cristina stood up and locked eyes with the woman. "This man is a distinguished professor at Sapienza. He has a brilliant mind, and you will show him some respect."

"*Was*," the nurse replied with a hint of relish. "He *was* a brilliant mind. Now he can't even control his bowels."

"There is always hope," Cristina said. "The mind is more powerful than any of us can imagine."

The nurse shrugged. "This is a hospital. We spend most of our time cleaning up faeces and blood. Not much time left for hope."

"Then perhaps you should study the Islamic philosophy of medicine."

Sourness spread from the nurse's mouth to engulf her whole face. "This is a Christian institution. You'd do well to keep your heathen thinking out of it."

Cristina realised there was nothing more she could say to this woman. It was impossible to engage with ignorance. "Just do your job. And keep him alive," she instructed, then strode past the nurse and left the *Incurabili*.

21: MYTHOLOGY

"You had two weeks." Pope Julius rubbed his brow, hoping to ease away the stress. "That deadline passes tomorrow. Yet today you ask for a private audience. It can only mean one thing: you have failed."

Cristina watched as Pope Julius lined up a dozen stubby bolts on the wooden table, so they could be swiftly loaded into his crossbows. She knew that he hated being disturbed while hunting, but she had been too impatient to wait for him to return to the Vatican so she persuaded Domenico to bring her here, to the wooded hills above Palestrina, twenty miles east of Rome.

"It is true, Holy Father, I have not located the bones of St Peter," she began, "but now I realise that is not necessary."

"You told me it was imperative," he loaded a bolt into the first crossbow and drew the string into the locking mechanism. "'The collapse in confidence will be devastating. It will be as if God has turned His back on Rome.' Your exact words."

"That is all true," Cristina admitted.

"So what has changed? We cannot conjure the bones from nothing." The sound of dogs barking on the ridge caught the Pope's attention. He turned and studied the woodlands, trying to pinpoint the precise location of the hunting pack.

Chasing through the forest on horseback was fraught with danger, which is why it had become customary for popes to indulge their love of blood sports with tower hunting; while they occupied the platforms of specially constructed lodges built up to the tree canopy, teams of beaters and huntsmen traversed the woodland with dogs, thrashing the underbrush and driving prey towards the papal position.

"Holy Father, how many people have witnessed first-hand the things they revere?"

Pope Julius loaded a bolt into the second crossbow. "Was that a rhetorical question?"

"Look at papal authority. You are revered throughout Christendom, millions of people follow your edicts and proclamations, but how many of those people have *seen* you with their own eyes?"

Pope Julius held the stock up to his shoulder to check the alignment of the sights.

"Christ's divinity," Cristina pressed on. "Why do we believe in His divine powers when no-one alive today has actually witnessed His miracles?"

"If we only believed what was in front our eyes, the world would be a very ignorant place," Pope Julius replied.

"Precisely. And that is where the solution to our current problem lies. We don't need St Peter's bones, we just need the mythology of the bones. If we can create that with enough conviction, people will believe in the existence of the relics."

Pope Julius was getting irritated. "You cannot simply fabricate a mythology."

"Why not?"

"Because beliefs are rooted in truth. Christ walked through Palestine. He preached. He performed miracles. He healed the sick and was crucified at Calvary. Our faith in Him is rooted in the truth of His life. We cannot just fabricate any reality we desire."

"With all due respect, given sufficient resources and intelligence, that is exactly what we can do, Holy Father."

Pope Julius turned his unforgiving gaze on Cristina. "They warned me you can be a very arrogant woman."

"Forgive me, but all we need is a grain of truth, and we have that. We discovered St Peter's tomb during the excavation of the northwest pier. That is an absolute fact, and it is all we need to grow the mythology."

The sound of the hunting dogs was close now, the trees and bushes nearby were rustling as frightened animals tried to find safety. Pope Julius picked up one of the loaded crossbows, stepped over to the railing at the edge of the platform and raised the stock to his shoulder.

Suddenly a deer burst into the clearing next to the tower. The Pope spun to his left, took aim, depressed the trigger and unleashed the bolt. It flew wide of the mark and embedded itself in a tree. *Thunk!* Startled, the deer spun round, then darted into the thicket.

"Holy Father!" one of the beaters shouted. "Over here!"

Pope Julius grabbed the next crossbow and hurried to the opposite side of the platform. Five dogs were harrying a wild boar. "Stand clear!" he commanded.

The beaters backed away as Pope Julius tried to find a clean shot, but the dogs were in a frenzy now, snapping at the boar who veered wildly from side to side.

He found his moment and pressed the trigger. There was a sharp whistle of air…

Then one of the dogs yelped as the arrow almost struck it.

"Damn!" Pope Julius muttered.

The other dogs fell silent, confused by the turn of events, and the boar seized the moment to break free and hurtle into the dense undergrowth.

Pope Julius reached for a bolt to reload. "It will never work. The truth will escape. Just like that boar."

"Holy Father, it has worked in Venice for over six centuries. They have shown us how to do this. The crucial thing is to keep a tight control of the narrative."

Pope Julius started to reload the crossbows, until all five of them were lined up on the table, ready to kill. "If I did agree to your proposal, which I am loath to do, how would it work?"

"You would give me the authority and the resources. I would assemble a small team. Together, I believe we could create a religious fervour in Rome that would leave no-one in any doubt about the power of St Peter's bones."

The bushes below rustled violently as three deer burst into the open, desperately trying to work out where to hide. Pope Julius grabbed a crossbow from the table and fired. The bolt missed, but sent the deer running in the opposite direction. Pope Julius grabbed the next crossbow and tried again, but he was in too much of a hurry and didn't take proper aim. The bolt embedded itself in the dirt, allowing the deer to escape.

"The church already harnesses the power of ritual," Cristina went on, ignoring the Pope's careless shooting. "We have magnificent architecture to instil awe, plainsong and incense to transport worshippers away from the mundane reality of daily life, sunlight streaming through stained glass to intimate the presence of the divine. All these are tools used to translate the mystery of God into something ordinary people can understand. Holy Father, allow me to use the power of imagination and intelligence to secure the foundations of St Peter's Basilica."

"God gave us intelligence so that we might understand the world."

"But we can go further than that. We can use our intelligence to *create* the truth of the world."

"Yet that is not reality, is it?"

"We need to create the conditions where it would be irrational to doubt the existence of St Peter's bones."

Carefully, Pope Julius put the crossbow back on the table. "Once we start to rule by deception, how will we know when to stop? It will be a Pandora's Box."

"This is not deception, Your Holiness. We are merely separating truth from accuracy. The truth is that St Peter lived and died in Rome. Compared to that, the details of where his bones found their final resting place is immaterial."

22: ANALYTICA

Domenico's worries started the moment Cristina came down from the hunting tower, having secured the Pope's backing. He only needed to look into her eyes to know that a new obsession was taking root in her mind, and his sister's obsessions could be a double-edged sword.

He remembered when, as a fearlessly inquisitive nine-year-old, Cristina had set out to discover whether fish slept. She built a special observation hide next to the pond at the family's country villa in Frascati, and another two on the banks of the streams that fed into it. But when a week of non-stop observation yielded no firm conclusions, Cristina decided to study the pond at night, and ended up nearly drowning herself.

Domenico studied his sister now, as she arranged her library for the first briefing session of the newly created Bureau of Relics. She may have been twenty-five years older and wiser, but her obsessions still had the capacity to be perilous.

Cristina unveiled a large sheet of black slate that she'd secured to the wall opposite the windows, then picked up a box of chalk sticks. "I will start, but the whole point of this exercise is for everyone to participate." She handed a piece of chalk to each member of the Bureau: Isra, Castano and Domenico.

"Nine years ago, a group of fanatics called the Evangelicals of Light brought terror to the streets of Rome. They engineered a series of elaborate and horrific murders that made Pope Alexander VI believe he was cursed. Our aim," Cristina wrote the words Bureau of Relics on the slate, "is to do the exact opposite. We need to create a series of events that will inspire and uplift Rome. Events that will fill the hearts of ordinary people with wonder at the power of St Peter's holy relics, recently rediscovered during the construction of the new basilica."

"And there's the rub," Domenico said.

"Which is why," Cristina chalked the word *secret* on the slate and underlined it, "the work of this Bureau must remain absolutely confidential. The power of our project lies in its invisibility. Only the Holy Father can know the full extent of what we are doing here."

Castano gave a supercilious chuckle.

"Is there a problem?" Cristina asked.

Geometra Castano swept the fringe from his face and cast his gaze on Isra. "I really don't understand why the housekeeper is here. In what way do her concerns reach beyond keeping us fed and watered?"

Domenico winced.

Cristina focussed her gaze on Castano. "A comment that reveals just how out of touch you are," she said brusquely. "This project needs an understanding of ordinary people. How they think. What they believe. Book learning is no longer enough. If we are to succeed then we need street knowledge, and no-one is better qualified in that than Isra."

Castano opened his mouth to reply with some erudite quip, then thought better of it.

"This is how we will operate." Cristina started writing on the slate. "I will put a series of words here to trigger your thinking. Don't worry about being 'right' or 'wrong'. Say what comes into your mind. We are trying to get one idea firing off another, and so discover solutions."

She finished writing the word *attention* on the slate. "How can we attract the attention of ordinary people?"

"Well, that's really quite elementary," Castano replied. "We simply make an official announcement."

"Which is the surest way to make people stop listening," Isra countered.

"I don't see your logic."

"Proclamations. Decrees. Edicts. Ordinary people hear those words and are immediately bored."

"Perhaps that's why ordinary people remain in a state of benighted poverty," Castano replied sourly.

"No judging of each other's ideas," Cristina reminded them. "At this stage, all ideas are considered." She chalked the word *proclamation* on the slate.

Everyone stared at the word.

"Anything else?" Cristina asked.

Isra raised her hand.

"You don't have to do that. Just say what you're thinking."

"Most people are trapped in dull, routine lives. They long to be part of something that will give them … meaning," Isra said.

"Good." Cristina wrote *greater meaning* on the slate. "People long to be part of something bigger. That would grab their attention. What else?"

Domenico looked at the others — they seemed uneasy with this type of raw, unfiltered thinking.

"How about this?" Cristina wrote the word *mystery* on the slate. "A puzzle is the quickest way to get my attention. Give me a mystery and you will have me hooked."

"Yes, you're right," Isra agreed. "That's why people love miracles so much. Because they don't understand them."

Domenico shook his head. "Shouldn't we be explaining mysteries, not creating them? Isn't that what your whole life has been devoted to?"

"But we are not educating now. We are trying to influence. And to influence we need to engage people."

"Look." Isra went to one of the console tables under the window, picked up three cups and placed them upside down on the library desk. "This magic trick is over three thousand years old." She picked a cherry from the fruit bowl, placed it on top of the centre cup, then stacked the other two cups on top of that. "Abracadabra!" She tapped the cups with her finger, and lifted them up to reveal that the cherry had magically passed through the cup and onto the table.

Cristina gave a small round of applause, but Domenico and Castano seemed unimpressed.

"Why have people been fascinated by that trick since the beginning of time? Because it is a mystery, happening right in front of them. They can touch the cup, but they cannot understand the mystery."

"But we are not street hawkers," Castano said. "We are working for the Vatican."

"And what is at the heart of all the great paintings hanging in the Vatican corridors?" Cristina asked. "Mystery. Art that truly mesmerises us is art we only half-understand. The half-understood has great power." She chalked the words *enjoy bafflement* on the slate. "What else?"

Silence.

"How else can we engage with ordinary people?"

"People fear loneliness," Castano ventured. "No-one wants to be alone."

"Very good," Cristina said. She wrote *belonging* on the slate. "People want to belong to something. Which links back to Isra's point. Be a part of something. Not many of us are loners."

"Which is why we love being patriots," Castano replied.

"And why the power of the mob is so lethal," Isra added.

"I'm sorry." Domenico stood up abruptly. "I need to leave."

The others looked at him in bewilderment.

"But we've only just started," Cristina said.

"This isn't for me. I really don't feel comfortable with the idea of fooling people in this way."

"We need the co-operation of the Guardia Apostolica." Cristina was getting agitated.

"And you shall have it. But not with me." Domenico picked up his sword and fastened it back onto his belt. "I will send Deputato Tomasso to replace me. But I need to focus on my regular duties."

"Promise you won't block what we are doing?"

Now it was Domenico's turn to be disappointed. "Surely you know me better than that? In any case, Tomasso would love to work with you."

"But that means widening the circle further," Castano objected. "The more people who know about this, the less our chances of success."

"Geometra, I trust Tomasso with my life. And so should you."

The moment he left the library, Domenico felt he could breathe more easily. He didn't know why he had reacted so strongly against his sister's plan, but he had learnt the hard way, in the blood and chaos of war, to always trust his instincts.

PART TWO

23: PROCESSION

The first miracle began in the most mundane fashion.

At just after dawn the following Tuesday, a dozen women carrying baskets filled with fresh cuttings from Cypress trees, met in the shadow of the high-walled Passetto at the point where Via dei Corridori turns into Borgo Sant'Angelo. Without a word of conversation, they set to work, laying the green cuttings neatly on the cobbles to make a lush carpet roughly the width of an arm, and the length of … well, that was the strange thing, there appeared to be no limit to the length of their creation.

As the first baskets of cuttings were emptied, another dozen arrived to replace them, and the group of women split in two, with one heading west and the other east. When the ribbon of green carpet stretched for an entire block of buildings, more teams of women arrived with baskets full of flowers. This second wave started laying vividly coloured blooms on top of the bed of Cypress cuttings in geometric patterns. Circles of sunflowers were framed with concentric lines of brilliant red poppies; diagonal stripes of lavender were criss-crossed with pure white lilies; letters of the Greek alphabet were created from thousands of small daisies, and outlined with olive leaves. Each woman used only one type of flower, but the way they worked together without instruction, spontaneously creating the carpet of ever-changing colour, was mesmerising.

As word of this strange ritual spread, crowds started to gather in the narrow streets, and a detachment of Apostolic Guards arrived to protect the flower artists as they worked. People bombarded the women with questions — *What are you doing? Who is it for? How long will the flower carpet stretch? Where will it end?*

The women said nothing, they just focussed on their work, swiftly and silently extending the ribbon of colour east and west.

Aware that something unique was unfolding in front of them, passers-by spontaneously started to join in, even though they didn't know what it all signified. Men scoured markets and warehouses across Rome for fresh flowers and transported them to the Via dei Corridori, where their wives and daughters created tributaries and offshoots that wound in and out of the main ribbon. Everyone wanted to be a part of whatever this was, and soon hundreds of people were all working together, turning the dull cobbled street into a kaleidoscopic burst of colour. Those who couldn't take part lined the route instead, whispering excitedly and speculating about what was going on.

The Apostolic Guards assumed they would have to police the flower-carpet to prevent over-curious onlookers from destroying it, but no-one touched a single petal. It was as if there was a sacred aura around the ribbon, and even young children who you might have expected to start picking at the blooms, instinctively knew that they must not harm this exquisite creation.

At two thousand feet long, the route of the carpet started to become clear: in the west it would end at Old St Peter's Basilica, in the east at the Castel Sant'Angelo. But what did that signify?

Knowing that city officials would refuse to answer direct questions, children were dispatched to loiter innocently near groups of Apostolic Guards and eavesdrop on their conversations; it wasn't long before two young brothers were hurtling back to their parents with astonishing news. They had heard one of the officers talking to his troops — apparently the casket containing the bones of St Peter was going to be moved along the flower-carpet that very afternoon, from his recently uncovered tomb beneath the basilica to the safety of the Castel Sant'Angelo, where they would remain until the new basilica was finished.

The news spread through the crowd in all directions, picking up embellishments as it went, until Rome was awash with wild rumours: St Peter had been found alive and well after fifteen hundred years underground; the construction workers who had opened the saint's tomb had been transformed into angels; Christ had appeared in the Vatican and was going to walk along this carpet of flowers to bless the people of Rome. Everything was possible, and nothing was too outrageous.

At three o'clock in the afternoon, just as the final flowers were being placed, a flock of white doves was released from the bell tower of the Old Basilica. They swooped and wheeled above Rome, arcing in great circles, before scattering.

And at that precise moment, a choir started singing inside the basilica. All those who hadn't managed to jostle a space near the flower-carpet now pressed into the small piazza in front Old St Peter's, but the doors were shut and guarded by the Apostolica. It was a closed service, for the Pope and the cardinals only, no-one else was allowed inside.

But the more people were told to disperse, the more desperately they wanted to remain, and the more wildly they speculated.

Was Pope Julius conversing with St Peter?

Or was the saint's body now ascending to Heaven from inside the basilica?

Or perhaps this was the start of the Second Coming?

A bell tolled ominously, the Apostolic Guards pushed the crowds back as the huge doors creaked open and the choir emerged, singing a *Missa brevis*. The music mesmerised the crowd and everyone's gaze turned to the basilica doors as the holy procession emerged…

Behind the choir came the cardinals, heads bowed in solemn contemplation; Pope Julius followed them, a stream of prayers tumbling from his lips; and behind him, carried by a phalanx of Apostolic Guards, was a golden casket bearing the Latin inscription, *Super Hanc Petram*. From Matthew 16, *Upon this rock I will build My church*.

People in the crowd dropped to their knees. Some clasped their hands together and prayed; others gazed in wonder at the casket and wept; a few fainted, overcome with the raw emotion. Those who hadn't previously felt moved, now saw what was happening to their neighbours and allowed themselves to be overwhelmed by the febrile atmosphere. No-one wanted to be excluded from this most sacred of moments.

24: MURDER

Domenico had never felt so isolated. It seemed as if he was the only person in Rome not caught up in the religious frenzy.

He had studiously avoided personal involvement in the procession by delegating to Tomasso, and instead used the time to tackle the backlog of paperwork that had been steadily growing on his desk. He'd even gone to bed early, hoping that when he awoke, the whole bizarre episode would be behind him.

But sleep wouldn't come, and the darkness just made Domenico feel more alone. He worried he was becoming estranged from his sister, from the troops that he commanded, and even from the city that was his home.

Had he made a mistake by refusing to get involved with the Bureau of Relics?

Domenico understood the logic of what Cristina was doing, but his heart was uneasy, and that feeling grew more intense as he listened to the feverish excitement on the streets drifting over the walls of the Vatican and through the shutters of the Administration Building where his rooms were situated. People were not going home, they were spontaneously gathering to pray and sing hymns; priests were giving impromptu sermons, and where there were crowds there were the usual noisy hawkers selling food and drink.

Maybe Domenico was being too judgemental. There had been no direct lying, no proclamation declaring the existence of St Peter's bones; people had witnessed a mysterious spectacle and made assumptions. But it was clear to Domenico that the procession was not truthful. Worse, it was his own sister who had masterminded the deception. Cristina had always been a champion of truth, refusing to follow the crowd, adamant that a lone voice could be right. Yet now Domenico's was the lone voice, and his sister was on the side of the mob.

Swirling self-doubt kept Domenico awake through the long night…

Then just as dawn broke, the alarm was raised.

"Capitano Falchoni!" the woman's voice screamed. "Come quickly! Please!" Her fists hammered frantically on the door to his rooms.

Domenico threw a cloak around his shoulders, grabbed a sword belt and opened the door to see a terrified young woman standing in the gloom. "What on earth's happened?"

"He's dead!" the woman sobbed. "Murdered!" She struggled to catch her breath.

Domenico poured a glass of brandy and thrust it into the woman's hands. "Here. Drink."

She slugged it back, and he poured her another.

"Tell me what's happened."

"You have to come with me! Please!"

"Who is dead?"

"I can't say."

"Is the killer still in the grounds?"

"Just come!"

Domenico pulled on his boots then followed the woman down the stairs and across the gardens. She was one of the cleaners who started work each dawn, lighting fires and cleaning hearths, one of a small army of servants who kept the Vatican running smoothly, people who remained invisible until something went wrong.

The cleaner led the way across Belvedere Courtyard and down a narrow spiral staircase into the tangle of service corridors. But as she turned into the vaults where the firewood was stored, the woman stopped abruptly. "Down there." She pointed into the gloom. "The large storeroom. On the left."

Domenico peered into the corridor, where pools of flickering light from torches were struggling to drive back the darkness. "Show me."

"No. I ain't going in there again. Don't make me."

Domenico plucked one of the torches from the wall. "All right. Wait here."

With one hand clutching his dagger and the other holding up the flaming torch, Domenico pressed forward into the darkness … muscles tensed, ready for an attack … ears straining to hear anything other than the drip of water and the delicate scratch of rats' claws.

Finally he reached the largest vault, thrust the torch into the doorway, and saw a priest lying on his back in a growing pool of blood.

"Holy Mother of God," Domenico whispered.

He edged closer, careful to avoid stepping in the blood, and held the flaming torch over the corpse. The man's throat had been slit, and blood was still soaking into his cassock and seeping onto the rough stone floor. Yet the man looked eerily peaceful; there was no blood on his hands and no sticky red footprints, nothing to suggest that he had tried to escape. He had just laid there quietly and bled to death.

Hoping to identify the victim, Domenico bent down, gently tilted the corpse's grey face towards him … and saw the desecration. The priest's right eye had been gouged out and a small piece of paper had been rolled up and pushed into the bloody socket.

"Did you find him?" the cleaner called out from the end of the corridor.

"Stay back!" Domenico warned. "It's not safe."

Who would murder a priest in the Vatican? And with such calculated violence?

Part of Domenico felt sick at the studied ruthlessness of this killing, and yet there was a part of him that was relieved. Now he had something to focus on. While the rest of Rome indulged in religious hysteria, he could concentrate on catching a brutal killer; this was work that he understood, it was his job, and it gave him the perfect excuse to avoid any involvement with the Bureau of Relics.

He slid the paper from the priest's eye socket and unfurled it. Someone had written a prayer in beautifully neat handwriting. Domenico held the scroll under the torch and read:

Light of the World, Father of All Mercies, who has walked by my side through the years of darkness, I beseech You now to hear my prayer and forgive the blood I have spilled.

So many times did doubt fill my heart. So many times did I fear You had forsaken me.

Yet now I understand: in that silence You were always there, Lord, guiding me with your loving hands.

Some will not understand the terrible power of Your love. But I have faith in You to know the truth in my soul.

For twenty-three years, I waited.

Twenty-three summers of hope.

Twenty-three winters of despair.

And then You spoke to me, through the miracle of St Peter.

Domenico stopped reading. He backed away from the corpse. Fear clawed into his guts. But it wasn't the dead priest that frightened him now, it was those last lines of the prayer.

For twenty-three years, I waited.
Twenty-three summers of hope.
Twenty-three winters of despair.
And then You spoke to me, through the miracle of St Peter.

This was not a random killing.

This crime was linked to the procession of the saint's relics.

Religious hysteria had driven someone to butcher an innocent priest.

25: CORRELATION

By the time Cardinal Riario arrived in the cellars, Domenico had managed to wrestle some order into the horror. The vaults had been roped off and guards placed at either end of the corridor, a sheet had been draped over the body, and the large pool of sticky blood had been cleaned away.

"Do you have any idea who he was, Your Eminence?" Domenico lifted the sheet to reveal the victim's head.

Cardinal Riario gazed at the face, now faded to a ghastly grey. "Part of the Vatican bureaucracy. I've seen him around. I think his name was Coraggioso." Cardinal Riario bent down to peer into the corpse's clouding left eye. "Didn't really live up to his name. Rather timid, as I recall."

Domenico frowned. "Who would want to butcher a timid priest?"

"Surely, that is for you to discover." Cardinal Riario sat down on a pile of logs.

"Do you recall exactly what he did in the bureaucracy?"

Cardinal Riario tilted his head to one side to study the corpse's face. "Ah yes, it's coming back to me now. I think he dealt with requests from other countries who wanted to send their priests here to Rome, to study in the Vatican."

"There's a department for that?"

"Naturally." Cardinal Riario looked offended. "Rome is the centre of Christendom. We are overwhelmed with requests. Everyone wants to be here."

"I didn't realise."

"Poor Coraggioso spent most of his time saying no to people and writing elegant letters of rejection."

"That would certainly provide a motive." Domenico pulled the sheet up to cover the man's face again. "Perhaps he rejected the wrong person."

"The people he turned down were all foreigners. It's hard to believe that someone would travel to Rome just to exact revenge on a bureaucrat."

"People do bear grudges." Domenico took the bloodstained paper from his jacket and handed it to the cardinal. "This was inserted into his eye socket."

Gingerly, Cardinal Riario unfurled the small scroll and read, "For twenty-three years, I waited. Twenty-three summers of hope. Twenty-three winters of despair. And then You spoke to me, through the miracle of St Peter."

"A long-harboured grievance. But what's really worrying, is that the events of yesterday triggered this violence."

"Correlation does not signify causation," Cardinal Riario replied.

"But the lines in the prayer are quite specific. *And then You spoke to me, through the miracle of St Peter*. That is a clear reference to the procession of the relics."

"Is it?" Cardinal Riario shrugged.

"Obviously, Your Eminence. What else?"

"Rome is full of references to St Peter. Paintings, statues, inscriptions. Why should this refer specifically to the procession of the relics?"

"We all saw the religious fervour yesterday's theatrics whipped up. That was not healthy."

Cardinal Riario studied Domenico. "You don't approve of the Bureau of Relics, do you?"

"Perhaps this is why." Domenico glanced at the corpse.

"Be very careful, Falchoni. Do not jump to conclusions."

"Either way, we should warn Cristina. She needs to know what's happened."

"It would be very unwise to interfere with her work," Cardinal Riario advised. "The project she is undertaking is necessary to maintain the majesty and power of the Church. She must see it through."

"At any cost?"

"Her authority comes from the very highest level. You know that. You should respect it."

Domenico hated it when his work was compromised by Vatican politics. "Are you saying I cannot talk to my own sister?"

Cardinal Riario gave a benevolent smile. "Of course you can. If you don't mind incurring the infamous Papal Wrath."

"Father Coraggioso gave years of loyal service to the Vatican. He didn't deserve to end up with his throat slit and an eye gouged out."

"Only a fool is loyal to a dead man."

"Don't you want to catch his killer, Your Eminence?" Domenico couldn't believe that the cardinal could be so blasé about the murder of a fellow priest.

"Of course I do. Both for our own safety, and for the sake of justice. But Coraggioso must have done something to deserve this."

"Not necessarily."

"People are not murdered for no reason. And it is your job to uncover that reason. But if you jeopardise your sister's work, you will suddenly realise how few friends you have in the Vatican."

Cardinal Riario strode from the vault.

"Was that a threat?" Domenico called after him.

"A man of my position does not need to threaten." Cardinal Riario made the sign of the cross with his right hand. "In the name of the Father, and of the Son, and of the Holy Spirit."

26: SHRINE

On a gentle rise overlooking Vatican Orchard Number Twelve, two horses stood quietly, swishing their tails at the occasional fly. On the horses sat Cristina and Tomasso, watching a small figure in the distance who was hurrying back towards Rome.

"I think he's swallowed the bait," Tomasso said. "It takes a lot to make a farmer run."

They had worked through the night, spreading a carpet of figs under the farmer's apple trees, creating a new miracle of fruit from the Holy Land for those left unmoved by the earlier procession.

Cristina nodded. "I was worried he might look too closely at the figs we hung from the central tree."

"I think the wasps swarming the ripe fruit helped us."

"Cynical farmers are not the type to get excited about anything," Cristina said, studying the dust trail that rose behind the man. "But if we really have convinced him, we can convince anyone."

"Where do you think he's going first? Church or home?" Tomasso asked.

"We can't leave that to chance. Pick him up before he reaches the city gates, and take him straight to the Vatican."

"Understood." Tomasso spurred his horse and rode down into the valley to stage-manage the second miracle.

By the time Cristina arrived in Cardinal Riario's rooms, Alessio had already been babbling for a quarter of an hour. The farmer seemed incapable of giving a concise summary of what he'd witnessed; rather he felt compelled to recount the events of the entire morning step by step, exactly as he had lived them.

Finally, Alessio got to the end of his account and fell silent.

The cardinal scrutinised him. "Have you been drinking?"

"No, Your Holiness. I swear."

"Because what you have told me makes no sense. Figs don't grow in Italy, and they certainly don't grow on apple trees."

"Yes, Your Grace, you're right. But what I've said is true. Every word."

"How long is it since you were last at the orchard?"

"Just three days, Your Lordship. It's as if the figs grew, ripened and fell in just three days."

"Indeed." Riario glanced at Cristina. "How strange."

"I'm a farmer, Your Holiness. The soil and rain are what I understand. Things you can touch. But I know what I witnessed: thousands of figs. I even tasted one, just to be sure."

Riario turned to Tomasso. "Can you corroborate his story?"

"I brought the man straight here, Your Eminence. But I have put guards around the orchard to make sure no-one tampers with the trees."

"So you haven't seen these 'figs' with your own eyes?"

"No. I haven't."

"That is not helpful. Not helpful at all."

"Your Worship, is it..." Alessio looked up at Riario, "is it because St Peter has returned to Rome?"

"St Peter never left Rome," Riario replied tersely. "He has always been with us."

"I meant the procession, Your Honour. His relics. Uncovering the tomb. Are the figs ... is this ... is it a miracle?"

Riario shook his head. "I doubt it very much. That word is bandied around far too loosely."

"Oh." Alessio couldn't hide his disappointment. "But how else can it be explained, Your Lordship?"

"Only the Pope can determine whether something is a miracle, so I will discuss your claims with him. In the meantime, I assume you have plenty of other orchards to attend to?"

"Yes, sir. Thank you, sir."

Tomasso started to usher the farmer from the chamber.

"For future reference," Riario called after him, "when you address a cardinal, it's 'Your Eminence'. Nothing more."

"Yes, Your Holiness. Understood."

Isra ensured the rumours spread quickly. She made a point of accidentally bumping into servants from Rome's wealthiest palazzos and drip-feeding snippets of information about the Pope making a surprise visit to one of the Vatican farms to investigate 'some sort of happening'. It meant that by the time Pope Julius arrived in the hills, an excitable crowd had gathered at the gates of Orchard Number Twelve.

Cristina watched as Pope Julius pulled up in a simple carriage rather than the ceremonial one, to give the impression of spontaneity; he was accompanied by Cardinal Riario. As the two men emerged into the midday sun, people bowed their heads in a sign of respect. Pope Julius raised his hand to bless the crowd, then approached the orchard gates. Only he and the cardinal went inside, everyone else waited by the wall, even the Apostolic Guards.

The crowd swelled as the two men studied the carpet of fresh figs spread across the orchard. They watched as Cardinal Riario picked up a single fruit, pinched the bulbous end between his fingers and tore it open, revealing pink flesh ripened to perfection; and they watched as the two clerics delicately touched the branches of the apple trees, as if trying to understand this mysterious occurrence. Eventually, Pope Julius and Cardinal Riario disappeared from sight as they made their way to the centre of the orchard to investigate the tree that was at the heart of all this.

Heat ripples started to shimmer up from the hillside. The kestrels arrived, hovering on the high currents, searching for mice. Shadows lengthened as the sun sank lower.

Finally, Pope Julius and Cardinal Riario emerged from the depths of the orchard. They were walking on their knees as a sign of devotion and humility, hands clasped in prayer.

Immediately the entire crowd dropped to their knees as well and started reciting the Lord's Prayer.

When Pope Julius reached the gates of the orchard he stood up and opened his arms as if to embrace the people. "Today we have witnessed a miracle!"

Excitement rippled through the crowd.

"We do not know how," Pope Julius continued, "we only know that it has happened. Fruit from the Holy Land has miraculously appeared on the branches of these humble apple trees. No-one can hope to understand the mind of God. It is a boundless mystery to mortal men. All we can do is prostrate ourselves before His majesty, and protect the holy relics of St Peter who guards this city and the Church of Rome. Henceforth, Orchard Number Twelve shall become a holy shrine. A place of pilgrimage and worship. It will be St Peter's Orchard!"

The crowd broke into spontaneous applause.

27: SACRIFICE

It was everything Domenico had dreaded: another brutal murder in the heart of the Vatican. A sacrifice, thoughtful and cruel in equal measure, with a terrifying warning of more to come.

Thank God he was dreaming. Thank God this wasn't real, that he was only caught in the strange state between sleep and wakefulness, when you could direct your nightmares but never completely escape from them. Any moment now he would wake up and this horror would be over. Any moment...

"Sir?"

The voice jolted Domenico. He blinked and glanced up to see his sergeant staring directly at him.

"Are you ready to examine the body, sir?"

"What?"

"Before we move it."

Domenico glanced around the cold cellar. So this wasn't a dream after all. The horror in front of him was real. A middle-aged priest had been butchered and splayed on the crates of quince which his own blood had now turned red.

Domenico was back in the labyrinth of cellars under the Vatican, staring at another atrocity. The first body had only just been taken to the morgue, and already they had another one to deal with.

The sergeant looked at Domenico uneasily. "Is everything all right, sir?"

Pull yourself together. Focus. Do your job.

Domenico cleared his throat. "Who was he?"

"Another Vatican bureaucrat, by the look of it," the sergeant replied. "We've sent word to Cardinal Riario. As soon as he arrives, we should be able to make a proper identification."

"If it's bureaucrats they're killing, there's a lot more of this to come," Domenico muttered. "The place is full of them."

"And we found this." The sergeant handed Domenico a bloodstained paring knife. "It was on the shelf. No attempt made to hide it. Almost like the killer wanted us to find it."

Domenico took the knife and studied the smears of dried blood on the blade. "What did they cut off?"

Both men looked at the corpse, their eyes drawn to the curtain of blood that emerged from the priest's mouth, tumbled down his cassock, spread across the fruit and pooled on the cellar floor.

"Something inside, by the look of it, sir."

Domenico bent down, gently opened the priest's mouth and saw the scroll of paper that had been forced between the corpse's teeth. Carefully, he reached his fingers inside to retrieve the paper, but as he slid it out he saw the bloody stub of hacked tongue at the back of the priest's throat. "I think that answers the question."

"*Figlio di puttana,*" the sergeant whispered.

The floodgates of dread opened inside Domenico's heart. This had too much in common with the first murder: a mutilated priest, body laid out on display, no signs of struggle, no attempt to escape … and a message written on a scroll of paper.

Taking care not to damage the bloodstained document, Domenico opened the scroll and read.

Lord, I beseech You, be patient with a humble sinner.

My body had turned away from blood, yet in my heart I could find no peace.

I was a wretched and lost soul, until You reached out to me.

In Your wisdom, Lord, You showed me the way.

You commanded: "Of the tree of the knowledge of Good and Evil, thou shalt not eat."

But they did eat.

They gorged themselves, and their gluttony left me empty and starved.

I had only my faith to nourish me, until You came back, Lord.

Domenico hesitated as he came to the terrible warning buried within the piety.

When the tree bore its miraculous fruit, I knew that You would guide my hand so that I might satisfy my longing for Justice.

Who would not kill the Serpent to redeem all mankind?

You gave me the sign, Lord, and I have acted. The mills of the gods grind slowly, but they grind small.

The contrast between the spiritual gloss of the prayer and the visceral reality of the murder was sickening. And the link between this atrocity and the staged miracles that had captivated Rome, was undeniable. *When the tree bore its miraculous fruit.* The killer was leaving them in no doubt.

"Sergeant, put armed guards on all the entrances to the Vatican cellars. Day and night."

"Yes, sir."

"We haven't seen the last of this madman."

The sergeant glanced at the bloody scroll in Domenico's hand. "Do they threaten more killings?"

Domenico handed him the prayer to read.

The sergeant read it slowly. "Sounds like the killer is a woman."

"Not necessarily."

"Here — *They gorged themselves … the tree of the Knowledge of Good and Evil.*"

"Come on, Sergeant. You know how things are in the Vatican. Men can be violated as well as women."

The sergeant looked suddenly pale. "You think that's all started again?"

"I think we are reaping something that was sown twenty-three years ago. Remember the prayer with the first victim? 'Twenty-three winters of despair?' This is a long-held grudge, reawakened by the miracles of St Peter."

The sergeant's forehead creased. "It doesn't make sense. St Peter blessing Rome can only be a good thing."

"When you stimulate people to believe extraordinary things, who knows where their minds will wander." Domenico left the fruit cellar and started to walk away down the corridor.

"Where are you going now, sir?"

"To warn the people who can stop all this. If they're still listening to reason."

28: CONFRONT

Cristina had decided that the third miracle was going to be the most audacious of all, for it would be a *true* miracle. Why stop at illusion when you had the knowledge and skill to actually transform reality?

For inspiration, she had gone back to the writings of the Islamic scholar and physician, Abu Bakr al-Razi.

The library door opened and Isra entered brandishing a notebook. "Thirty-four patients. There must be one who's suitable."

"Listen to this." Cristian slid over one of the volumes she had been studying and found a passage she'd marked with a small clip. "Al-Razi was so far ahead of his time. When he was commissioned to establish a new hospital, he knew that the location was crucial, that some parts of the city were more conducive to health than others. So he had slabs of fresh meat hung at selected places throughout Baghdad and observed how long each one took to rot."

"Wouldn't they all rot at the same speed?"

"Far from it. And understanding that was his genius. They ended up building the hospital where the meat stayed fresh for longest, because the air was healthier."

"Well, let's see if he can work his genius on any of these." Isra sat down on the opposite side of the table and referred to her notebook. "Fifty-seven patients on the ward for acute melancholia. I've eliminated the patients who have been there for a long time as there's nothing to be done with them." Isra pointed to the volumes in front of Cristina. "Unless your man has written about surgery on the brain?"

"Not as far as I've read."

"Of the remaining patients we have thirteen diagnosed with hysteria, seven with acute melancholia, seven with possession, two with frenzy and four with non-specific disorders of the spirit."

Suddenly they heard the main doors rattle in the hallway downstairs. Cristina glanced at the library clock.

"Expecting someone?" Isra asked.

They listened closely — heard the jangling of keys, then a familiar step in the hall.

Cristina relaxed. "It's Domenico."

Isra poured a fresh glass of wine for him, but as she placed it on the table the library door flew open and Domenico strode in. Immediately it was clear he wasn't in the mood for wine.

"You have to stop all this, Cristina."

She blinked innocently. "'This' being?"

"Whipping up religious hysteria."

"But that's not what we're doing."

"Don't split hairs."

"We are building a narrative that reflects the deep truth of St Peter's unbreakable links to Rome and the Church."

"Well, I have two dead priests that say otherwise." Domenico snatched the wine glass and slugged it down in one.

"When? I didn't hear about this. How did it happen?"

"They were brutally murdered. One had his throat slit and his right eye gouged out. The other had his tongue hacked off with a paring knife."

Cristina looked down so as not to give anything away. Yes, she was shocked, but a part of her was also fascinated by the choreography of the killings. She pulled herself up; now was not the time to get sidetracked. "I'm sorry to hear that, Domenico. But correlation does not imply causation."

"So everyone keeps telling me."

"Then perhaps you should start listening."

"Don't patronise me, Cristina!"

"I'm not. I just want to know what on earth two dead priests have to do with a celebration of St Peter's relics."

Domenico took the bloodied pieces of paper from his jacket and put them on the table. "Read."

The prayers looked shockingly macabre sharing a table with so many erudite volumes. Instinctively, Isra took a tray from the sideboard and placed it under the documents, as if to prevent any blood from contaminating the learning.

"The one on the left was placed in the first victim's eye socket. The one on the right was stuffed in the second victim's mouth."

"Look, I don't doubt that you're dealing with a violent criminal. Disturbed, even. But I am dealing with the highest spirituality possible — the blessings of a saint. I don't see how these two can possibly intersect."

"Read them."

Reluctantly, Cristina picked up the stained documents and read the prayers in silence. When she'd finished, she placed them back on the tray.

"The link is obvious," Domenico said.

Cristina shrugged. "Not really."

"'*You spoke to me, through the miracle of St Peter.*'"

"That could mean many things."

"'*When the tree bore its miraculous fruit, I knew that You would guide my hand so that I might satisfy my longing for Justice.*' Whoever is doing this has been moved to murder by the miracles you've created, Cristina!"

"So the murders are my fault? And you're here to arrest me?"

"Don't be ridiculous."

"You're the one making the link."

Domenico hated it when his sister's arguments tied him in knots. "All I'm saying is that if you persist in creating a febrile, religious hysteria on the streets of Rome, there will be more savage murders. More dead priests in the morgue. And it will be on your shoulders."

Cristina drew a deep breath. "I did not wield the knife. Nothing we have done has incited people to violence. Quite the opposite."

Domenico crossed the library and gazed out of an open shutter. "Someone down there has a very different understanding. If they're prepared to kill two priests in the name of St Peter, who knows where they will stop."

"Christ preached love, yet despite that, countless thousands have been murdered in His name," Cristina said. "Would the world have been a better place if Christ had abandoned His ministry? Because that's what you are suggesting."

"How much longer will the Bureau of Relics be manipulating the population?"

"Until no-one can doubt that St Peter's bones are working their divine power in Rome."

"So you'll keep going until everyone has swallowed the lie?"

"It's not a lie. We are serving a greater truth."

Domenico closed the window shutter. "I don't see it that way. I'm sorry, I just don't."

"Because you have no vision." Cristina picked up one of the books from the table. "This man had vision, even though he was going blind. When a physician offered him an ointment to cure his blindness, al-Razi replied, 'My eyes will not be treated by one who does not know the basics of its anatomy.'

Likewise, Domenico, I will not take lessons from you about the ethics of the intellect."

Domenico put the empty glass back on the table and left the library without saying another word.

29: EXORCISM

Cristina gazed up at the intricate carvings on the portico of the Hospital for the Incurables. "I just can't seem to keep away from the place."

"Are you going to see Professor De Luca while you're here?" Isra asked, pushing open the heavy doors.

"No."

Isra followed Cristina as she strode across the worn marble floor of the atrium. "But he might be recovering."

"He's not."

"How do you know?"

"I left instructions for the hospital to send a message if there was any change in his condition."

"Still … it might be nice to see him."

"He's unconscious, Isra. What's the point of standing next to his bedside when he won't even know I'm there?"

"Well … it's what people do," Isra ventured.

"It's illogical." Cristina turned hard right and hurried up the flight of stone stairs which led to the wards for acute melancholia.

They had arranged to meet Geometra Castano on a balcony overlooking the courtyard containing the huge umbrella pine, and he was, as always, punctual.

"The physician in charge of the melancholia wards has given us permission to assess all his patients," Castano reported.

"Excellent," Cristina replied. "I'd like to start with those who are considered possessed."

Castano raised an eyebrow. "I have to say, I really don't see the point of all this."

"You will."

"You appreciate that we are now overreaching the remit of the Bureau of Relics?"

Cristina turned to face Castano. "In the West, those with illnesses of the mind are thought to be possessed by demons. But that is an ignorant way of thinking."

"With all due respect, I hardly think you are in a position to judge. You are neither priest nor physician," Castano replied.

"No. I am a scholar. And I know that the Arabic term for the mentally unwell is *majnoon*. Derived from the term *jenna*, which means covered. As in unable to differentiate between the real and the imagined. The Islamic scholar Avicenna defined mental illness as a condition in which reality is replaced with fantasy. The real world is obscured. To imprison such patients is to punish them twice, and is another example of the unenlightened savagery that persists in certain strands of Western thought. We are here to correct that. Now do you understand?"

Castano remained stony faced. "So now you're introducing heretical thinkers into the work of a Vatican committee?" he sniffed.

"If you recall, Christ was considered a heretic as well as a lawbreaker during His life. Revolution never comes from the conformist." Cristina pointed to the doors leading to the patients. "Shall we?"

A junior physician had been assigned to guide them through the ward, and as he showed them each patient, he provided a medical history of their maladies and the treatments that had been used.

Isra found it heart-breaking to see so many people tormented by illnesses that could be neither seen nor touched nor soothed with ointments, but Cristina set aside emotion and focussed intently on the facts of each case, asking detailed questions not just about the patients' behaviour, but the circumstances that had brought them into the hospital.

They spent hours working their way along the gloomy corridors, encountering one lost soul after another. Cristina seemed to be searching for something very specific ... and very elusive. Finally, just as she appeared to be losing hope, the physician stopped outside the cell door of Rosa Cielo.

"She is only seventeen," he explained. "The youngest on the ward."

"What happened to her?"

"She was engaged to be married. The whole family was delighted. Everyone was busy making preparations. Then two days before the wedding, they found Rosa in her bedroom, screaming hysterically, thrashing back and forth on her bed, calling out to demons that no-one else could see."

"Is there any history of breakdown in other members of her family?"

The physician shook his head. "Not as far as I know."

"Have you asked?"

"Rosa's family were convinced the mother of a rival suitor had put a curse on the poor girl. They appealed to the magistrates, but could offer no proof. Rosa was deemed a danger to the public and committed into our care."

"I'd like to meet her." Cristina tried to open the cell door, but it was locked.

"We'll need to wait," the physician explained. "The exorcist is administering to her."

"Exorcism? On a young girl?"

"Her family requested it. Personally, I wouldn't have given permission, but I was overruled by the hospital governors."

"It won't help the girl," Cristina insisted. "You'll just make her more frightened."

"It's the third attempt, and Rosa shows no sign of improvement," he confessed.

"Three times?" Cristina glared at him. "You have subjected her to the barbarity of an exorcism on three occasions, even though you know it doesn't help?"

The physician looked down. "Who can understand the mysteries of the mind?"

"Open this door and let me in."

"I would not recommend it."

Cristina held out her hand. "Give me the key."

Reluctantly, the physician took a large ring of keys from his gown and unlocked the door. "I warn you, do not interrupt the Holy Rites. It could imperil Rosa's soul."

Cristina pushed open the door.

Isra gasped in shock as she saw what was unfolding.

Rosa was sitting on the bed. Her feet had been strapped down and her hands manacled behind her back. Tears were streaming down her face but her torso was twisting left and right as she tried to free herself. A bull of a man, the exorcist, was looming over her, his meaty hands clamped around the girl's head.

"I cast you out, unclean spirit!" he declared. "Along with every Satanic power of the enemy, every spectre from Hell, and all your demonic companions. In the name of our Lord Jesus Christ."

Gently, he made the symbol of the cross on Rosa's forehead, then boomed, "Be gone! Stay far away from this creature of God!" He thrust the girl back violently onto the bed, then grabbed her by the shoulders and pulled her up again.

"Be gone!" he thundered. "For it is He who commands you. He who flung you headlong from the heights of Heaven into the depths of Hell. Be gone!"

Rosa screamed as the exorcist jerked her backwards then hauled her up again.

"Tremble in fear, Satan! You enemy of the faith, you begetter of death, you robber of life, you corrupter of justice, you root of all evil and vice. Be gone!"

The exorcist flung Rosa down onto the bed, but this time he pressed his hands onto her face as if he was trying to crush the demons out of her.

The girl writhed, trying to escape his suffocating grip. "*Vaffanculo!*" she screamed. "*Figlio di puttana! Cornuto!*" The more she abused him, the harder he pressed on her head.

Suddenly the whole pitch of Rosa's voice changed into a raspy growl. "*Tua madre succhia cazzi all'inferno!*"

Stunned by her outburst, the exorcist released his grip and stepped back. He picked up a small bottle of holy water, but as he removed the cork, Rosa threw herself wildly towards him, knocking the bottle from his hands.

Isra watched the phial arc through the air ... then smash onto the floor, spilling its precious contents across the flagstones.

The exorcist grabbed hold of Rosa's shoulders and shook her violently, commanding the evil spirits to leave. Rosa drew a huge gasp of air, then her body went limp and she slumped forward. In an instant, all the fight had gone from her.

The exorcist lifted Rosa's eyelids with his thumbs, but the girl was unconscious. He laid her back on the bed and turned to the physician. "There is nothing more I can do for her."

"Did it work?" the physician asked.

"I did not see the demons leave her body." The exorcist looked at the damp stain of holy water on the floor. "I fear Rosa is beyond redemption." Then he picked up his Bible and left the cell.

Isra watched as Cristina approached the bed cautiously and looked down at Rosa. She touched her hand to the girl's forehead, then held her wrist to feel her pulse.

"If ever there was a child in need of the wisdom of Islam, it is Rosa. This is who we shall cure."

30: AL-RAZI

Perched on the roof of the hospital was a once beautiful pavilion. Its origins were obscure, but after twenty years of neglect it had fallen into disrepair. The moment Cristina saw it, she knew it would be the perfect place to effect a cure.

The pavilion resembled a huge wooden dovecote as it had dozens of arched openings on all sides, yet it was far too large for the birds. Perhaps it had been built as a folly, or a retreat for meditation; no-one in the hospital could shed any light on its true purpose, so they were quite happy for Cristina to renovate the structure. Once the broken boards and rotten roof slates had been removed, it was clear that the fundamentals of the pavilion were sound, for it had been built from seasoned oak which had weathered beautifully. Castano diverted a small team of workmen from the St Peter's construction site to the hospital, and within two days they had repaired the shutters on all the window openings, fitted a new roof of cedar shingles, and replaced the rotten cladding. When they had finished, Isra set about hanging linen curtains from floor to ceiling, which billowed gracefully in the breeze; because the pavilion faced all points of the compass, fresh air and sunlight were always filtering into the room.

Isra brought Rosa up the access ramp in a wheeled invalid chair, and Cristina took great delight in showing the patient her new room. "No-one will harm you up here, Rosa. This is your safe place. Your sanctuary."

Rosa's eyes briefly flicked around the room, but she showed no emotion.

"Do you like it?"

Rosa hugged her arms around her own body.

"Would you like to stay here? It's better than the ward, isn't it?"

No response.

"Look … you can see all seven hills of Rome."

Still, Rosa said nothing.

"As I suspected, this was a waste of time," Castano pronounced.

"The treatment has only just begun. You must not be so quick to judge."

"But this is clearly dangerous," Castano sniffed. "There are no locks on the door, the girl isn't strapped to the bed. Anything could happen."

Cristina looked at the curtains billowing serenely across the space. "Who would want to escape from this?"

"What if she suddenly decides that she is a sparrow that can soar through the skies?" Castano objected. "What's to prevent her jumping off the roof?"

"It's a fair point," Isra said. "There's nothing to stop Rosa from harming herself."

Cristina knelt in front of the patient. "You're not going to doing anything like that, are you, Rosa? There's nothing to be afraid of here."

No response.

"We want to help you," Cristina continued patiently. "And this beautiful room is where you can heal."

Silence.

"You might get more sense talking to a sparrow," Castano quipped.

Cristina spun round and glared at him. "Don't ever do that. Don't ever talk about a patient as if they weren't present."

"But she isn't. Look at her."

"It is a cornerstone of al-Razi's philosophy that disorders of the mind should be treated as medical conditions, and that the physician should always speak gently, and with the utmost respect for the patient."

"Even if they aren't listening?" Castano replied.

"Patients hear everything. Sometimes they choose not to respond. Which is why we need to set Rosa free from the condition that binds her."

The initial phase of treatment was to soothe Rosa's nerves and undo the damage caused by the exorcist; they wanted to put her in a calm, relaxed state of mind. To this end, they worked on three fronts. The first was food — Isra prepared three delicate and delicious meals every day and brought them to the pavilion. The emphasis was on fruit and vegetables, with nothing too heavy and only very small pieces of meat and fish.

The second front was bathing. Cristina asked Castano to organise the construction of a hot bath inside the pavilion. It was a project that played to his strengths, and within two days he had directed workmen to construct a network of pipes leading from the water tanks on the hospital roof, through a specially built furnace, and into a large copper tub. Every morning and evening, Cristina would fill the tub with steaming water and encourage Rosa to bathe for as long as she wanted. At first the girl was suspicious, but once she was immersed in the hot water it was impossible not to relax.

"How does that feel?" Cristina whispered as Rosa closed her eyes and lay back. "You know, I think one day every house will have something like this."

Still, Rosa said nothing, but Cristina could see that her anxiety was gradually seeping away.

The third front was smell. "Scent is the key to the soul," Cristina explained as she led Isra into the perfumier's salon that was situated at the junction of the *tre vie*, where the old Roman aqueduct ended. Immediately they were confronted by thousands of small glass phials, neatly racked on cabinets that reached up to the ceiling.

While they waited for the perfumier to emerge from his laboratory at the back of the salon, Isra started reading the labels on the bottles of essence. "So, are we looking for something to help Rosa relax?"

"No. She is already relaxed, now we need to stir her soul."

"But not agitate it?"

"We must stimulate the finest parts of her mind."

"Maybe … a nostalgic scent?"

"Interesting. Yes, that might work. Help her remember a time when she was well."

"And long to get back to that state of happiness."

"It's a good start, Isra." Cristina rang the bell impatiently to summon the elderly perfumier. "What's taking him so long?"

That whole afternoon was spent testing different scents and discussing with the perfumier what they were trying to achieve, and eventually they emerged with three phials of essential oils: one was based on cedar, the second on bergamot and the third on jasmine.

When Rosa next stepped out of the bath, Cristina offered to massage the scented oils onto her feet and shoulders, surrounding the girl with a cloud of evocative memories. From the look on Rosa's face, it was clear that the therapy of aromas stimulated a wistful pleasure.

The next phase of treatment was all about hope. Cristina hired a trio of musicians who played mandolin, flute and violin, and briefed them carefully. "The aim is to play music that convinces Rosa of the possibility of a cure."

The musicians looked at her blankly. "So, cheerful tunes then?"

"It needs to be much more than that. Anyone can do cheerful, this needs to be … life-affirming, but in a spiritual way. Contemplative yet underpinned with emotion."

"Oh."

Words were evidently not the forte of these musicians, so rather than trying to articulate what she meant, Cristina had them play samples from their whole repertoire, and selected the most evocative pieces.

Cristina would sit with Rosa for hours in the afternoon, listening to music and watching shadows creep across the pavilion as the sun arced above Rome. It was deeply affecting for both of them, almost like entering a trance state, where time and space merged into a fluid whole, where you surrendered to forces that were powerful and primal.

As the sun edged lower on the third evening, Cristina paid the musicians as usual and watched them walk away across the roof. That was when Rosa spoke for the first time.

"Will they return tomorrow?"

Cristina could barely contain her excitement, and she had to try very hard not to make any sudden exclamations that might startle the girl. "Would you like them to?"

"Yes. I would."

"Then that's what we'll do."

It was the most understated of breakthroughs, but how could Cristina build on it? "It's so nice to hear your voice, Rosa. Your real voice."

"I am not the problem," Rosa whispered.

"Then who is?"

The girl curled up on the bed. "Some fates are sealed. And there is nothing you can do to change it. Nothing anyone can do. That is my fate."

Cristina sat on the edge of the bed and gently placed her hand on Rosa's hair. "Then it's just as well I don't believe in fate."

31: BODIES

Packed in ice, the two dead priests looked strangely comfortable in the morgue.

"You can see why I'm worried," Domenico said as he pulled the shroud back to let his deputy see the brutalised corpses.

Tomasso said nothing as he used a magnifying glass to study the gaping eye socket, the slashed throat and the severed tongue.

"These weren't opportunistic crimes. They were carefully planned and meticulously executed," Domenico added, with an unintended hint of admiration. "The only evidence the killer left behind was what he wanted us to see."

Tomasso put down the lens and stepped back from the slab. "Someone really hated these men."

"And yet, I have been unable to discover anything in their lives that could provoke such an attack. These were anonymous priests leading uncontroversial lives."

"How have you managed to keep all this quiet?"

"I don't want to keep it quiet, believe me." Domenico reached into a sack he'd brought with him, pulled out some large chunks of ice and started replacing those sections that were starting to melt. "I want to shout this from the rooftops, but Cardinal Riario has imposed an information blackout."

Tomasso was puzzled. "Doesn't he want you to catch the killer?"

"He insists that nothing can be allowed to distract from the 'religious euphoria' in Rome that my sister is creating." Domenico gave a snort of derision. "He says euphoria, I say hysteria."

Tomasso didn't want to get drawn into taking sides. "What do you know about the victims so far?"

"They're both the same age: forty-six. Both built their careers inside the Vatican." Domenico pointed to the first victim. "Father Coraggioso dealt with foreign priests coming to Rome. Victim number two, Father Maggio, worked in the Exchequer. He was responsible for reconciling all the rents from the Papal States."

"That's got to suggest a motive. All that money flowing under his nose?"

Domenico shook his head. "First thing I checked, but Maggio was incorruptible. That's why he got the job."

"No-one is above corruption," Tomasso replied. "The only question is the price."

"Maggio reconciled his accounts down to the last ducat. He was a notorious pedant."

Tomasso looked at the grey faces of the priests. "What about other forms of corruption? Women? Gambling debts? Addiction?"

"Nothing. And I went through every vice I could think of."

"Did they renege on bribes they'd taken?"

"There was no trace in their private correspondence."

"Have you considered rivalry in the Vatican bureaucracy?" Tomasso suggested.

"You really think the killer could be another priest?"

"Wouldn't be the first time a man of the cloth has murdered to get a promotion."

Domenico considered the theory. "The victims were in different departments. So that doesn't really fit. It's not as if the killer is trying to eliminate a chain of command."

"There has to be a motive."

"The lack of it is what's causing such fear inside the Vatican," Domenico said as he emptied the last of the fresh ice onto the corpses. "If there is no reason why these two were targeted, then every priest is in danger."

"Especially the forty-six-year-olds," Tomasso said grimly.

"Officially, no-one's allowed to talk about these murders, but in private, people are terrified. I'm getting anonymous letters threatening to have me sacked if I don't catch the killer."

"No Christian compassion in the Vatican, then."

"When priests don't feel safe, they really lash out."

Tomasso picked up the notes that were found at the murder scenes and reread the prayers. "These are so pious. The killer really thinks they are doing God's work."

"That's what makes this so baffling, the notes are deeply religious. They're not railing against the wealth or decadence of the Church. They're personal and devout, not political."

"So what's your next step?" Tomasso asked.

Domenico gave a wearily cynical laugh. "I know what *needs* to be done. We need to stop the Bureau of Relics from whipping up any more religious hysteria."

"It's not going to happen."

"But that is what's triggering the killings."

"What does Cristina say?"

"She's not listening to me. Or to anyone, for that matter. I thought she of all people would have more respect for the lone voice of reason. She's spent her whole life being an outsider, but now that she's at the heart of things … it's gone to her head." Domenico studied Tomasso's face, looking for a reaction. He knew how much his deputy liked Cristina, and how much his loyalties were now being pulled in opposite directions. "Has she even talked about the killings?"

"She's just focussed on the next miracle."

"What trick will it be this time?" Domenico sat down on one of the morgue slabs. "What bauble to dazzle the masses?"

"She says it won't be a trick, but a real miracle."

"The woman's deluded."

Tomasso shuffled awkwardly.

"Look, she's my sister, and I love her. But I'm telling you, Cristina is suffering from delusions of grandeur."

"We have been put on standby for this Sunday," Tomasso explained. "Apparently, she will reveal the miracle at the Castel Sant'Angelo, in the presence of the casket containing St Peter's relics."

"You mean the empty casket?"

"We shouldn't talk like that."

"But it's the truth."

"Not any longer."

"Tomasso, don't allow yourself to get caught up in this mass delusion. I need you to stay sane. And focussed."

"Yes, sir. I'm sorry. But..." A long silence followed.

"But?" Domenico prompted.

"What if Cristina really does perform a miracle?"

Domenico looked at his deputy in disbelief. "I saw her nappies being changed. I watched her milk teeth fall out. I saw her stumble and bleed and cry; I witnessed her have toddler tantrums. Cristina can no more perform a miracle than I can walk on water."

32: PULSE

Cristina chose the most serene time of day for the experiment, the hour just before sunset, when the low light caught buildings at a perfect angle and made their cold stonework glow.

"Do you trust me?"

Rosa nodded.

"You know I would never do anything to harm you."

"I know."

"Why don't you lie on the bed?" Cristina suggested. "In the most comfortable position."

Rosa did as she was told and lay on her back, her head cradled in the pillows, her arms resting on either side of her body.

"Now close your eyes," Cristina said, "and breathe deeply and slowly. Count to two as you breathe in, five as you breathe out."

Rosa started drawing deep, steady breaths.

"Yes, that's perfect ... keep going ... in ... and out." Cristina watched Rosa's body relax, then gently took the girl's wrist between her fingers.

"What are you doing?" Rosa asked.

"I need to feel your pulse." Cristina adjusted her fingers until she could feel the steady throb in Rosa's radial artery. She counted the beats, waiting until the pulse was steady, then without letting go, she started talking. "I want you to think of a time in your life when you were happy. Perhaps you were with friends, laughing and drinking ... or maybe it was on one of the feast days ... you were at ease with the world ... find a moment that could go on forever."

Fleeting expressions fluttered across Rosa's face as she remembered what it felt like to be at peace. Cristina focussed intently on the slowing pulse that was beating under her fingertips.

"Good. Excellent, Rosa. You're doing well. Now, I'd like you to think about your family ... your mother."

Still, the pulse remained slow.

"Remember when you were a girl, and your mother brushed your hair before bedtime ... how nice that felt ... her warmth ... the gentleness of her touch. You feel so close to your mother..."

"Yes," Rosa whispered. "I do."

"And now you hear the door open ... it's your father coming home from work."

Cristina felt the girl's pulse lurch.

"You haven't seen him all day ... you run down the stairs to greet him..."

Rosa's pulse raced faster, but there was an edge of irregularity in it. Cristina glanced at the girl's face and saw her forehead tense.

"He's pleased to see you ... he opens his arms to give you a hug —"

Suddenly, Rosa pulled her wrist from Cristina's hand.

"What's wrong?"

Rosa shook her head and sat up. "I don't want to do this."

"There's nothing to worry about."

"I don't want this!" Rosa swung her legs from the bed and escaped to the side of the pavilion.

Cristina gave her a few moments, then walked over and stood next to her. Together they gazed out across Rome, watching the dying sunlight wrap itself around the curves of the Colosseum, as if clinging to the ancient stones to avoid being consumed by darkness.

"I thought you wanted to heal me," Rosa said. "Not remind me of…"

She didn't complete the sentence, but Cristina knew that they were getting to the heart of it.

"The physician whose techniques we have been following, he believed that the mind and body are one. That they affect each other in complex ways and in every moment of the day. If you want to cure one, you have to cure both. A person's pulse is where the body reveals what the mind is feeling."

Rosa shook her head. "That doesn't make sense."

"You can hide things from me, but you cannot hide them from your own body."

No reply. Cristina had to do something to stop the girl from slipping back into silence. "You know, my own family is complicated. There are many things I have to keep hidden from my parents."

Rosa turned and looked at her. "They don't know you're doing this?"

"They wouldn't understand, so I don't tell them. My brother defends me, but he also frustrates me. It's as if he doesn't really trust me, as if I will always just be his little sister."

"Family can be difficult," Rosa muttered.

"I know what it feels like to be at odds with those closest to you. So I will not judge you, Rosa. But if you want to heal, we need to keep going." Cristina beckoned to the bed.

Rosa hesitated. "Without my family, I would be nothing."

"I know. But that doesn't make them right." Cristina guided Rosa back to the bed, made her comfortable, and took her wrist between her fingers.

"Tell me something that you like to do. Something that makes you happy."

Rosa closed her eyes and thought for a few moments. "Baking bread."

"Really?"

"It's like ... magic. You take the simplest ingredients, on their own they're nothing, but put them together and something happens. The smell of freshly baked bread ... that is happiness to me."

Rosa's pulse had settled into a steady rhythm — she felt secure in her memories.

"Can you imagine baking bread in your own house? For a family of your own?"

"Yes. One day ... sharing fresh bread with my children. Watching them dip it into a pot of honey."

"Someone once told me that a hot oven is the heart of a household."

"Yes ... it is."

"And when your husband comes home at the end of the day, perhaps he lifts the saucepan lids to see what's cooking?"

Cristina felt Rosa's pulse tense again.

"Maybe." Anxiety was creeping into her answers.

"You were going to be married, weren't you?"

Suddenly, Rosa's pulse started racing. She tried to pull her hand away, but Cristina gripped her arm. "What is it?"

"Nothing."

Her pulse spiked wildly.

"They said you wanted to get married. That everyone was so happy."

"Yes. But..."

"But what?" Rosa's pulse was throbbing between Cristina's fingers. "Don't you love him? Don't you want to get married?"

"I do!"

"Then what, Rosa?"

"I do want to get married ... but not ... not to him!"

Cristina's mind flashed back to what the physician had told her — Rosa's family accused the mother of a *rival* suitor of witchcraft. They claimed she had put a curse on the girl.

Finally, it all made sense. "Perhaps the man you really love is not the man your family wants you to marry?"

Rosa looked down and seemed to stop breathing.

"Is that the truth?"

The girl was terrified of doing anything that would reveal her innermost feelings.

"Your mother understands, but your father will not listen. He has forced you to give up your true love. And that has pushed your mind to break down. You were never possessed, you were simply unable to accept a reality that you didn't want."

Rosa's shoulders started to tremble as she fought back the tears.

"What's his name, Rosa?"

"I must not say it. They forbade it."

"Tell me the name of your true love."

"I had to give up everything that made me happy," Rosa stuttered. "It was in my hands, and I threw it away. I threw it away."

"Say his name, Rosa. Say it for me."

"Rodrigo," she whispered.

It was like plucking the cork from a barrel of wine. The relief at uttering his name unleashed a flood of emotions. Rosa cradled her head in her hands and wept. And as she cried, all the anger and confusion and hurt were released from her body.

Cristina said nothing, she just sat next to the girl; being there was enough. When Rosa's tears finally subsided, Cristina lifted her chin and gently dried her face with a handkerchief. "What if we could change your father's mind?" she said.

Rosa shook her head. "You don't know my father."

"That's the thing about miracles," Cristina smiled, "they can penetrate even the hardest of hearts."

33: GRACE

"You must not speak," Tomasso warned. "You can only listen, and watch."

Rosa's parents nodded. Even if they had been inclined to speak, they were too confused to say anything coherent. They had been awoken just after dawn by two Apostolic Guards hammering on their door, who told them they needed to come to their daughter urgently, but refused to elaborate. As they followed the guards through the chilly streets, Rosa's mother and father started to fear the worst, and by the time Tomasso met them at the gates of Castel Sant'Angelo, they were terrified.

"Is she alive?" the mother whispered. "Please, just tell me that much."

Tomasso held a finger to his lips. "Watch. And listen."

He led them down a dark, narrow corridor into the stone heart of the Castel, then pushed open a set of heavy bronze doors that led to the vault. Gently, Tomasso ushered Rosa's parents inside.

The room was filled with a shimmering light from hundreds of flickering candles that had been arranged in concentric circles around a stone plinth. Sitting on the plinth was a golden casket with the Latin inscription *Super Hanc Petrum*, telling the world that these were the bones of St Peter.

Four monks with cowls pulled low over their faces, knelt in deep, meditative prayer, like spiritual guards watching over their beloved saint. Overwhelmed, Rosa's mother and father sank to their knees and clasped their hands together.

After what felt like an eternity of waiting, a door on the far side of the vault creaked open, and Rosa appeared, slumped in an invalid chair that was being pushed by Castano.

The mother gasped when she saw her daughter. The girl's head was doubled over on her chest, her hair obscured her face and she seemed completely unresponsive.

"Rosa!" her mother cried.

Tomasso glared at the woman, urging her to remain silent.

"But the evil spirit is still on her."

"Be quiet!" Tomasso hissed.

Forbidden from talking, the woman expressed herself through tears instead; they trickled down her cheeks and plopped onto the stone floor.

Meticulously, patiently, Castano moved a segment of candles aside to create a corridor in the flickering light; then he wheeled Rosa's chair towards the golden casket, lifted her right hand and placed it on the lid.

"St Peter, First Bishop of Rome, who was ordained by Jesus Christ, who walked by the side of our Lord, and who witnessed His sacrifice on Golgotha, hear my prayer." Castano glanced at Rosa's parents to gauge the effect of his words before continuing. "We beg you to take pity on your servant, Rosa, who has been overtaken by darkness. St Peter, you showed us by your life that the power of light will always triumph over the power of darkness. As we live in the hope of forgiveness and eternal salvation, I beseech you now to have mercy on this child. Bring the Light of the Lord into this girl's heart!"

Castano fell silent.

Suddenly a gust of wind billowed through the vault. The candles flickered wildly, but stayed alight. And Rosa gasped. Her lungs heaved, like a swimmer coming up for air. Her body shook once, as if casting off an invisible shroud, then she was still again.

Castano knelt beside her. "Rosa? Have you come back to us?"

Slowly, Rosa raised her head and blinked. She looked around the vault, disorientated, then saw her parents kneeling on the far side of the casket. It was as if she had woken from the heaviest of sleeps. "What am I doing here?" Her voice sounded hoarse. "Where have I been?"

Unable to restrain herself any longer, Rosa's mother stumbled to her knees, ran across the vault and scooped her daughter into her arms. "I thought I'd lost you, Rosa! I thought I'd lost you forever..."

Castano was finally able to prize Rosa free from her mother's embrace long enough to usher the family out of the vault, and into an anteroom where Cristina was waiting.

"This is one of the physicians who cared for your daughter," he said.

The mother clasped Cristina's hands. "How can we give thanks?"

Cristina shook her head. "We are all humbled by the power of St Peter."

"Yes. Yes, we are," the mother agreed, reaching for her rosary beads. "St Peter has saved us all."

"And yet..." Cristina hesitated.

"If there is something we can do, tell us," the mother urged.

Cristina reached out and touched the side of Rosa's head. "When she was ill, in the depths of her delirium, Rosa spoke."

"She spoke? What did she say?"

"Much of it didn't make sense. Except, there was a name she kept mumbling."

"Was it us? Was she calling for her parents?"

"No. I think it was … Rodrigo," Cristina ventured. "Does that name mean anything?"

Awkwardness jolted the euphoria of the reunion.

Rosa's mother looked at her daughter. "You said that?"

"I don't remember. Everything is so confused."

The mother turned accusingly to her husband. "You see?"

The man shuffled uncomfortably.

"Whoever Rodrigo is," Cristina said innocently, "I believe the thought of him kept your daughter alive in the darkness. If you want to give thanks, perhaps it should be to him?"

Rosa's mother crossed the room and stood in front of her husband. She took his hands in hers and gripped them tightly. "We cannot lose her again. I won't let that happen. Do you hear?"

The man's heart was too full to argue. He opened his arms and hugged Rosa tightly. "Rodrigo has earned the right to love you. St Peter has willed it."

34: RUMOUR

Word of the miracle spread like wildfire.

When her parents took Rosa home, the whole street turned out to welcome the girl back, triggering an impromptu neighbourhood party. Huge cooking pots were rolled into the street and slung over freshly made bonfires; mothers and scullery maids rummaged in their larders to provide ingredients, and before long vast quantities of pasta were bubbling away next to dozens of smaller pots containing every sauce under the sun. Barrels of wine that had been put aside for special occasions were cracked open with relish, for what could be more special than a miracle? At noon, the butcher turned up with a wild boar that had been killed that very morning, even as the miracle was unfolding. The carcass was shaved, olive oil massaged into its skin, then herbs and seasoning were stuffed into every cavity; before long the tantalising smell of roast boar was drifting over the rooftops of Rome.

As the aroma spread, neighbouring Municipios started to feel left out of the festivities. Why should they work while their neighbours partied? So people downed tools, shuttered up their shops and started street parties of their own.

"What are we all celebrating?"

"A miracle! A young woman lost her mind. Just by touching St Peter's tomb, she was cured!"

"Saint Peter brought her back?"

"Yes! Back to her family, as if she'd never been struck down."

"A miracle!"

"Did you hear? St Peter brought a woman back from the dead."

"From the dead? Impossible!"

"I heard it from the baker who lives next door to the family."

"Are you sure?"

"St Peter's relics can cure anyone."

"Even the blind?"

"Especially the blind. And the sick, and the lame. One touch! That's all you need, brother. One touch and you are cured of all maladies."

"And forgiven your sins?"

"Forgiven and healed."

"A miracle! Rome is the City of St Peter's Miracles!"

So the rumours tumbled across the city, amplifying with each Municipio they touched, and they didn't stop at the city walls...

Within days, pilgrims started heading into Rome, thousands of them, from all directions of the compass, desperate to have whatever burden they bore eased by the blessings of St Peter's relics. At first, the city was delighted to welcome these new visitors. Taverns and shops, buskers, soothsayers and opportunist street hawkers all did a roaring trade.

But there was a problem.

The pilgrims didn't just visit the city then go home, they stayed, hoping for a chance to glimpse the saint's relics with their own eyes and receive a personal slice of Divine Grace. So when the lodging rooms were full, people started camping on the streets, turning piazzas into tent cities and the River Tiber into a bathroom. Rubbish clogged the walkways, piles of excrement appeared down every dark alley, rats and pickpockets flourished, and rising from all the filth came a wretched stench that hung over the city like a miasma.

Yet still they came. Wave after wave of euphoric pilgrims pressing into Rome, until finally the authorities were forced to close the city gates, just as they had when Rome was under attack from the Barbarian hordes.

Cristina's moment of triumph was turning very sour, very quickly…

"This is impossible!" Tomasso shouted above the clamour of the crowd. "Someone's going to get hurt. Seriously hurt."

He was standing next to Cristina on the castellated tower of the Porta Pinciana, looking down at the sea of pilgrims battering against the closed gates. It wasn't just the immediate area that was mobbed, the pilgrims were backed up for half a mile along the dusty road and were now spilling out into the vineyards on either side, trampling fragile crops in their religious zeal.

"You need to enforce the Dispersal Edict," Cristina said.

"How exactly am I supposed to do that? Look at them!" Tomasso pointed to the front section of the crowd where people were being crushed against the huge wooden gates.

"They can't just ignore the law, Tomasso. It's for their own good."

"What use is a few hundred men against ten thousand desperate pilgrims? It's out of control!"

"Then you need to get more troops here."

"There are no reinforcements!" Tomasso was getting exasperated by Cristina's naivety. "It's the same at every gate around the city. All eighteen of them! We're at full stretch."

Cristina gazed down on the masses. This wasn't how it was supposed to be. She had been aiming for the dignified stoicism of Santiago de Compostela, or the well-rehearsed order of the Pilgrims' Way from Winchester to Canterbury; none of the accounts she'd read of those pilgrimages had described any kind of anarchic frenzy.

"Help! Somebody, help!" A man's voice cried out from the heaving throng. "She needs a doctor!"

Tomasso pointed to someone in the centre of the crush. "There. Look … she's fainted."

An unconscious woman was being passed over the heads of the crowd, hand to hand, like a sack of grain.

"Open the gates!"

"She needs a doctor!"

Cristina watched as the woman seemed to float above the heads of the mob towards the Porta, and realised that this wasn't altruistic behaviour; the heaving mass had understood that this victim was their best hope of penetrating Rome's defences. If the gates opened just a crack to let her in, the weight of numbers would do the rest. "Don't open the gates," Cristina warned Tomasso.

"We can't just leave her out there!"

"As long as she's outside the walls, she is not your responsibility."

Tomasso looked at Cristina with incomprehension. "How can you be so cold?"

"They're using her as bait. Don't fall for it."

Tomasso looked at the surging crowd beneath him, so desperate for salvation, and just for a moment he wondered if this is what the Gates of Heaven were really like. Maybe all those paintings depicting choirs of angels and queues of humble souls were completely wrong. Maybe it was anarchy in the afterlife.

And then he saw them — an old couple caught up in the hysteria who looked just like his grandparents. They were frail and exhausted, and there was a desperate fear in their eyes. All they wanted was to go home, yet now they found themselves in the middle of a crush they did not have the strength to survive. Maybe they weren't even pilgrims … maybe they'd just come to Rome to visit their family.

"I'm opening the gates." Tomasso turned and started down the steps.

"If you do that you'll never close them again!" Cristina shouted after him.

"People are going to die down there!"

"Tomasso, wait! Imagine all this anarchy *inside* Rome. The city can't take any more people."

"I will not stand by while people get crushed to death."

Cristina watched as Tomasso ran down into the street behind the Porta Pinciana and instructed two soldiers to help him slide back the bolts on the wicket gates. He was trying to relieve the pressure outside whilst controlling the influx to prevent a stampede, but the moment the first small door was unlocked, desperate pilgrims surged through and started lashing out with fists and sticks, venting their frustration on the Apostolic Guards.

Tomasso and his troops tried to defend themselves, but the fury of the mob was vicious.

"Leave them!" Cristina screamed from the walkway. "They're just doing their job!"

The pilgrims weren't listening. While one group overwhelmed the guards, another pulled aside the huge iron drawbars on the main gates and stood back. The crack of light appearing in the city's defences triggered a fresh surge and people charged forward with a deafening roar.

Some of the guards were pushed backwards, trapped between the gates and the brick towers, others were trampled underfoot as the pilgrims stormed Rome in search of a miracle.

"Tomasso!" Cristina screamed. "Tomasso!"

He glanced up for a moment, then disappeared under the boots of the pious.

35: THREE

Why did the number three have such dreadful power?

When the first priest had been slain, Domenico hoped the murder would be an isolated incident, a terrible aberration. But when the second body was discovered, he knew in his guts that the violence wouldn't stop there, that this killer was obsessed with pattern, and that a third atrocity was inevitable.

Now he was staring at it…

The priest looked eerily peaceful, except for the ghastly grey death-pallor of his face … and the fact that he was bathing in a copper vat filled with his own blood.

Like the previous two victims, this ritual killing had been enacted in the heart of the Vatican, inside the complex of laundry rooms, which the murderer had taken great care to lock behind him after the deed was done. Yet again, it had been an unsuspecting servant who had discovered the body in the small hours, when he'd come in to light the fires under six huge water tanks that fed the laundry throughout the day. The killer had meticulously planned the theatre of his victim's discovery … so where was the third prayer?

Domenico leant over the body, put his fingers on the man's chin and pulled open his mouth. No scroll of paper, but at least he still had his tongue. Then Domenico ran his fingers through the priest's unruly mass of curly black hair, but nothing had been hidden there either.

With a dreadful sense of foreboding, Domenico gazed at the congealing vat of blood; what horrors lay beneath the surface?

"Sergeant, help me get him out."

"Do we have to, sir?"

"Can't just leave him in there."

"Perhaps we could scoop the blood out, sir? Won't be so messy."

"Since when did that bother you?" Domenico was puzzled by his sergeant's sudden reticence.

"It's just … the wife … this uniform was clean on today."

"Well, I hear the Vatican has a good laundry. I'm sure they'll be glad to help."

"Funny, sir. Very funny," the sergeant replied grimly.

The two men put their hands under the corpse's armpits and gripped his shoulders.

"One, two —" They hauled the priest from the vat of blood and flopped him face-down on the stone floor. Domenico grabbed the priest's torso and rolled it over.

"Jesus wept!" The sergeant turned away and threw up into one of the floor drains.

Domenico didn't flinch, but he was no less shocked. The priest had been castrated. Where his genitals should have been was a gaping wound, as if the man had been desexed. To compound the horror, it looked as if something had been stuffed into the newly formed cavity. Domenico peered closer, and saw the tip of a small scroll of paper. Other commanders would have delegated the job of retrieval, but Domenico was not that sort of leader. He reached out, pinched the paper between his fingertips, then delicately pulled the scroll out of the priest's groin.

The parchment had been coated in some kind of varnish or resin, for the blood wiped off it easily and the writing was still perfectly legible. Domenico glanced over to the sergeant, who was wiping the last traces of vomit from his mouth. "Are you all right?"

"Perhaps it's best you don't read it out loud, sir."

Domenico unfurled the scroll and read the chilling words of the third prayer. By the time he had finished, he was furious. He had warned people but no-one would listen; now the murderer had made it clear.

As I witnessed the healing of a mind through the power of St Peter,
So shall I now witness the healing of my own soul through this sacrifice…
This priest has been cut so that I may be whole.
You have shown me the power and dread of Your love.
Father, Son and Holy Ghost.
Miracle, Sacrifice, Prayer.
The Holy Trinity.

Now there could be no doubt: these murders were directly linked to the manufactured miracles that had mesmerised Rome. The butchered priests were collateral damage, unexpected and unforeseen, but now undeniable.

"You disgrace! You be sacked! The lots of you!" A man was shouting in the corridor outside.

"What's happened now?" Domenico couldn't hide his irritation.

"Sounds like trouble," the sergeant sighed.

Both men emerged from the laundry to discover a furious seminarian being forcibly restrained by one of the guards. He had a pale face, thinning red hair, and judging from his strong accent and poor Italian, was probably from England. "You rubbish! Idiots better jobs than you can be doing."

"Please, go away," Domenico said. "You're not helping."

"A man cannot feel safe! Inside Vatican walls a man should be safe, not dead!"

"Do you think we want any of this? Do you think we're not trying?"

"Resign! Give jobs to men who can detect."

Domenico turned away and muttered to the sergeant, "Just get rid of him. I can't deal with this right now."

"Pleasure." The sergeant strode towards the seminarian.

Confident that the protest was being managed, Domenico went back into the laundry room to contemplate the castrated priest.

The English seminarian may have been ignorant, but he had a point: if a priest wasn't safe in the heart of the Vatican, then he wasn't safe anywhere, and it was the Guardia Apostolica that would be blamed. But why should Domenico be fired because his sister was too stubborn and pig-headed to listen? He'd warned her and she had brushed him aside. Well, that wasn't going to happen again. He would force Cristina to look at the three violated bodies and confront the bloody consequences of her actions.

When she had unleashed miracles, she had unwittingly opened the door to demons.

36: CONSEQUENCES

Cristina ran behind the stretcher, praying that Tomasso's life would be spared. The guards on the Porta had reacted quickly, but the frenzy of the surging crowd was so intense it seemed to take an agonisingly long time to pull the deputy out from under their boots. He was barely conscious and covered in blood, but at least he was still breathing. For now.

A runner had been sent ahead to warn the hospital to prepare for emergency surgery, so everything that could be done was being done, yet that didn't make Cristina feel any better. Every time she saw Tomasso's arm flop down from the stretcher she feared the worst. She had warned him not to open the gates for precisely this reason … and yet if he hadn't, perhaps they would now be carrying the bodies of pilgrims to the morgue instead.

The stretcher bearers hurried up the hospital steps and Tomasso was rushed straight into the operating rooms, but when Cristina tried to follow, the lead surgeon blocked her path. "Not you."

"I need to stay with him," she protested.

"That's not possible."

"I'm a friend."

"You'll have to wait outside."

"No!"

"I'm not asking you, I'm telling you." The surgeon was losing patience.

"Well, how long will the operation last?"

"I cannot say."

"You must have some idea."

"It depends what injuries we find."

"Then at least let me stay while you examine him," Cristina pleaded. "I promise not to say anything, or interrupt —"

"Signorina!" the surgeon snapped. "If you want to help your friend, go away! Let us to do our jobs."

He pushed open a set of swing doors and strode into the operating rooms. As the doors closed again, Cristina peered through the shrinking gap and glimpsed a middle-aged man tied to a chair with leather straps, blood streaming down his face. He was writhing violently as if trying to escape, while two orderlies reassured the man that the worst was over. The doors clicked shut just as the surgeon reached for a bone saw.

Cristina recoiled from the violence of the scene — this was not how operations were depicted in surgical textbooks. Perhaps she was better off waiting outside until it was all over.

Doing nothing was not something Cristina found easy, so she decided to visit Professor De Luca. He had been moved to a different room in the hospital since she last saw him and this one overlooked a courtyard which echoed with the peaceful splash of a fountain. Someone had even gone to the trouble of dressing the room with fresh flowers. Yet despite the improved aesthetics, De Luca remained completely unresponsive.

Cristina pulled up a chair next to the bed and held the professor's hand. "How are you feeling, old friend?"

There was not even a flicker of acknowledgement on the man's face.

"Are they treating you well?"

The professor's hand felt smooth and cool in her clasp, and she noticed that someone had trimmed his nails. Gently, she squeezed his hand, but he did not reciprocate.

"He spends most of the time in a deep sleep."

Cristina looked up and saw a nurse enter the room, carrying a jug of warm water and some linen cloths.

"Most of the time, but not all?" Cristina asked.

The nurse washed De Luca's face. "Sometimes his eyelids flutter, as if he's dreaming, but he never properly wakes up. And he never speaks. You just get the occasional mumble."

Cristina looked at the professor, remembering the eloquent and powerful intellect that had inspired her for so long. "Is it all right if I just sit with him for a while?"

"Stay as long as you want. He's in no hurry."

Cristina waited until the nurse had finished washing De Luca, then she took his hand again. "I wish you were here with me. This is turning out to be a difficult experiment. I mean, it's working. People are convinced. No-one doubts the miracle of St Peter's relics. But things have become messy." Cristina could feel her eyes tingling as she remembered the horror of the scene at the Porta. "It was terrible to witness. It was like … like watching a monster devour someone alive. And we were powerless to stop them. Completely powerless."

She watched De Luca's chest rise and fall as he drew breath; even though he was so ill, there was something strangely comforting about the steadiness of his breathing. Cristina closed her eyes and gently rested her head on the side of the bed. She imagined that the professor was just taking an afternoon nap and would sit up at any moment and ask for a glass of port.

Perhaps if she waited here long enough, holding his hand, that would all come true.

But how long was long enough?

The sounds of the professor's breathing mingled with the splash of the fountain outside, until Cristina felt the heaviness of sleep start to settle on her like a film of dust…

"He's out of surgery now."

Cristina opened her eyes and sat up, momentarily disorientated. She turned and saw Domenico standing in the doorway.

"The doctors said it was a complex fracture, and he was lucky not to lose a leg. That would have been his career finished."

"I need to see him." Cristina hurried towards the door, but her brother grabbed her.

"Feeling guilty won't help him recover."

Cristina disentangled her arm. "What do I have to feel guilty about?"

"I warned you to stop this madness, but you wouldn't listen."

"You're blaming me? For what happened to Tomasso?"

"Who else should take the blame?"

"An ignorant mob! People had whipped themselves into a frenzy —"

"And why was that?"

"It could have been for any number of reasons," Cristina replied. "On a different day it could have been a crush to receive the Pope's blessing. Or to get to the markets early."

"But today it was because of lies *you* spread." Domenico locked his gaze on her. "At least have the courage to admit it."

Cristina was stung by her brother's vehemence. "Domenico, have you ever considered the chaos that would have erupted if the truth about St Peter's tomb had become public knowledge? That there are no bones?"

"People must learn to deal with the truth."

"Ordinary people can't deal with that kind of truth!"

"A very patronising thing to say."

"It's not my fault people are ignorant!"

"Just because someone doesn't speak half a dozen languages is no reason to belittle them."

Cristina felt uncomfortable with where this was leading. "I don't know why we're arguing. You said Tomasso is going to recover."

"But the priest won't."

"Which priest?"

"The one who was castrated last night and left to bleed to death in a copper vat."

Cristina flinched at the image.

"Three dead priests in total. All with confessions by the killer." Domenico held out the bloodstained prayers. "All inspired by your 'miracles'."

"Correlation does not imply causation," Cristina replied quickly, although this time there was little conviction in her voice.

"Forget your fancy sophistry. This is what's happening in the real world." He forced the third prayer into her hand. "It leaves no doubt."

"I'll look at it later."

"*Now*. Read it now."

Cristina knew it was pointless arguing with her brother when he was being this stubborn. Reluctantly, she took the prayer over to the light spilling through the window, and started to read.

"A murderer is on the loose because of hysteria that you have created, Cristina. You have a moral obligation to stop him."

She drew a long breath. "It's not a him. It's a her."

"Not necessarily."

"'*This priest has been cut so that I may be whole.*' That points to sexual abuse."

"Abuse victims are both men and women."

"If the killer was a man, there would have been signs of violent struggle. But you said all the victims were found in peaceful attitudes."

"So you have been paying attention."

"To me that suggests they were drugged, then cut, then left to bleed out. That is how a woman would kill a man who is much stronger than herself."

"It still leaves half of Rome as suspects."

"Give me all the evidence you have. Let me study it this evening, then first thing tomorrow, perhaps I can examine the bodies?"

Domenico breathed a sigh of relief. "I thought you'd never ask."

37: COHORT

The three dead priests made a strange brotherhood in the morgue. Similar in age and appearance, yet each bearing their own catastrophic injuries, they reminded Cristina of the Three Wise Monkeys: see no evil, speak no evil, hear no evil. The pattern almost worked, a missing eyeball and a missing tongue, but instead of taking the third victim's ears, the killer had castrated him.

Cristina took her time examining each of the corpses but found nothing that Domenico hadn't already noted in his autopsy dossiers.

"You've done a good job preserving the bodies," she said, standing up straight again to stretch her back. "They can be released for burial now."

"Before we've caught the killer?" Domenico was puzzled.

"The families must be getting impatient. And we have what we need."

"But the unusual methods of killing ... surely we have to link any suspects we find directly to these bodies?"

Cristina put her magnifying lens back in its leather pouch. "Now the only thing we need are the prayers. All the clues will come from those."

"So you admit the link between your staged miracles and the murders?"

"I admit nothing, Domenico. And I have only agreed to help solve these crimes because the killer needs to be caught. That does not make me culpable."

Domenico held his tongue; now was not the time to get back into this argument. "Cristina, I've read those prayers a thousand times but cannot find a clear lead. Show me what I've missed."

"Actually, I don't have the prayers anymore."

"What? But I gave them to you."

"And I sent them to Venice."

"Venice? That is crucial evidence. We need it here!"

"Don't worry. I've made a copy." Cristina pulled a single sheet of paper from her folio case and handed it to her brother.

Domenico looked at the neat, cursive handwriting — Cristina had copied all the prayers exactly and compiled them into a single text.

"But the words aren't what's interesting," she added.

"They're confessions. It is damning evidence."

Cristina shook her head. "The prayers are what the killer needed to say. But they're not what we need to catch her."

"You're not making any sense. Again."

"The killer had control over the words, and she is too intelligent and resourceful to volunteer anything that might reveal her identity. But what she could not control was the paper she wrote on."

"The paper?" Domenico was starting to wonder if he wouldn't have been better pursuing the investigation on his own after all.

"I sent the original prayers post-haste to Edoardo Boschi, a publisher in Venice who has an unhealthy obsession with paper. On this occasion that is precisely what we need."

Domenico frowned. "And what will he do with the paper?"

"Analyse it."

"To discover?"

"If I knew that, I wouldn't need Boschi." Cristina picked up her bags. "While we wait for a response from Venice, perhaps you can show me the dossiers you've compiled about the victims."

It was a relief to get out of the morgue and into the open air of Rome, for no amount of ice could prevent the slow putrefaction of flesh and its pungent aroma. Not that the air in Rome was particularly sweet at the moment, for the immense throng of pilgrims had lit bonfires on every corner, and when they weren't cooking street food they were chasing away rats that their own unsanitary habits had attracted in the first place.

"Will we ever get our city back," Domenico grumbled as he tripped over a tent that had been slung across the end of an alley.

"We should be grateful there are so many credulous people," Cristina replied. "Their faith is saving the new basilica."

"There must have been another way. One that would have spared us all this chaos."

"Progress always causes disruption, Domenico. We shouldn't fear it."

Although he had failed to make any useful deductions, Domenico had gathered copious biographical information about each of the victims. But the more he found out, the more baffling the murders became for there was nothing about these priests that was noteworthy.

"It's points in common that we're looking for," Cristina said, her eyes darting across the pages; she seemed to be reading only one in every ten words so that she could assimilate their meaning more quickly. "Where did their lives overlap?"

"They were all harmless bureaucrats," Domenico suggested.

"The Vatican is full of those. But why pick on these individuals?"

"They were all forty-six years old."

"Perhaps the number is significant." Cristina wrote it down in her notepad.

"The killer waited twenty-three years to exact revenge on forty-six-year-olds. It's an exact doubling."

"So numbers are important to the killer. Order and numbers." Cristina wrote the word mathematics in her pad and underlined it.

"Or..." Domenico started pacing the room as a fresh idea bubbled to the surface. "Perhaps the choice of number is irrelevant. Perhaps it's the equivalence that really matters."

"Go on."

"It's like soldiers of a certain age who all end up fighting in the same campaigns. They experience the same situation *because* of their ages."

Cristina liked this line of thinking. "Except ... it could be even simpler. Perhaps, instead of enlisting as soldiers, they went to the same school or university. Maybe that's where they met. And just like soldiers bonded by battle, they bonded in training."

Domenico flicked through the notes; he only had the education information about the first victim. "Coraggioso trained at the Gandolfo College of the Holy Cross."

"Then let's see who else is an alumnus."

They tracked down the yearbooks for all the Papal States' seminaries in the Vatican Library of Administrative Records, and quickly located the list of students who had matriculated at Gandolfo College in 1483. Cristina took out her magnifying lens and scanned the list of names. Suddenly her hand stopped.

"There they are…" Cristina handed the folio to her brother. "Coraggioso, Maggio and Banche."

Once they had shared a page in an enrolment register, three young men full of hope and ambition; now they shared a cold slab in the city morgue.

38: CALM

Cristina had left clear instructions to guide the Bureau of Relics while she was on secondment to the murder investigation: there were to be no more miracles for at least ten days. Rome simply could not take another wave of religious zeal. Instead, Isra and Castano were directed to monitor the situation and find discreet ways of calming passions. The hope was that pilgrims would start to get bored of living in squalor and gradually drift away.

Isra ventured onto the streets every morning and afternoon to listen to market traders, gossip with servants who worked in the grand *palazzos* on the Tiber, and count the makeshift tents in the piazzas; the numbers remained worryingly high.

Castano, meanwhile, did a circuit of key churches to monitor the mood of their congregations, then spent his afternoons in various upmarket salons to judge how far the religious euphoria had permeated the aristocratic classes.

In the evening, they met in the library at Cristina's house to compare notes and enjoy a light supper that Isra had left simmering on the stove. But by the end of the second day, Castano was getting anxious.

"When is Cristina going to return to her proper duties?" he grumbled, pushing his bowl of risotto aside.

"You mean get married and have children?" Isra suggested.

"We need the woman here. At the Bureau. Working to ensure that the sanctity of St Peter is never questioned."

"I think catching a serial killer might also be pretty important." Isra looked at the flecks of grey appearing in Castano's hair. "Especially for middle-aged priests."

Castano poured them both another glass of wine. "But why her? Why can't the Apostolic Guards look after that? It is their job, after all."

"Because no-one's insight is quite as sharp as Cristina's."

"So what has she found in this case?"

"I don't know. She hasn't discussed it with me."

"But you talk about everything. You share each other's private thoughts without paying any heed to the propriety of class or station. I've seen you."

"Isn't that what friends do?"

Castano studied Isra for a moment, as if considering the best line of attack. "I'm sure she finds your friendship very useful."

"Useful?"

"Although Cristina takes the credit for solving crimes, you are the one with your ear to the ground, Isra. I daresay without your knowledge she would not be nearly as effective."

"What Cristina does, goes far beyond listening to gossip. Logic is how she tackles problems. Logic and reason."

"Indeed? Fascinating. So how would that work in the case of the three murdered priests?"

Isra drew a breath, ready to enlighten Castano with a list of all the steps she knew Cristina would be taking right now to catch the killer … when suddenly, she hesitated. Castano was studying Isra a bit too intently. He was normally so dismissive of the lower classes whom he regarded as ignorant and unworthy of his time, yet now he really wanted to know what Isra was thinking.

She decided to deflect. "Where would you start, Geometra? If you were conducting the investigation."

Castano flicked the fringe away from his face. "The thing you have failed to understand is that people are imbued with a strange and often unhealthy fascination for priests. I remember vividly the moment I was ordained, immediately people started reacting differently towards me. Even my own parents. People who before the service might clap me on the shoulder or share some tavern humour, after ordination, they wouldn't dare be so casual. It was quite extraordinary. Ordination elevates a man. Sadly, it also makes us lightning conductors for people's emotions. Their fears and disappointments can all become focussed on the figure of their priest. So, if I were conducting the murder investigation, I would start by looking at the little people the victims encountered in their day-to-day lives."

"But these were not parish priests," Isra replied. "They were bureaucrats who had no congregations."

Castano hesitated for a moment. "You have missed the point entirely. You see, priests are never off duty. And those working inside the Vatican, in such proximity to the Holy Father, they are often seen as even more mysterious and potent than other priests. The killer could well be someone in their social circle. Or a lonely concierge who looks after one of the buildings where they had rooms."

"So that is where you would look?" Isra replied. "The 'little' people?"

"Most definitely. It does not take a genius to realise those poor priests were most likely killed by someone they knew."

Isra nodded but said nothing, because it was always interesting to observe how people reacted to silence.

Castano pulled the cheese board towards him and started cutting some slices of Parmigiano Reggiano. It was remarkable how much more at ease he seemed now that he had broadcast his own particular take on the murders.

What was really going on inside his patronising mind?

Little more was said over supper, but after Isra had shown Castano out, she hurried through the small courtyard at the rear of the house, left through the iron gate and double-backed along the side alley so that she could follow him without being observed.

Castano had told her he was going to meet a friend to enjoy an evening stroll along the left bank of the Tiber, but that turned out to be a lie. Instead, he went straight to his lodging house in Trastevere. Isra watched from the shadows on the opposite side of the street as he lit an oil lamp in his rooms, then started moving around with a great sense of purpose. A few moments later, he emerged wearing a cloak and clutching a travelling case. Striding quickly, he made his way to the Piazza di Santa Maria; as the city clocks struck eight, a black carriage pulled up, he climbed inside and they sped off.

It was a risky time of day to start a journey. Where was Castano going with such haste?

39: SIX

Three hours of solid riding brought Cristina and Domenico to the spectacular seminary at Gandolfo. Perched on a wooded hill, the college dominated the entire valley, although the sharp slate spires that topped off its towers made it look as if it would be more at home in Bohemia than the Papal States.

Even more impressive than the building itself was the view it enjoyed across the shimmering blue circle of Lake Albano. Domenico paused his horse on the winding track to gaze across the huge body of water that was encircled by an unbroken ridge of hills.

"Why does the sight of water always make you feel calm?" he pondered.

"It's strange, isn't it?" Cristina stopped her horse next to his to share the moment. "It must be something very ancient in our souls."

"And this lake is such a perfect circle … it looks as if it was dug by hand."

"It's the remains of a volcanic crater that has flooded," Cristina explained, "hence the shape. But it's baffled people for thousands of years. Sometimes the water level rises spectacularly even when there's no rain. The Etruscans believed it was a sign from the gods, foretelling whether they would triumph over the Roman legions."

Domenico frowned. "I've had enough miracles to last a lifetime. I really don't need another."

"I suspect the true explanation lies in volcanic activity deep beneath the surface, but until someone invents a machine that can travel underwater, we won't know for sure."

"Sounds like the stuff of nightmares. Imagine if something went wrong and you were trapped down there." Domenico snapped the reins and turned his horse back up the hill.

They finally reached the gates of the Gandolfo College of the Holy Cross just as the bell was tolling for lunch. A young seminarian arranged for their horses to be stabled, then led them along seemingly endless corridors that led to the Rector's office. En route, they passed numerous classrooms; some were full of students listening intently to lectures on scriptural analysis, while others hosted lively debates about arcane aspects of canon law.

Most notable of all were the paintings — everywhere they looked, the whitewashed walls were covered with thousands of portraits of priests. It wasn't the faces per se that were interesting, it was the backgrounds against which they posed, which featured everything from snowcapped mountains to Japanese pagodas to the dense tangle of jungle trees.

"It's one of our traditions," the young seminarian explained. "Alumni donate portraits of themselves as their careers progress. It's to inspire the next generation to spread the Word of God across the globe."

The rector of the seminary was Father Marrone, a kindly old man who had prepared a small table on the balcony so the three of them could bathe in the spectacular views of the lake while they dined. He wore a thick pair of corrective glasses which made his gentle eyes look large and owl-like, and Cristina was glad they hadn't told him this was an investigation into how three of his former students had been murdered in the most horrific circumstances. The news hadn't yet made its way up the mountain, and for the time being Cristina was happy to leave it that way.

"The atmosphere at your college is not at all what I expected," Cristina said as she tucked into some spicy lamprey that had been marinated in its own blood.

"You were braced for miserable and oppressive?"

"I'm afraid I was."

"People forget that seminaries are full of energetic young men with minds hungry for knowledge, and souls eager to fulfil their destiny."

"It reminds me of military academy," Domenico added, "except your students are being trained to save souls rather than kill enemies."

"That's quite a difference," Cristina muttered.

"But the comparison is valid," Father Marrone added. "It's a good observation, Capitano Falchoni. Just because they're seminarians doesn't stop them being young men. Sometimes we must be firm disciplinarians to guide them onto the right path."

"What strikes me," Cristina said, "is how inquisitive they all seem. Quite a contrast to older priests who are loath to stray from church dogma."

Father Marrone refilled their glasses from a carafe of Trebbiano. "What we do here is not unlike breaking in horses. You want to preserve the men's energy, yet they need to emerge from Gandolfo as God's ambassadors. It can be a difficult balance to get right. Too much shaping of their minds, and you crush them; not enough and they will become anarchic priests, useless to anyone."

"Do any of them rebel against your authority?" Cristina pressed.

"The best priests always start out as the most argumentative students. And I would be lying if I said they didn't struggle, but that's why the bonds formed here last for life. Decades after leaving Gandolfo, the men still support each other."

"That surprises me," Domenico said, "given how scattered they are. Those portraits on your walls come from across the world."

"Scattered in body, but not in soul." Father Marrone smiled. "The friendship between priests is one of the unacknowledged pillars that gives the Church strength. Everyone leans on the priest, but who can the priest lean on? They can only truly be at ease with one other, which is why there is sometimes a dark humour between priests that ordinary people will never understand."

"How dark?" Cristina asked. "As dark as corruption?"

Father Marrone stopped eating. "Is that why you're here?"

"We are trying to trace a particular cohort," Cristina dodged, "some of whom have mysteriously vanished."

"Vanished?" Father Marrone looked concerned.

"The 1483 intake," Domenico replied. "We're keen to find out as much as we can about them. Perhaps their portraits are hanging on your walls?"

Father Marrone nodded. "Let us finish lunch, then I will take you to their corridor."

After consulting a map, Father Marrone discovered that memorabilia from the class of 1483 was curated in the corridor that led to the seminary's wine cellars.

"It's quite appropriate, really," Father Marrone observed as he led them down a narrow flight of steps. "They were a lively year."

"Good lively? Or bad lively?" Cristina asked.

"Why are you really here?" Father Marrone's tone hardened as he studied Cristina.

"As I said, we are looking for some missing priests."

"Specifically?"

"Do the names Coraggioso, Maggio and Banche mean anything?" Domenico asked.

There was an immediate glint of recognition in the rector's eyes, which his strong glasses magnified.

"I'll take that as a yes," Cristina said.

"Their group had a certain … notoriety. But we were able to … contain their excesses."

"What do you mean by group?"

"Or excesses?"

Father Marrone led them to an arched window under which hung a group portrait of six priests, posed as if sitting on either side of Christ at the Last Supper. "Rather than wait until they were established in their careers, the Thursday Six as they were affectionately known, commissioned this portrait in their final year at Gandolfo."

"That was very arrogant." Cristina studied the painted faces, brimming with confidence.

"Arrogant? Or enthusiastic?" Father Marrone pondered. "Sometimes it's a fine line. They were the life and soul of their year. Everyone loved them. Hard to imagine them now as sober, middle-aged priests."

Memories of the three men lying on the mortuary slab flashed across Cristina's mind, but she said nothing.

"Point them out to me," Domenico said, his gaze locked on the painting. "Who exactly were the Thursday Six?"

"Starting on the left, Father Banche, then comes Father Coraggioso, then Father Maggio. All now working in the Vatican hierarchy if I remember correctly. Then on the other side of Christ is Father Giacomo, a cardinal in Paris. Next to him is Father Cerchio, who went to the New World as a missionary. And the one on the far right is now a very senior official in Rome, the geometra working on the construction of the new St Peter's Basilica, Father Castano."

The revelation changed everything.

Father Marrone had arranged overnight rooms in the seminary and offered to retrieve academic records relating to the Thursday Six from the secure archives, but Cristina was reluctant to waste time combing through paperwork when she had a living witness to question back in Rome. So they left in the middle of the afternoon with fresh horses, giving themselves just enough time to get back to the city before sunset.

"Geometra Castano needs to be put under protection, day and night," Domenico said as they rode away from Gandolfo.

"Protection? Or surveillance?" Cristina asked.

"Protection. The last thing we want is another dead priest on our hands."

"Don't you think it's suspicious that Castano never mentioned the murders? All that talk of lifelong friendships and the deep bonds forged between men, yet three of Castano's closest friends are butchered and he barely mentions it?"

"I was told to suppress the news," Domenico replied. "Cardinal Riario insisted that nothing should be allowed to distract from St Peter's miracles."

Cristina shook her head. "Nothing escapes Castano's beady eye. The killings would have shaken him to the core, yet he said nothing. He knows he is in the killer's sights, yet he never asked you for a bodyguard. His silence can only mean one thing: guilt."

"About what?"

"I don't know, but the Thursday Six must have done something to become victims."

Domenico frowned. "It's unlike you to jump to conclusions."

"I'm following the logic."

"Not really. You are falling into the 'guilt by association' fallacy."

"Are you trying to out-logic me, Domenico?"

"I'm just saying, I worked under a corrupt and immoral Borgia pope, but that does not make me guilty of his crimes. Castano knew the victims; it is interesting but not incriminating."

They rode on in silence for a few minutes as Cristina tried to marshal her thoughts. "I just get a very bad feeling about the Thursday Six," she said finally. "They looked so arrogant in that painting."

"Feeling?" Domenico couldn't help chuckling. "So it's not really about logic at all. It's about gut feelings. Now you're talking my language."

"I cannot believe that such brutal violence would descend on people for no reason."

"So you think the priests deserved to die?"

"The killer clearly thinks so. Look at all the care she put into composing those prayers. And what exactly were the 'excesses' that had to be managed when they were students? Father Marrone was very cagey about all that."

"One way or another, we'll have to get the answers directly from Geometra Castano."

"What if he doesn't cooperate?"

"We won't give him a choice," Domenico said grimly.

Cristina's suspicions were confirmed the moment they arrived back in Rome and Isra told them that Castano had mysteriously fled the city.

"He didn't tell anyone he was leaving?" Domenico asked.

"Not a soul. And he left no message or note."

"Did you ask at his lodgings?"

"He's paid his rent a month in advance, and that's all the landlady cares about."

"Sounds like he's on the run, or in hiding," Domenico speculated.

"And yet he clearly intends to return," Isra said. "Why else would he keep his landlady sweet?"

"We'll check all the city gates." Domenico strode across the hall towards the main doors. "Perhaps the journey was logged somewhere."

"And you should talk to Cardinal Riario," Cristina called after him. "Castano might be on Vatican business. It could be an official trip."

"Leaving at that time of night? Unlikely."

"But worth eliminating."

As the doors clattered shut, Cristina turned to Isra. "Any word from Venice? We should have heard by now."

"More than a word. A person. Boschi himself has turned up."

"What? Where?"

"He was in a very excited state. Said he had the results of the paper analysis."

"And?"

"I warmed a pot of stew for him, and insisted he had a bath. It was an arduous journey —"

"Isra! Stop playing games. Forget the sweat, what has he discovered?"

"Ask him yourself. He's waiting in the library."

40: BLANK

Cristina bowled into her library to find Edoardo Boschi scrutinising the shelf where the Greek manuscripts on geometry were kept. "Well? What did you discover?" she asked eagerly.

Boschi straightened himself up and gave a small groan. "Ah, it was a most arduous journey, but I survived. Although there is now an ache in my lower back which refuses to shift. And my right foot still feels a little numb."

"I didn't ask about —"

"Perhaps you should."

Cristina blinked in momentary confusion.

"It's the small lubricants in everyday life that mean so much to people," Boschi continued.

"Did you really travel all the way from Venice just to reprimand me?"

"What would be the point? Since you clearly don't care." The publisher plucked Euclid from the shelves and sat down at the long table.

Cristina had seen this type of behaviour before and knew exactly what to do. She took the decanter from the sideboard and poured Boschi a generous glass of sherry, then she sat next to him and clasped his hand. "Edoardo, it's so good to see you again. And you look well — such a healthy glow. You know, it makes you look very handsome. Truly, I'm sorry to hear about the pain in your back, but now that you're my guest and can enjoy healthy food and sound sleep, it will soon pass." She looked at him with large, innocent eyes. "Is that better?"

Boschi gave a grim laugh. "For a moment I almost believed you."

"We both know you didn't come all this way to be flattered. You have made a discovery that is burning your soul and you can't wait to tell me about it. Am I right?"

"Of course you are," Boschi admitted.

"Then let's forget the trivia and get straight to business."

Boschi unbuckled his satchel, took out four sheets of blank paper and laid them neatly on the table. "The thing I love most about paper, is that in reality, it is just a large number of holes enclosed by a network of fibres. And the holes are just as important in determining the properties of the paper as the physical characteristics of the fibres themselves."

Cristina settled back in her chair; she knew better than to rush Boschi to a conclusion.

"In Europe, the fibres used for making paper are extracted primarily from pulped rags." Boschi picked up one of the blank sheets and felt its texture between his fingers. "When soaked in water the fibres swell, and it is in this state that they are spread across the sieve, allowing most of the water to drain away. As the fibres dry they cement themselves together to form a coherent sheet." He took a large, powerful magnifying lens from his satchel and studied the paper. "If you look closely, you can see the pattern made by the mass of fibres."

Boschi handed the lens to Cristina who examined the four sheets.

"But here's the trick: every batch of paper has its own unique fibre pattern."

"So paper tells its own story before anyone has written a word on it?" Cristina said.

"There is more." Boschi bent each of the sheets in two, but stopped short of folding them. "See how differently each sheet behaves when twisted out of shape? Elasticity is another defining characteristic that differentiates batches of paper, since the mechanics are determined by the particular mix of fibres."

Cristina experimented with bending the paper into different shapes and watching it snap back. "It had never occurred to me that paper could be so different."

"Hold it up to the oil lamp," Boschi suggested. "A similar story emerges when we assess the opacity and subtle changes in colour."

While Cristina held each of the sheets up to the light, Boschi pulled a small bottle of ink and a quill from his satchel. "Now for the real magic," he said, and started to drop blobs of dark ink onto the blank paper. "Do you see the different ways each variety of paper absorbs the ink?"

Cristina was surprised to see the difference; one sheet soaked the ink up quickly to form a fuzzy blob, while on the next sheet the ink sat on the surface and was only taken up slowly; the last two managed to absorb the ink quickly but without blurring. "Is that also because of the fibres?"

"That is because of the holes!" Boschi exclaimed with delight. "Ink dries because the water in it disappears into the pores of the paper, leaving a layer of pigment on the surface. How rapidly this happens tells us about the structure and size of the holes. Who would have thought empty space could be so significant?"

Boschi leant back in his chair with a serene look on his face. "Paper is a miracle, yet so many take it for granted. They scribble on it, screw it up and toss it away without a second thought. Such ingratitude. One day I shall draft a book all about paper. A story about paper, printed on paper; how beautiful would that be?" He closed his eyes and fell silent, contemplating the genius of the blank sheet.

Cristina waited a few moments, then gently nudged him back to reality. "So, Edoardo, how does all this relate to the three prayers I sent you?"

"Ah, yes." Once again, he rummaged in his satchel, but this time produced the bloodstained prayers. "These are all from the same paper batch, of course." He held each of them up to the candlelight and studied the fibre patterns through the lens. "Completely predictable."

"But?"

"Here's the crucial point: when batches of paper are sent to the wholesalers, they are accompanied by control sheets which are retained. Should a customer complain about smudging or fading or any other instability, the wholesaler can prove whether the problem is with the paper he supplied, or the customer's ink. Now, I have discovered that the whole of Rome is served by just one paper wholesaler. It's a rather unhealthy monopoly which I suspect was acquired through nefarious means, but for our purposes that is irrelevant. The point is —"

Cristina leapt to her feet. "We must go to the wholesaler, check all the control sheets against the paper on which the prayers are written, and determine which batch they came from. Then we can produce a list of clients who bought that particular batch and thereby narrow the field of suspects. Am I right?"

Boschi stared at Cristina in silence; disappointment clouded his face. "Do you always finish other people's stories? It's a very bad habit."

The *Nove Draghi* paper warehouse was in the semi-rural rione of Monti, just north of the Colosseum, where ramshackle houses still jostled with vineyards and vegetable gardens. Being that little bit further from the Vatican, property prices were considerably cheaper, which was significant when you were trading in something as bulky as paper.

Cristina didn't need to explain the details of their investigation to the owner of *Nove Draghi*, all she had to do was show a Warrant of Authority that bore the Pope's seal, and moments later they were ushered into the main storage warehouse that still smelled of lemons from its former life.

Patiently, Cristina and Boschi worked their way through the control sheets of dozens of batches of paper, comparing the properties of each to the bloodstained paper on which the prayers had been written.

Just as their eyes were starting to go blurry, and they felt as if they couldn't look at another tangled fibre pattern, Boschi found the perfect match. Everything tallied: the texture, the colour, the fold patterns, the ink absorption.

Checking the sales inventories, they drew up a list of every client who had purchased paper from this batch over the previous three months. Half were sent to Ostia for export, there were also large shipments to various printers in the city, as well as the Rome branch of the Monte dei Paschi banking house. But the order that caught Cristina's eye was a shipment of eight hundred quires to a single convent in the centre of Rome, the House of Eternal Grace. "Why on earth would a convent need so much paper?"

Boschi rubbed his temples thoughtfully. "Perhaps they still copy religious texts by hand."

"But why would anyone do such a bizarre thing in the age of the printing press?"

"Speaking as a publisher, I couldn't agree more. But some people find it hard to let go of the past."

Cristina held up one of the prayers next to the control sheet. "And you're sure these are a match? There's no room for doubt?"

"There's always room for doubt, but I would stake my professional reputation on this judgement: those blood-soaked prayers were written on the same batch of paper that was shipped to the House of Eternal Grace."

41: CONVENT

From the outside, the convent was the epitome of tranquillity. Quietly industrious bees bobbed in and out of great swathes of honeysuckle that grew across the ancient stone walls; colour-splashed butterflies floated from blossom to blossom without a care in the world, and a family of swifts had made a secure nest up in the belltower. It was as if a small tract of Eden had been transplanted into the middle of Rome.

As they walked around the perimeter wall, Cristina and Domenico both wondered the same thing: how could brutal violence have originated from inside such blissful surroundings?

A handwritten note had been pinned to a scullery door that was built into the wall at the back of the convent. Cristina leant closer to read it. *Please ring the bell and wait. If no-one answers, don't leave the delivery on the porch. Try the front door instead. Bless you.* Beneath it was a diagram illustrating the same message for the benefit of the illiterate.

Cristina pulled one of the prayers from her pocket and held it next to the kitchen note. "Different handwriting. But the paper..." Using her magnifying glass, she studied the texture of the note, then held it up to the light to check the opacity. "The note and the prayer are from the same batch of paper."

Domenico gazed up at the chestnut tree whose branches were hanging over the wall as if attempting to clamber to freedom. "Perhaps the tree knows there's a killer in there," he mused.

"We think the murders were committed by a woman. We know from the content of the prayers that she had a deep spirituality; it all fits."

"Yet I still can't believe it," Domenico said. "The life of a nun is about contemplation and selfless devotion to God. How do you move from that to castrating a priest and letting him bleed to death?"

Diagonally opposite the main gates of the House of Eternal Grace was a small wine shop with a side-kiosk selling fresh olives; on the pretext of having a lunchtime *aperitivo*, Cristina and Domenico occupied a table to study the comings and goings of the convent. Although this was not an apostolic order working in the Rome community, it soon became clear that it was far from being a cloistered order, for there was a steady trickle of nuns through the gates. Most seemed to be on market errands, for they would return with food or candles and other small domestic items.

"That gave the killer plenty of opportunity," Domenico said. "She would have found it much harder in a closed order where people rarely leave. But we still have no motive. And without that, we'll never catch her."

"Any news on Geometra Castano's whereabouts?" Cristina asked.

"Not so far. He left no trace. Which is worrying."

"I think we need a two-pronged approach, Domenico. You should team up with Isra and search for any links connecting members of the Thursday Six. How have their careers intertwined? Have they been involved in any business transactions together? Dig around in church records and city archives — find out if they had any links to this convent."

Domenico scribbled down the list on his notepad.

"Twenty-three years ago they were in their final year at Gandolfo. The rector won't tell us anything that might damage the reputation of the college, but perhaps the people in the town remember things differently. Some scandal involving the students, maybe?"

"We can cover all that," Domenico said, snapping his notebook shut. "And the second prong?"

"I shall go undercover in the House of Eternal Grace."

"What?"

"I'm going to present myself as a novice and infiltrate the sisterhood."

Domenico started to laugh.

"What's so funny?"

"You can't just pretend to become a nun."

"Why not?"

"Because no-one will believe you!"

"A thirty-four-year-old woman. Unmarried. Living alone in the city. I think I fit the profile perfectly."

"Someone in there will recognise you. I doubt you'll last a day."

"The sisters spend their lives in contemplation of God. Why would they have the slightest inkling about who I am?"

"The abbess will know. Rome is smaller than you think, and you are not always as discreet as you imagine, Cristina."

"Then it's just as well I have some powerful friends."

Cardinal Riario's diary was blocked out for the entire day, as he was entertaining a delegation from England that included the rising young star, Thomas Wolsey. After pleading relentlessly with Cardinal Riario's private secretary for a whole hour, Cristina was finally able to win a brief audience. But when she told him of her plans, the cardinal's face creased with concern.

"That is the only way?" he asked.

"No. But it is the best way." Cristina was adamant. "In the close confines of the convent I can observe people and behaviour patterns. They won't suspect me, yet I will suspect all of them. Imbalances of power invariably produce rapid and radical results."

Cardinal Riario gave a derisory snort. "It seems to me that you are mocking the gravity of the order. Being a nun is not simply a question of wearing a habit. It is a calling from God, and should be treated with respect."

"Your Eminence, I expect to be treated just like any other novice. I will perform whatever duties are expected of me, and will require no special provisions. All I need is for you to smooth the way by setting an introduction using my alias. You could say that I am the daughter of a family friend who has heard the calling. The abbess won't have any doubts if it comes from you."

"And who will know the truth about your identity?"

"Inside the convent, no-one."

"Is that wise?"

"The sisters must not know since they are all under suspicion. At this stage, even the abbess. Only you and Domenico will know the truth."

"You do understand that you could be putting yourself in mortal danger, Cristina? Locked in a convent with a serial killer?"

"That is a risk I am prepared to take, Your Eminence."

42: NOVICE

Abbess Beatrice ran her hands through Cristina's thick hair, sweeping it away from her face. "I think we'll start on the top." She gathered a bunch of hair between her fingers, lifted it clear of Cristina's scalp and cut through it with a pair of scissors.

Both women watched the curls drift to the stone floor of the convent's sacristy.

"It's surprisingly quick once you get started," the abbess said with calm reassurance, as the scissors flashed around Cristina's head, effortlessly sheering off long, dark locks.

Cristina watched the hair gather round her feet, dismayed by how much grey was starting to appear. Not that it mattered now, for in a few minutes she would have precious little hair left to worry about. It was shocking how easy it was to remove something that had taken so many years to grow. She wondered how old the oldest hair on her head was. How much had she learnt in the time it had taken that hair to grow?

"Better," Abbess Beatrice said, stepping back to survey her work. "Now, be sure to hold still for this next part." She put down the scissors, picked up a straight-edge razor and unfolded the copper blade.

"Will it hurt?" Cristina asked.

"Not when I do it. Though not all the sisters are as gentle." She lathered some soap onto Cristina's head, then carefully started to shave the stubble clean.

Without warning, emotion welled up inside Cristina, and tears pricked her eyes. It wasn't regret, she had never been a woman to preen herself; rather it was a sense of liberation that overwhelmed her, as if she was being freed from the constraints of womanhood.

"Losing your hair is a powerful moment, isn't it?" Abbess Beatrice said.

"Is that why nuns do it, Reverend Mother? To free themselves?"

"In a way. It's a symbol. A woman's hair is a sign of beauty, so by cutting it she gives all of herself to God, including her sexuality."

Cristina listened to the steady scrape of the razor moving across her scalp. For true novices this wouldn't have been so unnerving because they would have spent many months as postulants, learning about the demands and sacrifices of a life of devotion. But because Cardinal Riario had vouched for her, Cristina was able to sidestep the normal procedures and enter the novitiate. It meant she would be admitted to the community of nuns without making a permanent and irreversible commitment, and rather than being questioned by the sisters about her suitability for the order, Cristina would now be able to slip into the routines of convent life and start her search for the killer.

"All done." The razor flashed in a stray shaft of sunlight as the abbess folded it shut and placed it in a small wooden cupboard.

Cristina ran her fingers over her scalp, amused to feel smooth skin. "That must be a very sharp razor."

"We send it to the market once a month to keep the blade keen."

"And is the cupboard locked, Reverend Mother? Where the razor is kept?"

"Why on earth would we do that?" Abbess Beatrice frowned. "Trust is at the heart of this community." She handed Cristina a towel to wipe away the soap residue.

"Reverend Mother, do you have a mirror? I'm curious to see what I look like."

The abbess raised an admonishing finger. "There are no mirrors here. You should know that. Mirrors are a thing of vanity, and you renounced vanity when you entered the House of Eternal Grace."

"Forgive me." Inwardly, Cristina chided herself; if she was going to succeed here, she would have to keep her curiosity well hidden.

"Have you chosen your new name?"

"Can it not just be Sister Cristina?"

"I'm afraid not. We all take a new name when we start our lives here. It signifies our new relationship with God."

"Then, perhaps Sister Maria?"

"Oh, we have far too many of those already. I was thinking you should be Sister Clara. After St Clare of Assisi? She also came from a wealthy family, but chose the monastic life."

Cristina nodded. "Very well. Let it be Sister Clara."

The abbess supervised one of the junior nuns as she rummaged among the vestments to find clothes of the right size. Piece by piece, Cristina discarded her own clothes and changed into a long, black tunic, which was covered with a scapular that hung from the shoulders; her head was dressed in a wimple and veil leaving just her face visible.

"Now you're starting to look like one of us," Abbess Beatrice said with approval. She led Cristina across the neatly tended walled garden and into the chapter house on the far side, where fifty sisters, all with rosaries wrapped around their fingers, were gathered in silent meditation.

For Cristina, this was perhaps the most shocking moment, for immediately it was clear that there was a heavy spirituality here that pressed on your soul, and none of the sisters looked remotely beatific as they prayed.

More sinister was the uniformity: the women all looked the same, they clasped their rosaries with identical gestures, and were most likely running through the same prayers in their minds. The individual vanished when you walked through the doors of the House of Eternal Grace, and that, Cristina realised, was the true meaning of the rituals. With every snip of the scissors and every piece of clothing taken away, individuality was eroded, until what started on the outside had seeped deep into your soul. Cristina would have to be vigilant, if she let her guard down she risked being drowned in a quagmire where everyone thought the same way and questioned nothing.

The abbess beckoned to a sister in her late forties (though it was difficult to tell, for all the nuns looked older than they were), who hurried over.

"Sister Denise," Abbess Beatrice whispered, "this is Sister Clara. The one I was telling you about."

Sister Denise gave a frosty glance in Cristina's direction.

"She needs to be familiarised with our daily routines," Abbess Beatrice continued. "Meanwhile I shall find her a cell."

"Very good, Reverend Mother." Sister Denise beckoned Cristina to follow her into the garden.

Outside the convent walls, a pleasant conversation might have ensued as the two women got to know each other, but this was not the outside world.

"Listen to the tolling of the bell," Sister Denise instructed, "for that will now determine your whole life. We wake at four-thirty, get washed and dressed, and have a little time in our cells for quiet adoration of the blessed sacrament. At five the bell rings for Lauds and we gather in the chapel to offer the first prayer of the Divine Office. Six is Prime, where we celebrate Holy Mass, and at seven-thirty we have breakfast in silence. From nine o'clock until midday, we work, either in the gardens tending the vegetables, or in the kitchens, or sometimes on errands to the market. Then it is Terce, followed by lunch at one, again eaten in strict silence. At two o'clock we pray for the souls of those who have made bequests to the convent, and at three we resume our work, spinning and weaving, or illuminating manuscripts. Stations of the Cross is at four. Followed by Vespers, then an evening meal. We meditate until Compline, the last prayer of the Divine Office. And that is the day complete. Any questions?"

Cristina's mind was full of them, but she had to tread carefully. Illustrating manuscripts — that was interesting, and it explained the large quantity of paper the convent bought from the wholesaler. Two periods of work, when it would be possible for one of the sisters to slip away without being missed; and the sleeping hours between Compline and rising at four-thirty the next day — that was most likely when the murders were committed. Working in the kitchens meant working with knives, and there was still the question of who had access to that copper razor.

Cristina noticed Sister Denise staring at her impatiently. "I said, any questions?"

"No, Sister."

"Perhaps you find this too daunting?"

"A little."

"Well you will find no sympathy from me. I have committed my life to this convent. Ever since I was a young woman. While you were wasting your time in the wealthy salons of

Rome, indulging your appetites, I was praying for God to show mercy to mankind."

"You assume a lot, Sister Denise."

"How dare you speak to me like that."

"I only meant —"

"Have you forgotten the rule of obedience already?"

"No, Sister Denise."

"Inside these walls you are beyond the reach of your powerful patrons. Now you are just a novice. The lowest of the pecking order. And if you upset the sisters, your life in the House of Eternal Grace will be a living hell. Do you understand, Sister Clara?"

Furious, Cristina resisted the urge to fight back, to put this miserable old tyrant in her place; that was not why she was here. She was on a mission. She had to stay focussed. So Cristina bowed her head. "Yes, Sister Denise. Forgive me. I spoke out of turn."

"Yes. You did." Sister Denise turned her back on Cristina and returned to her religious devotions in the chapter house.

Domenico knew it was wrong to give thanks for someone else's misfortune, but in this case he couldn't resist.

Believing that the rector would be so protective of his seminary's reputation that he wouldn't fully co-operate, Domenico had taken a squad of Apostolic Guards to Gandolfo to question the residents of the town instead. If there had been some scandal or crime committed twenty-three years ago, a few of the older residents might still remember. But when they arrived, they discovered that Father Marrone had been unexpectedly called away to Perugia, where his brother had been taken seriously ill.

The assistants who had been left in charge of the College of the Holy Cross had neither the authority nor the confidence to argue with Domenico's Papal Warrants, and they agreed to give him full access to the archives. So while the guards made house-to-house enquiries in the town, Domenico and Isra plunged into the seminary's records, hunting for links between the Thursday Six.

It was painstaking work. They had to trawl through academic records and tutor reports, minutes from tedious administrative meetings, financial records, and mountains of correspondence between the students and the seminary. But even though the work was boring, they had to stay focussed as the smallest lapse in concentration might mean a vital piece of evidence was overlooked.

At the end of the first day, their diligence was rewarded: Domenico discovered a travel permit granting a one week leave of absence to every member of the Thursday Six. It was for the same dates right in the middle of term, allowing travel to Tivoli, some twenty-five miles north-east.

"What is so interesting about Tivoli that all six of them wanted to go there?" Domenico said.

"It can't be family. Not for all of them." Isra looked at the faded copy of the permit. "That would be too much of a coincidence."

"It's very strange. But the timeline fits — twenty-three years ago. We should check to see if there are any links between Tivoli and this college."

Suddenly the great bronze bell in the seminary tower started to toll, summoning the students to Vespers.

"Let's go to the service," Isra suggested. "It won't take long."

"We should really keep working."

"Domenico, we need a break. The archives will still be here afterwards."

Domenico nodded. "Very well. Perhaps we should get some food while we're at it. I'm starving."

Immediately the choir started to sing, Domenico felt the tensions in his mind ease.

"*Deus, in adiutorium meum intende.*" Their voices echoed through the space in complex harmony.

Domenico's instincts were always to keep going, to overcome all obstacles with hard graft, and he would routinely force himself to battle through fatigue and sickness.

"*Domine, ad adiuvandum me festina.*"

But Isra was right — doing nothing felt strangely productive. Domenico focussed on clearing his mind and not thinking about anything, yet somewhere deep down, a part of his mind remained busy sifting through fragments of evidence, trying to fit different pieces together to make coherent patterns.

Domenico looked at the candles flickering in the gloom of the college chapel, watching their little plumes of smoke spiral up and vanish into the vaulted roof. Then he closed his eyes and let the music of the psalm wash over him…

"*Gloria Patri, et Filio, et Spiritui Sancto.*"

A sharp nudge in the ribs brought him to his senses.

"Domenico!" Isra hissed. "Were you asleep?" She glared at him accusingly.

"Me? No. Not at all. Just … thinking." He looked around, trying to get his bearings — Vespers had finished and the choir was packing away its music.

"Look." Isra pointed to a small side chapel built into the south wall, where the seminary students had formed an orderly queue. One by one, each of them lit a votive candle, then inscribed something in an impressively bound ledger that was chained to the altar rail.

"What are they writing?" Domenico whispered. "Confessions?"

"I doubt it. Too public."

"Maybe it's some kind of attendance register."

"No-one takes a roll call that seriously."

"You've clearly never been in the army, Isra."

They waited until the chapel had emptied and they were alone, then they crossed the nave and examined the book. Embossed on the front cover were the words *Liber Spei — Book of Hope*. Inside, each of the students had written a small, aspirational prayer. Some were wishing for success in their examinations, others were thinking about their families; one student prayed for an aunt who was about to give birth, while another asked to be favoured with a fat, juicy benefice after ordination. There were thousands of prayers written over hundreds of pages.

"The hopes and dreams of young men," Isra whispered.

Domenico turned to the frontispiece. "This is volume one hundred and ninety-one. It must be a tradition going back a long time."

"I wonder what the Thursday Six prayed for," Isra mused. "Perhaps that would explain the trip to Tivoli?"

All thoughts of food vanished, instead they went straight back to the college archives. In a bay next to the student yearbooks they found the complete collection of *Libri Spei* — all one hundred and ninety of them, dating right back to the inauguration of the seminary. After some trial and error, they found the volume relating to the period when the Thursday Six were inexplicably absent. On their return to the College of the

215

Holy Cross, all the men had offered prayers to the Virgin Martyr Philomena.

"Peace be unto you, Philomena. My devotion to you is boundless and unquestioned."

"May you protect us and forgive us, Philomena, for we know not what we do."

"Take pity on us, Philomena. Whatever the world may think, there is love in our hearts."

"Those are the words of guilty men if ever I saw them," Isra said.

"But why the sudden obsession with Philomena?" Domenico hurried back to the archive entrance where the indices and codices were racked. He plucked the *Roman Martyrology* from the shelf and searched through the pages until he found Philomena. "Also known as The Wonderworker," he said. "Philomena is the protector of infants and babies."

Connections flashed across Isra's mind. "There is an orphanage in Tivoli."

Domenico looked askance. "How would you know something like that?"

"They wanted to send me there when I first arrived in Rome. Until your sister saved me. But that is why the Thursday Six went to Tivoli. It has to be. Why else would they all come back and pray to Philomena?"

43: YSABELLA

The tolling bell was a tyrant, and the rigid timetable it enforced hampered Cristina's efforts to investigate the sisters of the House of Eternal Grace.

If she was going to identify the killer, Cristina needed to get beneath the skin of the convent, and to do that she needed language. Yet two thirds of each day were spent in prayer, meditation, or devotions in the chapel, and all meals were taken in silence, which severely limited the opportunities to strike up conversation.

The afternoon hour set aside for work also offered little hope — you were either copying manuscripts, a task carried out in silence to avoid careless errors, or you were in the cloth workshop. This should have been more sociable, but the creak and clatter of the treadles and battens, and the incessant whir of spinning wheels made normal conversation impossible.

That only left the morning work session. Those sisters who did errands in the city went out in groups of two or three, which would have been the perfect time to talk, but novices were never assigned these tasks. Which meant that Cristina's best hope was to volunteer for kitchen duties. As she had relied so heavily on Isra's domestic talents for the past decade, Cristina had no culinary skills to offer, so she ended up being assigned the lowliest jobs in the kitchen, scrubbing vegetables, scouring pots and mopping the floors.

Although being a kitchen porter was gruelling, it gave Cristina plenty of opportunity to move around the cooking stations; now she could observe the sisters at close quarters and study their different characters.

There were the Timid Sisters, who were nervous of the heat and flames, and perpetually startled by the clatter of knives. It was clear that the Timids did not have the strength of character needed to take a man's life, and Cristina could rule them out as suspects.

Then there were The Frail, who performed their duties with trembling hands and slow, confused movements. It was hard to imagine them overpowering anyone.

Most of the remaining nuns, including Sister Denise, were The Angry, who seemed to harbour a brooding resentment about their lot in life. Their faces rarely lit up, and their sense of grievance was palpable. These were the ones who Cristina would need to focus on.

It was clear there were no kindred spirits here, no-one who Cristina could ever imagine becoming a friend … with perhaps one exception…

Sister Ysabella was bright. You could tell that from the way she peeled fruit and chopped vegetables. Faced with the tedious task of processing a pile of onions, she would use a different cutting pattern for each one, and never tired of experimenting with new knife techniques. No-one else noticed, of course, and it was done purely for her own amusement, but this was just the sort of ally Cristina needed to help her narrow the list of suspects.

When she next came to take away the cutting boards for washing, Cristina pointed to a neat pile of apple pieces that had been cut into pentagons. "Where did you learn that?"

"Never the same cut twice," Ysabella replied playfully.

"But why?"

"It's a little prayer in action. My way of thanking God for the bounty He provides."

Sister Ysabella was about forty years of age, but had none of the usual sourness that clouded many of the older nuns. Expressions danced quickly across her face.

"How are you settling in?" Ysabella asked.

"To be honest, it's hard," Cristina replied.

"Took me eight years to stop hating the bell. Now I love the order it brings."

"But it's a lonely life, being a nun, isn't it?"

Ysabella picked up a piece of apple and offered it to Cristina. "You'll find that silence is your friend. But it will take time."

"Thank you." Cristina took the apple and started chewing.

Sister Ysabella turned to a basket of plums, picked one up and bounced it in her palm, wondering where to make the first incision.

Cristina returned to the sinks. She didn't want to appear too eager, and knew that everything in the convent had to unfold at its own pace. But that evening, as the nuns dispersed after Compline, Cristina made a point of taking the long way back to her cell; as she passed Ysabella's door, she heard the sound of gargling coming from inside. She paused to listen: *gargle … spit.* Then more gargling. Intrigued, Cristina knocked gently and pushed open the door.

Ysabella was standing over her washing bowl cleaning her teeth, but this went far beyond the usual rubbing with a linen cloth; she had laid out an array of equipment on a small table to help with the task.

"I see it's not just the fruit that gets special treatment," Cristina ventured.

Ysabella stopped gargling and spat into the bowl. "It's the same thing, Sister Clara. A little prayer. What could be Godlier than a clean mouth?"

"Do all the sisters do this?"

Ysabella laughed. "The others mock me for it. But I don't care."

"Good for you." Cristina glanced at the small table. "It looks complicated."

"Are you genuinely interested?"

"Of course."

Sister Ysabella hurried to the door, checked no-one was in the corridor, then ushered Cristina into the room. "Let me show you."

Ysabella positioned Cristina in front of the bowl. "Caring for teeth begins long before you clean them. I'm convinced that certain types of food are better than others, but we do not get a huge choice here in the convent. Which makes cleaning all the more important." She pointed to a set of five sticks that she had shaped into toothpicks of assorted sizes. "These are to remove any food that has become trapped between your teeth."

Cristina looked at the sticks. "Which one do I start with?"

"That depends. Different teeth have different sized gaps between them."

Cristina picked up the smallest one and tried it out between her front teeth.

"No, no. Start at one side and work your way round, one tooth at a time. It's important to be methodical or you'll forget where you were."

"Do I spit as I go?"

"Of course."

Cristina concentrated as she cleaned each gap carefully, dislodging all sorts of tiny food particles that were hiding in the warmth of her mouth.

"Now, a quick gargle." Ysabella handed her a bottle.

"What is it?"

"Water and vinegar. Very invigorating."

As Cristina gargled, Ysabella selected a stick that was about the length of a quill; one end had been chewed until it formed a tuft of bristles. "This tooth-brusher is far more effective than a cloth. I put some pumice paste on the end, then scrub each tooth in turn." She handed the brush to Cristina.

"Who taught you all this?"

"It was a process of trial and error. You want to see some of the instruments that *didn't* work."

"I'll take your word for it." Cristina got to work with the brush, and was astonished at how effective it was. When she had finished, she couldn't stop running her tongue over her teeth. "They feel so smooth."

"Amazing, isn't it? I'm sure it brings us closer to the Divine."

"And another wash with vinegar to end?"

"If you like. Or you could chew one of these." Ysabella offered her a dish with some anise seeds. "They really prolong the feeling of cleanliness."

Cristina popped one of the seeds in her mouth, and Ysabella did the same. They sat for a few moments, chewing in silence, enjoying the sensation.

"I'm impressed by what you've invented, Sister Ysabella. This complete system … it's really something."

"Everyone thinks I'm mad, but I don't care. That's why I keep my door shut when I clean."

"People always ridicule what they don't understand. But that is their problem."

Ysabella reached out and clasped Cristina's hand. "Thank you. That is a kind thought."

This was more than Cristina could have hoped for — she had the trust of one of the sisters, which would be invaluable in her mission. But when she stood up to leave, Ysabella gripped her hand tighter, refusing to let go. "I know why you're here," she whispered.

Cristina blinked. "I'm sorry?"

"I know why you've come to the convent. The true reason. I know."

"What do you mean?"

"You're not who you say you are."

"The abbess made me change my name, but —"

"I don't mean that." Ysabella pulled Cristina back down into the seat. "I mean the charade of you being a novice. You are pretending. You are a fake."

44: TIVOLI

Domenico and Isra arrived in Tivoli to find the place in chaos. Five days earlier a flash flood had inundated the town, and the residents were still trying to dry out what could be salvaged, and burn what could not.

The River Aniene was the lifeblood of Tivoli. For two thousand years it had been used to ship locally quarried travertine to Rome, and its beautiful riverbanks drew the wealthy to build their summer villas here. But the Aniene could be a fickle mistress, turning from seducer to tormenter in minutes by sending torrents of churning water crashing through the homes of unsuspecting residents.

Situated on Via Sossi, just yards from the riverbank, the orphanage had caught the full fury of the flood. Yet despite the chaos, *Direttore* Scudo remained in good spirits.

"These things happen," he sighed. "It's not the first time, it won't be the last." His amiable face sat atop a body that was staggeringly obese, which meant progress through the flood-damaged building was frustratingly slow. "See here? That's how high the water came." His chubby finger pointed to a grey tidemark on the wall of the corridor that led to the back of the building.

"And there was no warning?" Domenico asked.

"Nothing," Scudo declared. "A massive storm broke on Monte Tarino, next thing the flood was heading down the valley. I hear Subiaco was hit worse than us."

"How long will it take to dry everything out?"

"Honestly? Months. Fire is less damaging than flood. If you can stop the flames in time, you can rebuild quickly. But water … it seeps into everything."

"I doubt I'd be as calm as you, Direttore," Isra said.

"None of the children were hurt, and that's what really matters."

"So where have you put them all?"

"They're squeezed together on the top floor. It's chaos. They love it," he chuckled.

"Well I'm sorry to add to your burdens, but this is urgent," Domenico explained.

"The burden isn't mine, it's yours."

"I don't follow."

"You will. The files were floating in five feet of dirty water by the time we got to them. Had to wait for it to drain away before we could even start to salvage anything." He turned right and led them down a steep flight of steps.

"Is it really wise to keep archives in the basement when you live next to a river?" Isra asked.

"The rooms down here are too damp for the children. And we did instal flood defences. Look." He pointed up to one of the windows — set into the frame were some horizontal wooden planks that were supposed to keep out floods, but they had cracked and disintegrated under the weight of water. "The carpenter who sold them to us promised they would last a lifetime. Turns out he was just another lying *stronzo* trying to make his commission."

Finally, they reached the basement archives. "Brace yourselves," Scudo warned as he pushed open the door.

The smell hit them in the back of the throat — a pungent, mouldy stench as if something sinister had died down here.

"These will help." Scudo handed them a couple clean handkerchiefs to hold to their mouths. "I sprinkled them with lavender oil."

As Domenico steadied his breathing, he took in the chaos — ledgers and document folders that had once been meticulously maintained were now strewn across the basement floor, mired in mud. Order and systems had been overturned, which meant the only way to find what they were looking for would be to inspect each document in turn and hope for a stroke of luck.

"The man you sent ahead started over there." Scudo pointed to a mushy pile of books in the far corner. "Not sure if he found what he was looking for."

Domenico suddenly lost interest in the files. "What man?"

"From Rome. He's been searching for a couple of days."

"We didn't send anyone."

"But you're from the Vatican? So was he."

"What was his name?"

"Domenico Falchoni."

Domenico and Isra exchanged a stunned look.

"But that's *me*." Domenico felt his guts tighten. "*I'm* Falchoni."

Scudo shrugged. "That's what it said on his Letters of Authority."

"They must have been forged!" Domenico insisted. "How closely did you look at them?"

"Capitano, I have a hundred and sixty-two boys living in rooms meant for fifty. I have mushrooms growing in my wardrobe and a fallen tree wedged in my office. Bureaucratic confusion in Rome is really not my problem."

"Where is he now?" Isra asked.

Scudo shrugged. "He comes and goes. Works to his own hours."

"So he must be staying close by?"

"There's a tavern just up the hill. Maybe he has lodgings there."

Il Fantasma di Cesare was a few hundred yards up the street, safely beyond the river's reach. Rather than use the main tavern door, Domenico and Isra went through the brick arch and entered the stabling courtyard. There were three storeys of rooms, all with windows looking out onto the yard.

"Where do we begin?" Isra said.

Domenico didn't reply; he was studying each window in turn, working his way along the line.

"There." He pointed to a window on the first floor. Isra followed Domenico's gaze and saw the silhouette of dozens of sheets of paper hanging from a rope that zigzagged across the bedroom.

"Looks like he's drying out documents. Do you think it's the same evidence we're hunting?" Isra asked. "The reason the Thursday Six were absent?"

"Almost certainly. But we'll have to go carefully. If he knows we're coming, he might destroy the papers." Domenico's gaze darted around the courtyard and landed on a ramshackle line of storage sheds built against the tavern walls. "Isra, you go into the main building, find a way upstairs. Pretend you work here and knock on his door. While you keep him talking, I'll get in through the window to secure the documents."

"And then?"

"We improvise."

The tavern was crowded with people displaced by the flood, so no-one paid any attention to Isra; she cleared some empty tankards from one of the tables and went through the doors leading to the service area, but instead of going into the kitchens, she turned right and made her way up the stairs.

Il Fantasma had been here a long time; all the woodwork had gone black from countless layers of beeswax polish, and the crooked floors creaked with every step. Fortunately, Isra's job was to be the distraction, so noise was her ally. As she approached the bedroom door, she glanced out of the window at the end of the corridor and saw Domenico clamber into position on the wooden roof slates of the storage sheds. When he was poised, he gave the signal and Isra knocked on the door.

"Go away!" a muffled voice called from inside.

"It's about your dinner order, sir." She knocked again.

"I'm not hungry."

"Sir, I really need to —"

SMASH! The sound of glass shattering inside the room.

"Sir! Is everything all right?" She tried the door handle, but it was locked. "Open the door, sir! Please!" She could hear the grunt and thump of two men wrestling inside.

Isra stepped back, raised her boot and kicked the lock. The door shook.

She kicked again and heard wood splitting.

One more jab with her heel directly onto the lock and the door burst open.

She saw Domenico crouched on the floor, his knees pinned on the chest of a man who was struggling to break free.

"Enough! It's over!" Domenico yelled.

The struggling man turned his face towards the door, and Isra realised that it was Geometra Castano.

"Get him off me!" Castano yelled.

Isra was too stunned to move.

"Help me! It's not what you think!"

Domenico snapped the shackles around Castano's wrists. "I beg to differ."

45: BLOWN

Cristina disentangled her hand. "You are mistaken." She moved towards the door, but Sister Ysabella moved faster and blocked her exit.

"Please let me leave," Cristina said.

"Why the hurry?"

"It's late, and I'm tired."

"You're also a fake," Ysabella whispered. "It's the only rational explanation."

"You're wrong."

"Look at the evidence."

"I don't know what you're talking about."

"No-one joins the House of Eternal Grace as a novice. Everyone must go through postulancy, but not you, Sister Clara. Why is that, I wonder?"

"Ask the abbess."

"I'm asking you. And here's another thing: I think your mind is focussed on the sisters, not God. I've seen you studying us during worship. What are you looking for?"

Cristina struggled to find a way to deflect the interrogation; anything she said might be compromising.

"And then there is the matter of your other life," Ysabella continued, "in the outside world."

"That's all behind me. This is a new beginning."

"I wonder how true that is?" Ysabella started to circle Cristina as if she was studying a specimen. "I've seen you before. When they first broke ground for the new St Peter's, there was a dedication ceremony. The calligraphy for the Inauguration Charter was done here, in the convent, and I was part of the delegation that presented it to the Holy Father. I saw you there, not hobnobbing with the painted wives of the dynastic families, but standing with the architects. You are clearly an independent woman, yet now you are in a convent, about to take vows of obedience." Ysabella gave a dry smile. "I don't think so. Now, Sister Clara, are you going to start being honest with me?"

Cristina studied Ysabella's face; she was a sharp-witted and observant woman who would make a bad enemy, but a good ally. Exceptionally good. In carrying out her crimes, the killer would have left ripples of irregularity in the meticulous routines of the convent, and who better to detect them than this bright woman?

"I'm here to catch a killer," Cristina confessed.

"What?" Ysabella was bewildered.

"Three priests have been murdered inside the Vatican in the past weeks. The killer is still on the loose."

"Murdered?" Ysabella stumbled backwards and sat on a small stool, her face pale with shock. "But we haven't heard anything about this."

"News of the killings has been suppressed."

"Why?"

"That's … complicated," Cristina sidestepped. "But we must catch the murderer before they strike again."

"Those poor men," Ysabella put her hands to her face as if wiping away tears.

Cristina crouched down and put an arm around her shoulders. "I'm sorry you had to learn about it this way. I didn't mean to be so abrupt."

"But what does this horror have to do with our convent?" Ysabella looked at Cristina earnestly.

"A vital clue was left at each of the murder scenes: a prayer."

"That is blasphemous! To conflate the taking of a man's life with a prayer."

"Not if it helps us catch the killer."

"You mean she gave herself away by accident? With something written in the prayers?"

Cristina hesitated. "Why do you say 'she'? I didn't say the killer was a woman."

"Why else would you be in a convent, Sister Clara? There are no men here."

"The paper on which the prayers were written has been traced to this convent," Cristina replied.

"Traced? How is that possible? Paper is paper."

"Not true. The evidence is arcane and technical, but compelling. It means that the killer is one of the sisters in the House of Eternal Grace."

"No, no..." Ysabella stuttered. "I cannot believe it. Not one of the sisters. Your evidence must be flawed."

"You don't *want* to believe it. But that is where the logic leads, and that is why I am here: to unmask the killer hiding amongst you."

Cristina watched emotions flicker across the nun's face. There was fear, there was confusion, but there was also anger Did Ysabella feel that the whole convent had been betrayed? That this safe haven had been violated? Did she now fear for her own life?

"I realise this is difficult," Cristina said, "but it is better that you know the truth."

Finally, Ysabella's confusion resolved into determination. "Let me help you, Sister Clara. I know these women. I have watched them all my adult life. Together we can catch this monster."

"Who among the sisters is capable of such violence?"

"Let me see the prayers she left," Ysabella replied. "Maybe I can recognise her voice."

It was only a short walk through the dark corridors to Cristina's cell, but they had to be careful not to be seen. Fortunately, having risen at four-thirty, most of the sisters were fast asleep, and quite a few were snoring loudly.

Cristina closed the door softly and lit a candle, then she picked up a framed engraving of the Virgin Mary she kept by her bed. She undid the clasps and removed the backplate, to reveal the three prayers hidden behind the picture.

"You can imagine the violence from the blood." Cristina handed over the prayers.

Ysabella studied each one in silence. She read the words slowly, as if meditating on them; then she ran her fingers over the red stains that bloomed across the paper. "The woman who wrote these is deeply spiritual."

"Why do you say that?"

"Life in a convent changes you. It alters your horizons, until you come to believe that God is talking to you through everyday things. Because life in here is all about God, it becomes *only* about God. The miracles Rome has witnessed in these past weeks were for all of us, for the whole of Christendom. But this woman," she handed the prayers back to Cristina, "she thought they were only for her. Loss of perspective is one of the risks of convent life."

"Yet you have kept your reason, Ysabella."

"To have harboured revenge for twenty-three years … that is quite something. And there are certainly women in here who have a brooding anger."

"Like Sister Denise?" Cristina suggested.

Immediately, Ysabella dismissed the idea. "It's not her."

"How can you be certain? She is not a woman to cross."

"Sister Denise is too cynical and dried up. Those prayers were written with passion."

"So how do we narrow the list of suspects?"

Ysabella started pacing the cell as she wrestled with the problem. "The paper may have been taken from the manuscript room, but the prayers were not written there."

"Why not?"

"It's too public. Someone is always looking over your shoulder. But we are forbidden to have quills and ink in our rooms. Which means whoever wrote the prayers has smuggled quills into her cell and hidden them. Why not search all the rooms?"

Cristina shook her head. "That would alert the killer that we are closing in on her. She might have time to destroy the evidence, or even escape. Who knows how she will react when backed into a corner."

They lapsed into silence again, trying to find a different way through.

"What about access?" Cristina suggested. "The killer had to leave the convent to attack her victims."

"We are not a closed order."

"But movement is restricted. No-one goes out alone. And as a novice I'm not allowed out at all."

"Yes ... you might be onto something. There is a register kept in the gatehouse that records everyone's movement in and out of the convent."

"Is it possible to leave without being seen?"

"There are windows facing the street on the first and second floors. You could climb out and drop to the street, but the only way back in is through the gatehouse."

"Well they certainly didn't sign in and out."

"I'm not so sure…" Ysabella fell silent.

"What are you thinking?"

"Nothing. It's only a half-thought. And I don't want to defame any of the sisters."

"Half-thoughts are often the best place to start, Ysabella."

"You have the dates of the murders? And the times?"

"Dates, yes. Times … all we know is that the murders happened at night."

Ysabella nodded. "Good enough. Finish breakfast early tomorrow. Leave the dining hall as if you need to use the toilet, and meet me in the gatehouse. No-one is there between breakfast and nine, when the sisters going into the city must be signed out. We can check the register against the dates of the murders."

"The very last thing the killer would have done is sign the register," Cristina frowned.

"Not necessarily," Ysabella's face was alive with the pursuit. "The killer could never have imagined that they would be traced back to this convent. The knowledge you used, about the paper, that is without precedent. So they wouldn't have known that the register could be something to fear. The killer made a mistake with the prayers. Perhaps that wasn't her only mistake."

46: DOCUMENTS

Securing the room in *Il Fantasma di Cesare* was almost impossible; there were too many nosey people coming and going and the landlord wouldn't stop complaining about the window Domenico had smashed. So while Isra stayed behind to go through the papers that were hanging up to dry, Domenico removed Castano to the more secure environment of the orphanage, where he turned one of the water-damaged rooms on the first floor into a detention cell. Its window looked down onto the courtyard where the children were playing, but their joyous cacophony was in sharp contrast to the grim business of interrogation.

"You have no right to detain me!" Castano said furiously. "This is wrongful arrest."

"That depends on what we find." Domenico slid a stool across the room for Castano to sit on. "But if you've done nothing wrong, why are you so reluctant to talk?"

"I don't answer to you."

"Why did you sneak out of Rome without telling anyone? Why come here to Tivoli? Why use a false identity?"

"It's none of your business," Castano replied.

"I have Papal authority to investigate the murder of three priests —"

"And I am your superior! In rank, in class, and in the church hierarchy."

"Then act like my superior," Domenico replied. "Not like a common criminal."

"You will answer for these slanders."

"Tell me about the Thursday Six."

Castano shrugged, then started waving his hands around in a display of innocence as he hunted for an answer. "I vaguely remember some student society when we were at seminary."

"Vaguely? Strange choice of word."

"I am a busy man. I have a lot on my mind."

"The rector at Gandolfo remembers you vividly. You made quite an impression all those years ago."

"And that is a crime?"

"Three of the Thursday Six are dead. Brutally murdered in the last eight weeks, yet you never stepped forward with information that might help? That is very suspicious."

"Can a man no longer grieve in private?"

"Grief is not the issue. Nor is it a crime. But withholding information is."

The muscles in Castano's face tightened, and for a moment Domenico glimpsed the ruthless survivor.

"You have picked the wrong man to frame," Castano warned.

"I am just trying to discover the truth."

"And I promise you, Capitano, this case will be your last investigation. One does not become the Vatican's geometra without knowing how to deal with small, jealous men who long to drag you down to their level."

Domenico rubbed his brow. "Why would I be jealous of *you*?"

"Because you are nothing. And deep down you know it. The sense of power you get from investigating crimes ... that is all you have. It's pathetic."

A fist banged on the door outside. Domenico swung it open to reveal Isra, who had returned with bundles of documents retrieved from the room in the tavern.

"What did you find?"

"He was burning documents in the fireplace."

Domenico looked accusingly at Castano. "A strange way to treat official records."

"They were ruined in the flood. I was doing the orphanage a favour."

Isra handed Domenico the surviving papers. "These were the ones he was still going through. They're all from 1483."

Domenico leafed through the pages. They were records detailing the movement of children in and out of the orphanage, simple lines that belied untold stories of sadness.

Left on the church step at Montecelio.

Abandoned by his mother who ran away last Friday.

Found in a basket next to the fountain in Palestrina.

But there were also happier entries, children from the orphanage being adopted by grateful families, or securing apprenticeships and finding their feet in the world.

Domenico looked at Castano. "Why were you destroying these?"

"I don't owe you an explanation. I am the victim here, of your defamatory accusations."

"Then set the record straight. Tell me the truth. What happened all those years ago?"

Castano turned his back on Domenico and walked to the window. He gazed down at the children screaming with delight as they chased a ball around the courtyard in a chaotic game of *pallapugno*.

"Geometra, the truth always comes out in the end."

Domenico's words were met with sullen silence.

"Very well. Perhaps solitude will give you time to reflect." Domenico placed a wooden bucket in the corner of the room. "Have a comfortable night."

"You cannot treat me like this. I am the Vatican's geometra."

"Don't we all know it," Isra muttered.

"I am a man of authority, a senior priest!"

"Then behave like one." Domenico ushered Isra from the cell, then locked the door behind them.

"Just the bucket? No food or water?" Isra whispered.

"Let him go hungry."

47: LAUNDRY

"How could I have been so blind?" Sister Ysabella stared at the register. "May God forgive me."

"What have you found?" Cristina was waiting by the gatehouse door, keeping watch through the small, barred window. It was getting worryingly close to nine o'clock, and she knew that once the bell struck, whoever was on register duty that morning would arrive promptly. But this was not a task that could be rushed; all the comings and goings of the nuns had to be cross-referenced against the dates of each murder, and a single missed line might mean the killer would slip through their fingers.

"One of the sisters *doesn't* follow any of our routines," Ysabella explained.

"Why not?"

"Sister Angelica runs the convent laundry, so she works to a different timetable."

"I don't understand." Cristina crossed the gatehouse to look at the register entries. "Show me."

"Here. And here. See?" Ysabella leafed through the register, pointing to various entries. "The Laundry Sister leaves the convent every day, but always at a different time. And sometimes twice or three times a day."

"Why would she leave at all?" Cristina asked. "The linen to be cleaned is already here. Is she getting supplies of lye?"

Ysabella hesitated. "I should not say. This is supposed to be a closely guarded secret."

"So is my presence here, but I trusted you."

Even though they were alone, Ysabella lowered her voice to a whisper. "Sister Angelica does all the laundry for the Holy Father, Pope Julius."

"What? That's absurd."

"But true. The Pope doesn't want anyone in the Vatican to see his most intimate clothing. Not even his servants. So he entrusts this task to the House of Eternal Grace. We are sworn to obedience, and are forbidden from ever disclosing … details."

Cristina was struggling to make sense of this bizarre revelation. "I just don't see the logic of it."

"Because you've never seen the Holy Father's underwear. Or his bed linen."

"And you have?" Cristina said.

"Oh yes," Sister Ysabella confessed. "And once seen, there are some things that can never be unseen."

"Is the Holy Father unwell?"

"Frequently. And the nature of his ailments is … written on the bed linen. That is why discretion is paramount. If the Pope's most intimate laundry were to be done inside the Vatican, his servants could be bribed to reveal details to ambitious cardinals who are jockeying for position. No-one must ever suspect the Holy Father has any weakness."

"It had never occurred to me that laundry could be so revealing."

"You obviously have a housekeeper."

Cristina nodded. "Little wonder she is always one step ahead. I thought it was down to finely tuned empathy, but maybe she just knows how to read my laundry."

"So you see, this task gives Sister Angelica the perfect cover. She comes and goes at various times of the day and night, summoned to the Vatican whenever the Holy Father's needs demand."

Cristina was struggling to picture exactly what went on in the Pope's bedchamber to warrant the immediate attendance of a laundry woman.

"Look at these entries." Sister Ysabella was like a bloodhound on the trail. "All three dates of the murders…" Her finger ran down the register. "Sister Angelica left the convent after Compline. So there would be no record of what time she returned."

Cristina studied the register. The correlation was too strong to ignore. She turned to the pages immediately before each murder — on every occasion, Sister Angelica left the convent early in the morning and didn't return until mid-afternoon. Was she planning the final details of the killings? Was she following her victims to track their precise movements?

"What about the prayers? Could she have written them? Is she that spiritual?"

Ysabella hesitated. "Spiritual is not the first word that comes to mind when you meet Angelica. But who knows what goes on inside a woman's heart?"

"When she leaves today, we need to search her rooms."

"You think she's hidden quills and ink?"

"Can you find a reason to take me off kitchen duty for a few minutes? One that won't arouse suspicion?"

"Setting fresh baits for the mousetraps is always a good one," Ysabella smiled.

"Mousetraps?"

"My speciality. Mice are a perennial problem in the convent. Trapping them is distasteful, but it provides the perfect excuse to go anywhere, as most of the sisters are terrified of mice."

There was precious little to search in Sister Angelica's cell, for it contained just a crucifix, a washstand, a bed, a simple chair and a small lectern for reading scriptures. After a few minutes, Cristina and Ysabella had checked everything but found nothing. They gazed at the whitewashed walls, hoping for inspiration.

"Could she have hidden quills in the laundry room?" Cristina suggested.

Ysabella shook her head. "They're here. I can sense it."

"Intuition is an unreliable partner."

"Trust me." Ysabella closed her eyes as if meditating, then slowly ran her hands over the wooden chair. She moved over to the bed, her hands skimming the thin mattress and lumpy pillow. Suddenly, she stopped, as if locking onto something.

"Is it hidden in the bed?" Cristina whispered.

Ysabella stood up abruptly, spun round and clamped her hands on the large mahogany crucifix that hung on the wall. There was an identical one in every room so that no-one would feel more favoured than the others, and they were so ubiquitous it was easy to forget they were there. Ysabella gripped the crucifix with both hands, lifted it from the wall and placed it on the lectern. She muttered a brief prayer, then slowly turned the crucifix over to reveal a hollowed-out section. Hidden in the recess were two quills and a small phial of black ink.

"God has guided my hand to catch the killer."

Suddenly, they heard footsteps approaching down the corridor.

"We have to get out!" Ysabella was panicked.

"No. Let's confront her with this now."

"Are you sure?"

Cristina picked up the quills and turned to face the door. They listened to the approaching sandals slapping on the stone floor of the corridor, then the iron handle rattled and the door swung open to reveal Sister Angelica.

"What are you doing here?" she demanded.

Sister Angelica's mannerisms reminded Cristina of a large chicken: her head darted from side to side in jerky movements, and she spoke as if she was pecking at each word.

Cristina held up the quills. "The real question is what are these doing here?"

Sister Angelica's head twitched forward to take a closer look. "Never seen them before."

"Come now, that's a pretty poor response."

"It's the truth."

"They were hidden behind your crucifix, in a specially carved hollow."

Sister Angelica's eyes darted to the crucifix, then back to the quills. "Never seen them. Not mine," she pecked.

"May I see your hands?" Cristina asked.

Sister Angelica's head jerked backwards. "What business is it of yours?"

"It would help us discover the truth."

"About what?"

"Please." Cristina reached out her own hands.

Reluctantly, Sister Angelica extended her stubby arms. Cristina took the fingers in hers and examined them, then turned to Ysabella. "No sign of ink. Not even under the nails."

"She spends all her time up to her elbows in hot water. Any ink residue would have been washed away."

"What am I supposed to have written?" Sister Angelica clucked. "What's all this about? Tell me. Somebody tell me."

She strutted back and forth as if limbering up to lay an egg out of sheer anxiety.

"Sister Angelica, can you write?"

"Of course. All the sisters can write. How else could we work in the manuscript room?"

Cristina took a blank sheet of paper from her tunic pocket and laid it on the lectern. "Would you mind writing The Lord's Prayer for me?"

"Why? What is this?" She glared at Ysabella. "What has she been saying about me?"

"That there is no-one in Rome who can wash linen as perfectly as you can," Cristina soothed.

Sister Angelica seemed thrown. "She said that?"

"Please. If you wouldn't mind." Cristina dipped one of the quills into the phial of ink, then offered it to Sister Angelica. "The Lord's Prayer."

48: DESIRE

Domenico and Isra returned to the makeshift prison cell after breakfast to find Geometra Castano huddled on the floor next to the bucket.

Isra placed a jug of milk and a plate with three slices of bread in front of him, but Castano didn't react.

"Well?" Domenico said.

"Listen to the sound of children's voices echoing through this orphanage." There was a humility in Castano's voice that Domenico had never heard before; it had been stripped of arrogance and pride. "And Jesus said, 'Suffer the little children, forbid them not to come unto me: for of such is the Kingdom of Heaven'. Perhaps I now understand what that really means." Castano raised his arms to embrace the room. "Listen..."

Filtering through the walls and ceiling was the irrepressible chatter of children.

"The world is pitted against them. Abandoned by their parents, strangers to family life, flooded from their place of refuge, and yet ... they remain so full of life, and hope. Listen to their laughter."

Castano closed his eyes. Domenico and Isra listened with him, enjoying the yelps and anarchic giggles of children playing on the floors above them.

"You rarely hear laughter in the Vatican," Castano lamented, "and when you do, it is never innocent. It is political laughter, designed to wound. Or score points. Or display one's intellect."

Castano fell silent. Domenico drew breath to speak, but Isra put her hand on his arm to stop him. She sensed that silence might coax a confession.

"How can children love so unconditionally?" Castano's brow furrowed as he tried to understand. "They cannot choose their parents, yet they love in spite of that. Sometimes I see them on Rome's streets, clutching the hand of a mother who is too harassed to care, or a father whose only interest is hurrying to the nearest tavern to get drunk. Yet still the child loves them. Follows them. Trusts them. And even when they are abandoned, put two or three children together, and soon they are laughing and playing. Children heal each other. It is a miracle. God's miracle. When did we lose that?"

The question hung in the silence.

"What happened all those years ago?" Domenico asked.

Castano looked at him with eyes searching for forgiveness. All his defences had broken down, now he needed to find peace. "That final year at Gandolfo was our last hurrah before taking Holy Orders. Every Thursday, the six of us would head into town to indulge our appetites. Food and wine, and…" He struggled to complete the sentence.

"Say it," Isra urged. "Name it."

"What fires burn in the hearts of all young men? It didn't matter that we were training to be priests. We had not learnt to control our desires. As the time for ordination drew closer, we resolved to lay our demons of lust to rest in one last indulgence. I know now that it was a terrible mistake. A wickedness that had tragic consequences. But at the time… We had come to know the women who worked in the taverns of Gandolfo. One woman in particular … Eva. And that night, when we were drunk, we cast off all restraint."

"You raped her," Isra said with disgust.

"No! We would never!"

"You're a liar."

"She was our friend," Castano pleaded. "She enjoyed the attention."

"So it was *her* fault?"

"That's not what I said. But … neither was it our fault."

"Someone was to blame."

"It was complicated."

"Coward! You don't even have the courage to admit what you did."

"What we did is what young people do!" Castano insisted. "Including Eva. How were we to know the consequences? We loved her!"

"You don't know the meaning of the word," Isra said with contempt.

"We didn't want to harm her. I swear on my life."

"How many of you abused her?" Domenico asked.

"It was not abuse —"

"How many?"

Castano lowered his head and stared at the cracked slabs on the floor. "All of us. All six." Then his face sank into his hands and he started to sob like a child.

49: LOOPS

With the writing sample now in her grasp, Cristina was desperate to carry out an analysis to compare the laundry sister's calligraphy with the handwriting used in the three murder-prayers. But Abbess Beatrice was prowling the corridors of the convent that morning ensuring the sisters were busy with their assigned tasks, forcing Cristina and Ysabella to hurry back to the kitchens. It was maddening.

"We'll just have to wait until tonight," Cristina said as they crossed the courtyard.

"It can't wait that long!" Ysabella fretted. "She might escape."

"Why would Sister Angelica run? She doesn't know why we wanted her handwriting."

"Of course she knows!"

Cristina folded the writing sample in half and put it safely in her tunic. "She didn't behave like a guilty woman."

"Because she's a good liar. A dangerous liar."

"Even if that's the case, if Sister Angelica really is the killer —"

"She is," Ysabella interrupted. "I know it."

"If you're right, and she runs, how far will she get on the streets of Rome?"

"Sister Angelica is more worldly than she presents. If the murders are even half as grotesque as you describe, her 'devout washerwoman' act is nothing but a veneer of deceit."

"If we are to accuse someone, we have to be sure of their guilt," Cristina insisted.

"Arrest her now. If we're wrong, you can apologise later."

"Listen to me!" They had reached the door to the kitchens and could already hear the clatter of pots being taken from cupboards. "If I call the Apostolic Guard to arrest Angelica and it turns out she's innocent, my cover will be blown and the real killer will slip away. You have to trust me on this, Ysabella."

"You're making a mistake. I know this convent better than you."

"We'll do the analysis tonight, after Compline. Come to my cell."

Time seemed to slow down. It was as if the convent bell that normally nagged the sisters from task to task, had succumbed to a bout of sweating sickness that drained it of energy and enthusiasm. Finally, the bell tolled to signal the end of the day's worship, and the sisters retired to their cells for the night.

Ysabella lit three candles and lined them up on the lectern, while Cristina rummaged under the mattress and pulled out her beloved magnifying glass. She placed the first murder-prayer on the lectern, smoothed it out, then laid the Lord's Prayer that Sister Angelica had written that morning next to it.

"Let's uncover the truth," Cristina said as she held the lens over the two pieces of paper, moving swiftly from one to the other and back again.

At first glance the samples looked identical, for both were written in the neat, copperplate hand that all the nuns were taught. But a different story lay in the idiosyncrasies.

"Look at *Hallowed be thy Name*," Cristina said. "The vertical strokes in the prayer are all straight, but in Angelica's hand they are slanted a little to the left."

"It's very slight," Ysabella said, looking over Cristina's shoulder.

"The letter size is also different." Cristina put the glass down for a moment and narrowed her eyes as she assessed the samples. "Sister Angelica uses larger letters, but in the prayers the letters are smaller, more closed down. You see?"

"But she had more to write when it came to the murder-prayers. More words to fit on the page."

Cristina picked up the lens again and continued the scrutiny. "*Our Father, which art in Heaven.* Look at the location of the 'i' dot. The killer's dot consistently drifts away from the letter, but Sister Angelica's is more accurate."

"This seems so pedantic." Ysabella was getting frustrated.

"But a person's hand is directly connected to their heart. The quill traces the soul. We do not consciously guide our hand, which is why writing is so honest." Cristina moved the lens further down the samples. "Here's another tic: look at the location of the 't' bars. Now compare them with *For twenty-three years, I waited*. The bar is higher up the downstroke on the killer's prayer. And it's consistent. It happens again and again." Cristina sat up straight. "I'm afraid it's not her. Sister Angelica is not the killer."

"This is absurd!" Ysabella exclaimed. "All the evidence points towards Angelica, but you obsess over these minute details of a few hastily written words?"

"Even if you don't agree with the study of handwriting, surely you can see this must give us reason to hesitate?"

Ysabella shook her head. "I think you should summon the authorities immediately. Let the magistrates decide on the strength of the evidence. That is their job."

Cristina understood Ysabella's frustration, but she also knew from bitter experience that when you forced the evidence in a predetermined direction, miscarriages of justice invariably followed. "We'll skip breakfast and perform another analysis tomorrow, with fresh eyes," Cristina suggested. "Let's see how we feel after a good night's sleep. We'll make a firm decision then."

But sleep wouldn't come to Cristina. The moment she blew out the candle, her mind started racing over the conflicting evidence.

How could it all be reconciled?

And there was another question that kept bobbing to the surface: why was Sister Ysabella so convinced that Sister Angelica was guilty? Why was she fighting the evidence of the handwriting analysis?

Could Sister Ysabella be trying to protect someone else?

The records from the gatehouse register showed a clear correlation between Sister Angelica's movements and the murders, but as Cristina had told other people time and again, correlation was not the same as causation. Perhaps there was another pattern lurking deeper in the register that they had failed to see, a pattern that implicated a different sister.

With that thought, all hopes of sleep were doomed. Cristina pulled the tunic over her head, slipped on her sandals and crept out into the deserted corridor.

It was just as well she had acted swiftly because the abbess had not yet completed her final patrol of the convent before going to bed, and the gatehouse door was still unlocked.

Cristina moved the register into a pool of moonlight filtering through a small window, and started to turn the pages.

Where to look for patterns in such a mass of information? Sisters coming and going, day after day … how would a murderous pattern hide itself beneath these routines?

Cristina flicked back and forth across the pages, comparing the days of the murders to the other days. What was different? What only happened on the days of the killings?

She heard a door slam shut in the courtyard, and the faint slap of leather sandals on the cobbles — the abbess was heading this way.

Think, Cristina, think!

As names and times started to slip into a blur, Cristina screwed her eyes shut and threw her head back.

Think!

When she snapped her eyes open, Cristina found herself looking at another list of names. Pinned to the wall above the gatehouse window was a rota setting out which sister was on gatehouse duty on which days. She stood up and examined the rota more closely. It was drawn up in blocks of three months on a repeating cycle. Cristina ran her finger down the list … checking the crucial dates…

There it was. The pattern that she had missed.

On each of the murder days, the same sister was on duty in the gatehouse, signing the nuns in and out. The same person controlled the record of who was where. That person was Sister Ysabella.

Keys rattled in a door close by. The abbess was nearly here. Cristina lifted the iron latch and drew open the door, trying not to provoke a squeak, then hurried away in the direction of her cell.

As she ran through splashes of moonlight illuminating the dark corridor, pieces of evidence fell into place in Cristina's mind. It was like tossing a deck of playing cards into the air and watching them fall in perfect suit order on the floor. Everything made sense if Sister Ysabella was the priest killer.

On the day of each murder, Ysabella must have signed Sister Angelica out to perform her laundry duties at the Vatican, but in the evening she left the convent herself, *without* signing the register. No-one would know Ysabella was absent because according to the register she had not left the convent walls. Anyone wondering why they hadn't seen her would assume she was on mousetrap duties. Ysabella must have hidden a key to the main gates somewhere in order to let herself back in, but hiding things was clearly one of her specialities. The crucifix with the secret recess containing quills and ink must have been Ysabella's, but she had switched it at the last moment to implicate Sister Angelica.

So not only was Ysabella the killer, but all along she had been setting up Sister Angelica to take the blame. Hence the suggestion to search her cell, and the insistence that Angelica was guilty despite the conclusions of the handwriting analysis. If Cristina could find the key Ysabella used to get back into the convent in the dead of night, the case against her would be watertight. But where would someone as cunning as Ysabella hide a large, iron key?

As her mind focussed on this one final point, Cristina pushed open the door to her own cell and stumbled in shock.

Sister Ysabella was standing in the darkness of the room, facing the door; she held a large wooden crucifix in her hands, gripping it like a club.

"What are you doing here?" Cristina whispered.

"I think we both know the answer to that." Sister Ysabella's face contorted with rage and she swung her arm.

There was a dull thud. Cristina felt her head jerk to the left. A searing pain shot down her neck.

Her vision swam … then she blacked out.

50: REPUTATIONS

Isra grabbed Castano's hands and yanked them from his tearstained face. "How dare you indulge in self-pity?"

"Can a man not show remorse?" Castano cried.

"You're weeping for yourself!"

"That's a lie!"

"Where were your tears these last twenty years? Did you spare a thought for the woman you raped?"

"For the last time, it was not rape."

"You're crying because you've been caught. Not for any other reason." Isra snatched a towel rag that was hanging next to the door and tossed it at Castano. "Dry your eyes."

Domenico watched Castano dab his face, then fold the cloth with the carefully cultivated pedantry that had come to define his life.

"What happened to the young woman?" Domenico asked.

"She fell pregnant. But we didn't walk away," Castano added hastily. "We knew that we had a moral responsibility for what had happened. On the other hand..." He glanced warily at Isra, trying to find words that wouldn't enrage her further. "We were about to be ordained, so any thought of marriage was impossible. Which left us no choice, the whole matter had to be covered up."

"The coward's way out," Isra scoffed.

"How else could we protect her reputation?"

"*Her* reputation?"

"Who would want her if the whole world knew about the scandal? Her life would have been blighted."

"The only reputations you were protecting were your own," Isra said. "Don't pretend otherwise."

Castano opened his mouth to justify himself, then caught the look of contempt on Isra's face and changed his mind.

"So what did you do?" Domenico asked.

"We brought the woman here, to Tivoli, and she was cared for until she gave birth. We paid all the bills, naturally. Then the baby boy was taken into the orphanage, where he could grow up without the cloud of scandal hanging over him."

"And without his mother's love," Isra said accusingly.

"The way is hard that leads to life."

"How dare you quote scripture to justify your behaviour?"

Domenico put a restraining hand on Isra's shoulder. "Don't let him provoke you further." He turned back to Castano. "What happened to the woman? Did she return to Gandolfo?"

"That would have carried too much risk. She was still … fragile after everything that had happened. So we used our contacts to have her admitted to a convent in Rome, where the sisters could help her rebuild."

"The House of Eternal Grace?" Domenico said.

Castano nodded. "It was the best thing. They had experience of helping fallen women."

"Fallen?" Isra was aghast. "She was pushed! *You* pushed her!"

"Everyone had to move beyond blame," Castano insisted. "Or there could be no healing. It was the right thing to do."

"And did she heal?" Domenico asked.

"For a while. When she entered the convent she changed her name to Sister Ysabella, and with that new identity began a new life."

"So she was punished for your behaviour?"

"It was not about punishment. There had been no crime, just a terrible mistake. The mistake that young people have always made."

"But it doesn't end there, does it?"

Castano looked down at his shoes.

"Does it?" Domenico demanded.

Castano shook his head. "Two years later, we made a fatal mistake."

Isra stepped closer until she was looming over Castano. "You abused a young woman, then forcibly separated her from her child. What mistake could possibly be worse than that?"

"We sheltered Ysabella from the truth. And that triggered a catastrophic chain of events."

51: STRENGTH

Pain pulsed through Cristina's head. It felt as if someone was hammering into her brain with a stonemason's chisel.

At least she was alive, but what had happened to her? Where was she now?

She opened her eyes but that revealed nothing — she was in pitch black. She tuned into her other senses. She was lying face down on a stone floor that smelled musty, like a cellar. That would explain the darkness. Her fingers moved up to her head to try and ease the pain and she felt a sticky patch of half-dried blood on her right temple. And then she remembered the blow. Sister Ysabella had struck her with the wooden crucifix. Hard. Knocking her unconscious.

How long had she been down here, wherever 'here' was? She had to move, raise the alarm about Ysabella, prevent another murder … save her own life.

With enormous effort, Cristina braced her muscles and hauled herself to her knees. As she moved, her hand slipped on something sticky pooling on the floor. She touched her fingers to her nose and smelled blood. It must have seeped from the wound on her head. It hadn't dried yet, so she couldn't have been down here for more than a few hours.

Another huge effort was needed to get to her feet. Cristina counted to three, then hauled herself up, but as she straightened her back, her head clunked agonisingly into the ceiling.

"*Figlio di puttana!*" she cursed. She rubbed the top of her head but that only made the existing pain worse.

Calm down. Take control. Panic never helps.

She drew a breath and started feeling her way through the space. Above her felt like a vaulted ceiling made from bricks, but it was only four feet high, forcing Cristina into a painful crouch. She edged forwards until she came to a stubby pillar supporting the ceiling. Instinctively, she wrapped her arms around it and held tight, taking comfort from the solid stone.

The rasp of a tinderbox striking broke the silence.

Cristina turned her head and saw the glow of an oil lamp balloon into the darkness. The first face it found was Sister Ysabella's.

"What have you done to me?" Cristina's voice was hoarse. "Where are we?"

"This is my sanctuary," Ysabella replied. There was a note of pride in her voice, as if she were an elegant hostess welcoming guests into her palazzo.

Cristina's gaze followed the light as it tried to push into the darkness. Dozens of stubby pillars supported a low, vaulted ceiling that extended in all directions. "Are we under the convent?"

"We are. But there's no point crying out for help. There are no buildings above us."

"I don't understand."

"The original plans for this convent had an ornate fountain in the middle of the quad. This undercroft was built to carry all the water pipes, but when the money ran out, they just cobbled over the space instead. The whole courtyard is floating above this space. I discovered it by chance, fifteen years ago."

Cristina peered into the dark recesses of the undercroft, half expecting to see the skeletons of Ysabella's previous victims, but instead she saw a stack of seven cages containing dozens of mice who were scrambling over each other in excitement.

"Yours?" Cristina asked.

Ysabella smiled. "As long as the House of Eternal Grace has a mice problem, I am free to roam the buildings at will. But I need a good supply to keep the system working."

"So you breed mice and release them?"

"Then excel at catching and killing them."

Cristina felt a shudder of unease at the casual talk of killing. Her eyes darted across the walls, searching for a way out, but there were no doors, only a hatch panel in the far wall — that must be how Ysabella got in and out.

"What are you going to do to me?" Cristina asked.

"Set the record straight."

"You didn't have to imprison me to do that. I would have listened."

Ysabella scoffed. "It's funny how people become suddenly reasonable when facing their own killer. When you returned from the gatehouse you were like a bloodhound following a fresh scent. You weren't in a mood to listen."

"Then tell me now, Ysabella, or whatever your real name is." Cristina squatted on the floor, resting her back against one of the pillars. "Explain everything."

"Have you ever had a child?"

Cristina shook her head.

"I thought not. Even though I was hidden away and my pregnancy was clouded with shame, it was the most wonderful thing. To feel life growing inside me. It changed everything. They said they were caring for me, but I knew they were hiding me from the world to protect themselves."

"Who, Ysabella? Who treated you like that?"

"The men from Gandolfo. The six young priests. But if you've found me, you must have already found them."

Cristina's mind pulled the fragments together and grasped what the Thursday Six must have done to her all those years ago.

"The pain of childbirth, the fear and agony," Ysabella continued, "that was all washed clean by the wave of love that flooded my heart. Unconditional love. I remember looking into his eyes in those first few moments, his face creased in a frown, trying to work out why he had been pulled from his warm darkness into the light and noise of the world. To hold him … to feel his heartbeat fluttering against mine…" Ysabella fell silent, remembering those blissful moments.

Then reality jolted the joy away. Her face clouded. "They took him from me. I tried to fight them off. I cried, screamed and begged, but they told me this was how God had ordained it. That I had sinned and God demanded penance. I wept for the entire journey from Tivoli to this convent. I wept for the first three months as a novice. Nothing could console me for the loss of my son. Grief had cracked my soul. Yet just when I thought I would shatter and die, they came back to the convent. All six of them. And they gave me hope. They told me that God had revealed His intentions to them, and that He was pleased with the contrition in my heart. They told me that if I served God in this convent, when my son grew into a man, God would bring us together again. We would be reunited."

"How could six young priests possibly know God's mind?" Cristina bridled at the calculated deceit.

But Ysabella had moved beyond rage. "I was young and naïve, they were priests. I had no education; they could read Latin and Greek. Why should I doubt the word of ordained men?"

"Because they are men first. With all the failings of men."

260

"Nevertheless, it was the hope of being reunited with my son that gave me the strength to turn back to life. I had to survive for his sake. Nothing else mattered. So I embraced my duties in the convent and became a good sister. Yet every day I thought about my son growing up, I imagined his life outside these walls, the friends he was making, the games he was playing, what he might be learning in school. Even though I had only been with my little boy for a few hours, he never left my heart. And I knew that when my penance was complete, we would be reunited, and all the pain and sacrifice would be over.

"Some years later, on the anniversary of my son's birth, those six men returned. They were building their careers in the Church, becoming men of importance. They were astonished by my recovery. They told me that I was truly blessed, that God was looking kindly on me, that it was His strength that was flowing through my heart. You cannot imagine what it feels like to know that God holds you close, that He watches over you night and day. It is the most extraordinary thing, like a physical sensation. It is what gave me the strength to survive … and the courage to kill."

"How can love inspire murder?" Cristina whispered.

Ysabella put her hand into a crack in the wall that was just above the mice cages, and pulled out a letter that had been hidden there. "See for yourself."

Cristina took the letter and looked at the small, neat handwriting. It had been written from one of the settlements in the New World, and the ink was splashed and smeared from its difficult journey to Europe.

With trepidation, she started to read.

52: LIES

"You see that bell tower rising above the roofline?" Castano stood at the window of his temporary prison cell, pointing up towards the centre of Tivoli. "That belongs to the church of Santa Maria Maggiore." He turned to Domenico and Isra. "That is where Ysabella's son is buried."

"He's dead?" Domenico gasped. "When?"

"He was just two years old. There was an outbreak of cholera. One of the risks of living in a town that is forever flooding. The outbreak took a lot of young children that year, including Ysabella's son."

"Convenient for you," Isra observed. "Nothing left to tarnish your 'brilliant careers'."

"The effect was quite the opposite." Castano turned from the window and sat down on the wooden stool. "The boy's death presented us with a sharp dilemma. You see, when she was taken in by the convent, Ysabella was inconsolable. To the point of hysteria. You'd think she was the only woman ever to have given up a child. Most get over it, but not her."

Isra looked at him in disbelief. "Do you have any idea how callous you are?"

"We all suffer. We all grieve. Compared to what people go through in war, Ysabella had a charmed life."

Domenico raised his foot and kicked the stool from under Castano, sending him tumbling onto the floor. "Do not presume to lecture either of us on the tribulations of war."

Castano picked himself up and brushed the dirt from his cassock. "Nevertheless. For the first three months she was in the convent, Ysabella's mind was crumbling. The abbess wrote to me, worried that the girl would die from grief. So we went to see her, and we gave her reason to live. We promised Ysabella that when her son had grown into adulthood, she would be reunited with him. We told her this would be God's reward for her penance."

"You presumed to speak for God?" Domenico couldn't believe the man's calm arrogance.

"That is what ordination means. I would not expect someone like you to understand. God works through His priests, and in this instance, we unleashed the astonishing power of hope. Ysabella's recovery began that very day. We saw her turn back to life. It was miraculous. Which is why, when her son died, we decided not to tell Ysabella straight away. At that stage she was still too fragile. The shock would undoubtedly have broken her."

"So you lied to her," Domenico said.

"What harm was there in letting her believe her son was alive and healthy?"

"A priest should not lie to those who trust him."

"In the short term it made no difference. She would not have seen him, so why snatch away hope?"

"The short term. That's the problem," Domenico replied. "What did you think would happen when the years passed? When the boy was supposed to have reached adulthood?"

"That was still far in the future, and we believed that time would heal Ysabella, just as it heals all wounds. Had she been a normal person, Ysabella would have mellowed as she got older, and forgotten about her son."

"Forget her own son?" Isra looked at him in disbelief. "You seriously think a mother could forget her own son? A child she carried for nine months?"

Castano shrugged. "We believed this was all part of God's plan."

"Because you are deluded!"

"Truly, there was something Christ-like about the fate of Ysabella and her son ... a mother making the ultimate sacrifice. The symbolism was striking."

"Except in this case," Domenico pointed out, "she was sacrificing herself so that the six of *you* could build successful careers."

Castano flicked a stubborn piece of fluff from his shoulder. "Whatever your moral judgements, the fact remains: Ysabella grew strong again. She built a life in that convent. The other sisters liked her, and she became a valuable part of their community." Castano's face suddenly clouded. "Until the last will and testament of Father Cerchio destroyed our meticulous plans."

"Who?" Isra said.

"One of the Thursday Six," Domenico explained.

"When he went to the New World, we all assumed we would never hear from him again," Castano recalled. "His friends advised him that such a venture was fraught with danger, but Cerchio wouldn't listen. He was desperate to save the Savage Soul in that strange and hostile land. Within a year, he had fallen sick with malaria. Unfortunately, as he lay dying, Cerchio became filled with remorse and tormented by guilt. He dictated a letter that was enclosed with his will. It was addressed to Ysabella, and it confessed the truth about her son. That he had died as an infant. It was sad to see a once proud man beg forgiveness with such desperation. Sad and rather humiliating."

"Who cares about him?" Isra said. "Did anyone go to Ysabella?"

Castano shook his head.

"In one terrible moment, she discovered that her entire life had been a lie, and you did nothing to console her?"

"I was concerned about what I would find," Castano admitted. "We all were. How would she react if she saw us again? It might have set her back years."

"So considerate of you."

"I prayed for her. I asked God to help Ysabella witness her rage in the privacy of the convent. But her grief could not be contained. And when the murders started, I knew that Ysabella had succumbed to the temptation of evil. She was exacting a terrible revenge for what she perceived were the injustices she had endured."

"Perceived? You think the hurt was all in her mind?"

"I didn't say that."

Castano tried to look away, but Isra grabbed his face and forced him to look at her. "At every stage of this tragedy, you did the wrong thing. You are a pathetic man, and a shame to the priesthood."

"*Figlia di puttana!*" Domenico strode towards Castano and punched him in the face. Castano fell backwards off the stool as blood exploded across his face.

Isra grabbed Domenico and pulled him back. "No! Let the courts punish him."

"You don't understand, he has put Cristina in mortal danger. She is in the convent right now, undercover, trying to identify the killer. But she has no idea what she's up against."

They burst into *Direttore* Scudo's office and instructed him to summon the local militia; acting on orders from the Apostolic Guard, the militia were to shackle Castano and take him to the Vatican. Then Domenico commandeered two of the best horses he could find in Tivoli, and he and Isra started the frantic race back to Rome.

53: FULFILLED

Cristina returned the letter to Ysabella, and watched as she tucked it safely into the crack in the masonry. It was as if anything to do with her son, no matter how painful, had to be preserved like a relic.

"I'm so sorry," Cristina whispered.

"Every Saturday, I had lit a candle for him in the chapel. Every week, for all those years. He was the focus of my life even though I had known him for just a few hours. And the light of those candles was the knowledge that one day we would be reunited. To have that snuffed out..." Ysabella's brow furrowed as she struggled to articulate her feelings. "I had this image in my mind of a fine young man, growing stronger with every passing day. And that letter cut him down. It destroyed him. Don't you see? I lost my son a second time."

"I cannot imagine the pain you must have felt."

"No. You cannot. No-one can." Ysabella wiped her eyes as rising anger coloured her grief. "But the worst sin of all, was that from the very beginning, those priests made me believe that what happened was my fault."

"You were just a girl when it happened."

"Which is why they used their authority to deceive me, to convince me that I deserved to suffer. Throughout all those years I blamed myself. So when I discovered they had been lying about my son, I started to question everything, and slowly I realised that they had been lying from the very first moment. Everything they had told me was a lie. The sin was not mine after all, it was theirs."

Ysabella gave the knowing laugh of someone who has just understood the secret behind a conjuring trick. "That realisation … it opened the floodgates of rage in my heart. I went to the chapel and demanded an explanation from God. How could He have stood by while I was so cruelly deceived? Hour after hour I knelt in prayer until my knees were bruised, and my hands cramped. And when no answer came, my rage turned into hatred. I hated God. For five long years I hated Him. Why had He let a young woman be tricked and abused? Why had He let His priests flourish whilst I had to languish in a convent? Why had He rewarded a mother's love for her son with betrayal?

"Silence. I heard nothing from God but silence. He gave me no answers. He had abandoned me. Until … in my very darkest hour, He finally spoke to me. Not in words or prayer, but through a series of miracles." Ysabella drew a deep breath, as if inhaling life itself. "When St Peter's miracles graced the streets of Rome, I knew that at last God had heard my lament, and sent His most beloved saint to give me strength."

Cristina felt nausea stirring in her guts as she saw how everything was connecting.

"St Peter's bones emerging after fifteen centuries buried in darkness, that was God reaching out to me, a woman who had been lost in the darkness of grief. The fruit miraculously appearing in the orchard, that was a celebration of fertility, reassuring me that I had nothing to be ashamed of. And the miracle cure of the young woman who had lost her mind, that was God's promise that He would heal me too. But I had to remain true to my heart and faithful to God. Which meant cleansing His Church of the men who had defiled it by abusing me."

"Ysabella, there was nothing in the miracles urging you to kill," Cristina said.

"*And he shall purify the sons of Levi, that they may offer unto the Lord offerings in righteousness.* You do not understand because God was not talking to you. He was challenging *me* to be avenged."

"But revenge is not a Christian virtue."

"Then why does Hell exist?"

"Ysabella, I am not a theologian —"

"And what do you think will happen on the Day of Judgement? The righteous shall be saved and the wicked damned. The sheep separated from the goats. That is written in the scriptures. St Peter's miracles spoke to me with the same strength as the Bible. That was their purpose. And their message was clear: just as the miracles defied the petty laws of men, so should I." Ysabella closed her eyes and tilted her head back, lost in her memories. "I know I am right, because the moment I passed the blade across Coraggioso's throat, I felt the most liberating sense of enlightenment. Nothing that felt so wonderful could possibly be wrong. There is no doubt in my mind that I have done God's work."

Guilt tightened its grip on Cristina until her lungs struggled to draw breath. This woman sitting in front of her, whose life had been destroyed by deception, had finally found truth ... in yet another lie. Ysabella deserved to hear the real truth, but Cristina was terrified to utter the words.

What demons would the truth unleash in Ysabella's wounded heart?

"Ysabella, you have been wronged in the most appalling way," Cristina began, "and nothing I am about to tell you is meant to diminish the suffering you have endured. But there is a truth that you need to know if you are ever to make peace with the tangle of sorrow that has choked your life. The miracles of St Peter that drew you to murder … they were not sent from God. They were created by mortal men. By me."

There was not a flicker of reaction on Ysabella's face.

"You need to find peace and forgiveness in God's eyes, but for that to happen, first you must accept that He was not leading you to murder. It was not His hand on the knife. You were not doing His will, Ysabella. Your mind latched onto something because you were in pain. I don't blame you, or judge you, but only once you accept the truth can you seek forgiveness and start the journey towards redemption. This horror must end, and you must face justice."

Still, Ysabella did nothing. She just sat in the flickering glow of the oil lamp, staring into the gloom of the undercroft.

"Ysabella," Cristina whispered. "Do you understand what I'm saying?"

Slowly, Ysabella started to shake her head, then her face creased into a smile and she laughed. "You are insane, woman!"

"I swear, what I've told you is the truth."

"Fake miracles? Why would anyone do such a thing?" Ysabella mocked. "It's absurd!"

"I cannot tell you everything. All I can say is that the Vatican has been terrified of people losing their faith."

"Rome is the centre of Christendom! Your claims are nonsense."

"I wish I could tell you the reasons why, Ysabella, but I am forbidden."

"How convenient."

"But unless you embrace the truth, you will never find salvation."

"People came from across Europe to worship St Peter's bones and witness his miracles. I saw it with my own eyes. Are you saying they were wrong? All of them? That they were fooled by you?"

"Yes."

"You can make figs grow on apple trees? You can heal the sick? You can persuade the Holy Father himself that the bones of St Peter have miraculous powers?"

"I know how strange it must sound, Ysabella."

"You are deluded about the powers you possess. *You* are the one who has lost their mind!" Ysabella cried. "But like a coward, you are trying to shift the blame onto me."

"There is a way out of this."

"Stop talking!"

"Listen to me —"

"No! You have said enough!"

"Why would I tell such an outrageous lie?"

"Stop! Stop! Stop!" Ysabella screamed. "You are trying to deceive me! Just like them! Just like the six of them. But I will not have the truth snatched from me again. I. Will. Not."

Cristina sensed that Ysabella's mind was about to shatter; she was now desperately trying to close down what she could not accept. She was so steeped in madness there was no turning back to reality, it would be too painful.

Somehow, Cristina had to escape from this undercroft. "I understand your anger, Ysabella, but I can get you proof."

"How can you prove nonsense?"

"I have the evidence in my room. Why don't we go there? Let me show you."

"I have a better idea," Ysabella whispered. She reached into the darkness of the brickwork and drew out a long knife. "This was the First Knife of Justice. One day it was carving meat in the convent, the next it was cutting Coraggioso's throat in an act of Divine Retribution."

"Please, Ysabella. You don't want to do this."

"Don't tell me what I want!" Ysabella lunged forward with rage.

Cristina raised her hands to protect herself and managed to grab Ysabella's wrists. For a few moments, the blade glinted dangerously close to her face as the women wrestled, then Cristina spun her body to the left, sending Ysabella thumping into one of the brick pillars.

But still she clutched the knife. And now she was galvanised with rage like a wild animal. "You will never understand, because God has never touched you!" Ysabella leapt across the space trying to plunge the knife into Cristina's heart.

Cristina lashed out with her foot to kick the weapon away but missed, and the knife slid up her calf which split open in a crimson gash.

She screamed as the pain shot through her body, but there was no time to stop the bleeding or even check the wound — Ysabella was coming for her again in another frenzied attack.

She stabbed wildly, left, right, left, right, forcing Cristina further into the darkness. But there was nowhere to escape, and all Ysabella had to do was follow the trail of fresh blood.

"Don't worry," Ysabella rasped as she closed in. "I'll write you a beautiful prayer as well. Perhaps it will lessen your time in Purgatory."

CLUNK! A brick slammed down on Ysabella's wrist with such force Cristina heard her bones crack. She howled with pain as Cristina yanked the knife from her hand and hurled it away into the darkness. "It's over, Ysabella! You cannot fight the world forever."

Ysabella's face contorted with pain. "You've broken my hand! You've broken it!"

Cristina knelt over her. "Let me see."

"Don't touch me!"

"Why wouldn't you do as I asked?" Cristina peered closer at Ysabella's wrist which was now lying at an impossible angle. Angry bruising had started to balloon under her skin. "Let me bind it," Cristina said. She pulled off her scapular and tore it lengthways. "And I must bandage my leg to stop this bleeding."

Suddenly, Ysabella's cry of pained melted into tears of remorse. "Forgive me for cutting you. Forgive me."

"Stay quiet. It's over now." Gingerly, Cristina started to slip the cloth under Ysabella's wrist, trying to disturb the fracture as little as possible. "Nearly done —"

Cristina felt a sudden, blinding pain, then slumped to the floor.

She forced open her eyes to see Ysabella looming over her, wiping the tears and snot from her face. Remorse had vanished. In her hand she clutched the stray brick.

"What … what did you do?" Cristina gasped.

"How many more times do I have to batter your head before you understand that you are simply not strong enough to defeat me?"

Blood trickled into Cristina's eyes, clouding her vision red as if she had been plunged into Dante's Hell. "Please … spare me."

"Oh, I won't kill you. That would be too easy." Ysabella let the brick drop from her hand. "No, you must have special treatment. You will be entombed, just like St Peter."

"No…"

"And maybe in a thousand years, someone will dig up the foundations of this convent and find your bones here and declare it a miracle."

"Please…"

"This will be my last act before I go to meet my son. Finally."

Through the blurry blood-haze, Cristina saw Ysabella scurry towards the small door in the far wall.

"Don't leave…" Cristina tried to follow, but she couldn't even crawl. Her limbs were impossibly heavy and her mind was being sucked into oblivion.

Focus. Stay awake. Focus!

But it was useless.

She heard the door open and close. The sound of bolts being drawn across from the outside. Padlocks snapping shut.

Now there was no way out. She couldn't move, she didn't have the strength to scream, even if there was anyone up there to hear.

She would die in this undercroft.

Cristina rocked her head to one side and watched her own blood pooling on the dusty floor.

Then she looked up at the mice in their cages who had stopped their frantic scurrying and were gazing down at her, wondering what this strange human was doing.

Cristina stretched out her hand, desperately trying to reach the cage door.

54: VANISHED

Having ridden non-stop from the orphanage at Tivoli, Domenico didn't have time for niceties. He stormed into the convent, with Isra and a troop of Apostolic Guards following in his slipstream.

While the guards secured the perimeter of the convent to ensure no-one came in or out, Domenico and Isra burst into the gatehouse, where they found the glacial Sister Denise on duty.

"Where is Sister Ysabella?" Domenico demanded.

"You cannot come barging into a house of God!"

Domenico slapped a Papal Warrant on the counter. "I too am on God's business. Where is Ysabella?"

Sister Denise picked up the warrant and started reading it.

"Where?" Domenico shouted.

"Let me fetch the abbess."

Sister Denise moved towards the door, but Domenico blocked her path.

"You're not fetching anyone. You're taking us to Sister Ysabella's cell without delay, or you will find yourself hauled in front of Cardinal Riario."

"You should learn some manners," Sister Denise retorted.

"Not the time or place."

Reluctantly, Sister Denise did as she was ordered. As she led them across the cobbled courtyard, nuns emerged from various cloisters to find out what was causing the disturbance.

"What in Heaven's name is going on?" Abbess Beatrice demanded as she marched from her office to confront them. "I order you to leave this convent!"

"Gather the entire sisterhood in the chapel," Domenico instructed, swerving past her.

"Didn't you hear me?" The abbess practically had to run to keep up with him.

"You are the one who needs to listen, Reverend Mother. Do as I say."

"Why? What for? With whose authority?"

Domenico stopped abruptly and glared down at the abbess. "There's a killer hiding in your convent. Three priests are dead, and if you don't do exactly as I say, my own sister's blood will be on your hands."

Abbess Beatrice recoiled in shock. "This cannot be true."

"Now please, do as I say. Gather all the nuns into the chapel."

By the time they entered the north wing of the convent, the bell was already tolling to signal the alarm. Sisters were hurrying from their cells in panic, wondering what could have shattered the peace of their cloistered life.

Sister Denise led Domenico and Isra, dodging and weaving against the flow of nuns. "She's in the next block."

But as they turned the corner, Sister Denise froze — there was a puddle of blood seeping out from under the door of Ysabella's cell.

Domenico pushed open the door. It was a ghastly sight: Sister Ysabella was lying on her bed, but the sheets were now saturated in blood that was oozing from her slashed wrists.

"No, no, no!" Domenico rushed over and lifted Sister Ysabella's eyelids. "Stay with me!" But her eyes had already rolled back into her head. Domenico put his ear to her lips, listening.

"Is she still breathing?" Isra asked.

"Barely."

"There's still time." Isra grabbed the towel that was hanging next to the wash bowl and started to tie it tightly round Sister Ysabella's wrists, trying to stem the flow of blood.

"Where's Cristina?" Domenico lifted her head, desperate to bring her back. "Where is she? What have you done to her?"

Sister Ysabella's chest heaved as she gulped in a deep breath.

"Where is Cristina? Tell me!"

Then Sister Ysabella's body relaxed and she breathed out … a long, slow exhale. There was a soft gargle in her throat, followed by nothing.

"Wake up!" Domenico shook her, but Isra could see that the blood was no longer pumping from Ysabella's self-inflicted wounds.

"She's gone."

They were still covered in blood when they entered the chapel, startling the sisters who were huddled together in the chancel.

"What's happened?" Abbess Beatrice asked.

"Who is missing?" Domenico demanded. "Have you counted everyone?"

"Sister Ysabella and Sister Clara are absent. Do you know where they are?"

Domenico's eyes hunted across the faces, frantically searching for his sister. "Ysabella is in her cell. But I'm afraid it's too late."

"What do you mean?"

"She's dead."

"God rest her soul!" Abbess Beatrice cried.

Immediately, the other sisters fell to their knees and started praying.

"We need to search this convent," Domenico said. "Every square inch. Stay in the chapel. Don't let anyone leave."

Domenico pulled guards from perimeter duty to make up search parties which scattered through the convent grounds. As they searched, they called out Cristina's name, creating a melancholy chorus that echoed off the ancient walls.

They searched every cell. They searched the manuscript room. They searched the outhouses where the gardening tools were stored, and they searched the rooms high up in the bell tower.

Then just as they were leaving the kitchens, Isra glimpsed a mouse hurrying into one of the pantries. With the sharp reflexes of a housekeeper, she picked up a glass jar and followed the mouse inside with the intention of removing it. But when she cornered the mouse she noticed something strange.

"It's all right," she whispered. "I won't hurt you." She cupped her hands and gathered the mouse up. She could feel it warm and wriggling in her grip, then she made a gap between her fingers to study it — there were smears of red all over its white body.

"How does a mouse get blood on its fur?"

Domenico hurried over and Isra opened her fingers wider to show him.

"Is it hurt?"

Isra stroked the mouse to soothe its fear; there were no wounds on its body. Her mind ran through different scenarios about how it could have become bloodied.

And then she realised…

"It's Cristina, isn't it?"

"What?"

"I think she's signalling for help."

They diverted two of the search parties into the cellars, and swiftly checked every alcove, locker and crawlspace; but all they found were barrels of wine and olive oil, piles of chopped wood, sacks of flour, and jars of fruit that had been pickled for the winter.

When there was nothing left to search, Isra turned to Domenico. "Order the men to be still. They mustn't make a sound."

Domenico nodded to the guards. "You heard her."

When everyone was still, Isra took the jar containing the mouse and knelt on the floor. She unscrewed the lid and whispered softly, "Time to go home." Then she released the mouse onto the cellar floor.

For a few moments it crouched, trembling with fright, terrified that it was about to be killed by one of the humans looming over it.

When nothing happened, it bolted across the floor and disappeared into a crack between two crates of bitter almonds.

"There," Isra said. "She has to be back there."

Domenico hauled the crates aside and discovered a small hatch-like door in the wall. It was padlocked and bolted.

He turned to the guards. "Break it down!"

55: DANTE

Two weeks later

His Holiness Pope Julius II, Supreme Pontiff and Leader of the Papal States, officially proclaimed that 'the Season of Miracles' was over. He spoke with great emotion of the vivid dream in which God had revealed His true will: henceforth, all efforts should be focussed on constructing the magnificent new St Peter's Basilica.

Now that the miracles had dried up, the pilgrims drifted away in search of fresh euphoria in other cities, and the citizens of Rome were left to clear up the mess left in their wake. The traders and tavern owners didn't complain too much, as they had made a small fortune from the zealous influx; rather it was the army of poorly paid labourers drafted into municipal service who felt aggrieved, as they were tasked with disposing of hundreds of mounds of refuse and excrement that had sprung up like a rash of urban molehills.

In the past, Cristina had always felt a sense of triumph at solving the murders which had afflicted Rome, but not this time. The sadness of Sister Ysabella's story weighed heavily on her, and the only comfort was knowing that Ysabella had chosen death at the moment when everything made sense. Had she lived any longer, she would have been forced to accept that the guilt for her crimes lay on her own shoulders, and not with God.

Cristina never tired of winding the verge-and-foliot clock that hung on her library wall. Every three days she took the special key from its drawer and used it to transfer energy from her own body into the heart of the mechanism. She loved keeping this clock alive, for as long as it ticked, there was one part of the world that made perfect, logical sense.

As usual, there was a large pile of books and manuscripts on the long library desk, waiting to be studied, but Cristina walked straight past them and instead gazed out of the window onto Piazza Navona. Catching part of her reflection in the glass, she raised a hand to her head. The surgeons had told Cristina to keep the wounds on her scalp clean of hair until they had completely healed, giving her an oddly asymmetrical appearance. Fortunately, Isra had found a charming, crocheted cap in the market to hide the temporary disfigurement whenever she left the house.

As she watched people hurrying about their business, Cristina tried to reassure herself that there were many reasons to be proud of what she had done. Geometra Castano was due to stand trial for obstructing justice, and would most likely be defrocked and expelled from the Church. The whole of Christendom now believed beyond doubt that St Peter's bones were encased in the golden casket, and would soon be reburied in the foundations of the new basilica. The way was now clear to complete the excavations for the four great pillars that would support one of the largest domes in the world, and construction work was already back to full speed.

And yet, Cristina felt a terrible emptiness that she had been unable to shake off since returning home.

She knew that there was no blood on her hands, but she couldn't help wondering what would have happened if she *hadn't* staged the miracles. Would Sister Ysabella have remained inside the convent, silently raging at God? Would the three priests still be alive? Or would Ysabella have latched onto something else to justify her violent acts of revenge? Either way, perhaps the Thursday Six were somehow doomed from the moment they tried to cover up their sin. It was impossible to know how these hypothetical timelines might have played out.

There was a knock on the library door, and Isra popped her head round. "You've got a surprise visitor."

"Really? Who is it?"

"If I told you, it wouldn't be a surprise. He's waiting down in the hallway."

As Cristina hurried from the library, Isra reached out and slipped the crochet cap on her head.

"Is he that important?" Cristina said, straightening the cap.

"You'll see."

Despite the season, it was a stormy day in Rome and the hallway was gloomy, so it was not until she was right at the bottom of the stairs that Cristina was able to make out the figure standing awkwardly by the front doors.

"Professor De Luca? Is that really you?"

His body was twisted at a strange angle, and he was supporting himself on a pair of crutches which he gripped tightly, as if in constant fear that he was about to topple over. Yet he was washed and shaved, and wore his formal academic robes.

"They told me you wouldn't be discharged for another month," Cristina laughed. "It is so good to see you. Come in, come in!"

She opened her arms to embrace the professor, but as she drew close, De Luca held up one of his crutches and pushed her away.

"Do not touch me."

Cristina was stunned. "What on earth's the matter?"

"Do not come near me."

The left side of his face had drooped from the stroke, pulling his mouth out of shape and making his speech difficult to understand. But it was immediately clear that behind the impairment, his mind was bitingly alive. "I am ashamed of what you have done, Signorina Falchoni. You are a disgrace to the intellectual ideals you claim to admire."

"Professor, I don't understand. What have I done to cause such offence?"

"I set you a test, and you failed."

"What test? I don't understand. You've been in hospital since —"

"A man came to this house. A blind monk, urging you to go to Venice. He was sent by me, in secret, as a test of your integrity. A test which you failed."

Cristina's mind was racing to keep up. De Luca's speech was hard to understand, she must have misheard him. "Professor, I think you are confused. Your illness —"

"Do not patronise me! Do not think that just because my words are mishappen, my mind is not clear."

"I'm sorry. I meant no offence."

"When Constantinople fell, a vast cache of letters and documents flooded west. I knew that Boschi wanted to publish some diaries revealing the shocking extent of Venetian deception. I needed to know if you had the integrity to understand evil when you saw it. You did not. I would have stopped your plan from being enacted had I not been cruelly struck down. My guilt comes from bad luck, but yours comes from arrogance."

"The first person I saw when I returned from Venice was *you*," Cristina said. "I was hiding nothing. I wanted to work with you."

"You think I chose apoplexy?"

"I had to do something!" Cristina exclaimed. "I did what I thought was right."

"That is not good enough." With great effort, De Luca manoeuvred a hand into his jacket pocket and pulled out a cotton cloth which he used to dab away the saliva that was dribbling down his chin.

"Please, let me help," Cristina moved forward, but De Luca shot her a look of such vehemence, it stopped her in her tracks.

"It is the duty of the educated *not* to exploit the ignorance of ordinary people. When you twist intellect around dishonest political ends, you betray everything that academia values. Your lies led to murder, and who knows what else. Thousands of pilgrims came to Rome, how many of those innocent minds have now been corrupted?"

"Stop this!" Cristina snapped. "You are in no position to pass judgement. I had to act. I had to make decisions."

"You care more about a pile of stones than the truth? The basilica is an extravagant conceit for vainglorious popes!"

"It's not just the basilica that was under threat. The authority of the Church itself would have been undermined if doubt had been allowed to spread unchecked. You know how high the stakes were. We were working together before you were struck down."

De Luca shook his head. "Do not contaminate me with your deception."

"You cannot deny that my plan worked, even though it was unorthodox. At least allow me that. However tarnished the means, we have achieved the right ends."

"Do you know what is found in the Tenth Ditch of the Eighth Circle of Hell?" De Luca demanded. "Forgers and liars. Condemned to suffer stench and filth for eternity, scrubbing and clawing at the scabs on their diseased skin. And do you know why Dante shows no pity for them? Because intelligence without truth is not just evil, it is the mother of all evils."

Cristina had never heard De Luca speak with such vehemence. Even through his impeded language, his fury was devastating.

"Please, Professor, try to understand the dilemma I was facing. If my actions have offended you, I am truly sorry. If I compromised our ideals, it was only to achieve a greater purpose."

"Selling your soul is not compromise. It is damnation."

"Then thank God that you are recovered, and can guide me in the future."

But De Luca shook his head. "I bitterly regret the years I spent teaching you, signorina. It was the greatest mistake of my life. From now on, there will be no more contact between us. I disown you."

He turned to the front doors and his right hand started to fumble with the latch. Cristina didn't dare move to help him, she just had to watch as he struggled with the lock, then finally managed to swing open the door and sway out of the house on his crutches.

Though sanity had been restored to Rome, Cristina could not feel normal again; it was as if she no longer belonged here, as if De Luca's rejection had made her an exile in her own city.

Fortunately, she still had a few powerful friends. The Holy Father expressed his personal gratitude for the work she had done both in underpinning the religious authority of Rome, and in putting an end to the horrific killing spree. Thanks to the Pope's patronage, Cristina was still able to study and have access to the libraries and archives of the city, but that wasn't the same as being accepted by academia.

Spurned by De Luca, she was now effectively excluded from Sapienza University. She could still enter the hallowed buildings, use their reading rooms and browse through their manuscript cases, but no-one wanted to talk to her or engage in debate. And if she couldn't argue intellectual points with bright minds, what was the point of studying anything?

After two weeks, Cristina wrote to Professor De Luca, offering a full apology, acknowledging her errors of judgement, and asking for a second chance. The letter was returned unopened.

The only place she could find solace was at the construction site for St Peter's, where she would sit for hours, watching the workmen dig ever deeper into the Roman bedrock. She wondered whether these were the biggest holes ever dug, and was endlessly fascinated by how the combined efforts of mortal men could create something on such a super-human scale.

But when the final bell of the day tolled, and the muddy-booted workmen clomped off site, Cristina had no choice but to return home to a library which now seemed to sit in silent judgement on her.

Even the normally sanguine Isra was starting to worry. She had seen Cristina experience difficult times before, but she had never known her lose interest in reading. For Cristina, to be tired of learning was to be tired of life.

"Maybe you're looking in the wrong place," Isra suggested, after serving up one of Cristina's favourite meals, *pappardelle alla Fiesolana.*

"I like watching construction workers. Every day they achieve something real, something you can point to."

"But it's not helping you, is it?"

Cristina shrugged and wiped a piece of bread around her plate, mopping up some of the creamy tomato sauce.

"Listening to crude humour and men complaining about their wives isn't enough for a mind like yours," Isra tutted.

"It passes the time."

"That's a terrible thing to say, Cristina. Wishing your life away."

"I just can't face sitting in that library again. Not yet."

"Then maybe you need to sit somewhere else."

Cristina looked up from her now spotless plate. "What do you mean?"

"Do you know why I enjoy cooking?" Isra waved a wooden spoon at Cristina. "Because it's impossible to do unless you use your hands. If you try to *imagine* preparing a meal, you get hopelessly confused, and then you lose confidence. It's the *doing* that keeps your mind focussed. I think that's what you need, to connect your hands to all the worries in your mind."

"But how do I 'do' anguish?"

"Isn't that what powers all great art?"

"I didn't think I would ever see you again," Abbess Beatrice said as she ushered Cristina into her office and drew a seat up next to the fireplace.

"But there is no bad blood between you and I, Reverend Mother. I only deceived you because I had no choice."

"Nevertheless, the House of Eternal Grace does not hold the happiest memories for you. I would understand if you never wanted to set foot in here again."

"How has the sisterhood been since…" Cristina struggled to pinpoint which part of the affair was the most shocking. "Since everything?"

"The whole convent is grieving."

"Me too, even now," Cristina confessed. "What have you done to make sense of it?"

"We cope as we have always coped." Abbess Beatrice picked up her rosary beads from a side table, and her fingers took on a life of their own as they shuffled from bead to bead. "Meditation. Prayer. Asking for forgiveness. Humbling ourselves before the mystery of God's will."

Cristina glanced at the abbess's hands, envying the unshakeable faith symbolised by the string of red beads. They were the perfect chart to navigate turbulent seas.

"What about you?" Abbess Beatrice could see how troubled Cristina was. "How are you coping?"

"I was wondering … I thought it might help if I wrote an account."

"Of what, exactly?"

"Of everything. From the very beginning. How I came to be involved in the rebuilding of St Peter's. The decisions it has forced me to take. How I ended up here."

The abbess's fingers stopped their progress along the beads. "It is … an interesting idea."

"And what I would really like, with your permission, is to write it here, in Sister Ysabella's own cell."

"But she tried to kill you."

"She was in her own torment. And if I could sit in her cell while I write, perhaps it will help me honour the truth."

"I'm not sure about the wisdom of all this, Signorina Falchoni. Have you really thought it through?"

"No. But that is precisely why I need to write."

"If that's what you truly want…"

"It is."

"Very well."

Abbess Beatrice pushed open the door to the cell, but didn't step inside. Cristina also hesitated on the threshold, looking at the whitewashed walls. Even though everything had been scrubbed clean and neatly set for a new occupant, Ysabella's deep sorrow still lingered.

Cristina glanced at the small desk, remembering the excitement of their shared detective work before she had understood the depth of Ysabella's trauma. For those few, short days, it felt as if they were kindred spirits.

"What will you do with it when you've finished?" Abbess Beatrice looked at the quires of paper tucked under Cristina's arm.

"Oh, I hadn't thought that far ahead. Writing is the important thing."

"And you know publishers?"

"I do," Cristina recalled the manic energy of Edoardo Boschi, "but I don't think people would accept such a narrative from a woman."

"Then change your name."

Cristina considered the idea, but shook her head. "I'm done with deception. And anyway, if I think about people reading it, I might alter the narrative."

"You mean make embellishments to entertain?"

"I think I should just write." Cristina entered the cell, placed the paper on the desk, then set a large pot of ink and two quills beside it. "Maybe … maybe the only way to truly make sense of the world, is to write about it."

"If that is what you want, then perhaps we can help in another way. When you are finished, I can lodge the manuscript here, locked securely in the convent. No-one ever has to see it, not until you're ready."

Cristina looked at the abbess. "Really? You would do that for me?"

"Of course. And we know about discretion in the House of Eternal Grace. After all, we do wash the Pope's underclothes."

"Then I'll be in good company," Cristina smiled.

"Well, I shall leave you to it. You're welcome to eat with the sisters. You know the routine."

"Thank you, Reverend Mother."

Abbess Beatrice closed the door and walked away down the corridor.

Cristina picked up one of the quills, dipped it in the ink, then stared at the blank sheet of paper...

Where to begin? Which words to start with?

She thought for a moment, then started to write.

The Basilica Diaries. First Folio...

A NOTE TO THE READER

When I was in the middle of the first draft of *Demon of Truth*, an article appeared in the press about an artificial intelligence drone 'killing' its human operator during a military simulation. According to reports, the AI turned on its human handler to stop it interfering with the mission. The US Air Force later denied all knowledge of the exercise.

The incident bears a striking resemblance to the rebellious HAL in Stanley Kubrick's *2001: A Space Odyssey*, and is a perfect illustration of one of the key problems that humanity will have to grapple with in the coming years — what happens when intelligence becomes detached from truth and humanity? Because left to its own devices, AI will get smarter and smarter, but not necessarily wiser.

It is a theme that this novel sets out to explore through the character of Cristina, as she becomes intoxicated with the power of her intelligence to manipulate others. She learns the hard way that intelligence has a momentum all of its own which is alluring, yet dangerous. While I was writing I often thought about the secret recordings of the (now disgraced) Cambridge Analytica executives boasting about how they had used data manipulation to turn black into white and win elections for the highest bidder, truth be damned.

I hope you enjoyed exploring these ideas through the filter of 16th century Italy, and would love to hear your thoughts.

I'm grateful for the feedback and reviews of the first two books that readers have taken the time to post. A lot of the feedback has been thoughtful and positive, although a few people have questioned the prose style of the novels. Why did

I choose to write historical fiction using clean, modern language? Let me explain the reasoning.

One of the first things you open when you become a screenwriter is the box of tricks for writing period dialogue.

For example, if you want to write 'Restoration English', you make each character repeat the last few words of the previous speaker.

"The previous speaker, you say? What an impudent trick."

"An impudent trick it may be, sir, but it can be most effective."

"Effective be damned! You are a bounder and a fraud."

"A fraud who has the measure of you, sir."

And so on.

Then there is 'Yoda-speak', where a simple change of word order gives the impression of wisdom. "Strong is the force, but great is the mystery."

And when you strip out the wisdom but keep the scrambled word order, you go straight to pompous chamberlain. "Amused, we are not. Humiliation is what awaits you." Compare the emotional feeling of that with, "We are not amused. You will be humiliated," which feels far less scathing.

I could have written *The Basilica Diaries* using these and numerous other tricks to give a faux period feel, but I chose not to for a quite simple reason. In the 16th century, people spoke to each other using language that to their ears would have sounded contemporary, rather than old fashioned. Their speech patterns would certainly have changed when they were in more formal settings, and I have reflected these changes — you wouldn't talk to the Pope in the same way you would talk to your brother. But in regular, everyday conversations, they would have sounded modern to each other, and I wanted to keep this freshness to help make the stories accessible and relevant. After all, there are only contemporary readers, and no-one from the 16th century is going to download *The Basilica Diaries* onto their Kindle!

I am now hard at work on the fourth book in the series, *Carnival of Chaos*, which sees Cristina returning to the fray with renewed determination to fight for justice. I do hope you are tempted to come along for the ride!

If you have time to post a review on **Amazon** or **Goodreads**, that would be great, or if you'd rather give me feedback through social media, here are the links:

Website: <u>www.RichardKurti.com</u>
Instagram: <u>RichardKurtiWriter</u>
X (Twitter): <u>@Richard_Kurti</u>

Either way, I hope you'll join Cristina and Domenico on their next thrilling investigation.

Sapere Books is an exciting new publisher of brilliant fiction and popular history.

To find out more about our latest releases and our monthly bargain books visit our website:
saperebooks.com

Printed by Amazon Italia Logistica S.r.l.
Torrazza Piemonte (TO), Italy

53011095R00167